WHEN TOTEMS FALL

WAYNE C STEWART

When Totems Fall

Series Design: Jerry Todd

Email: whentotemsfall@gmail.com

waynecstewart.com

facebook.com/authorwaynecstewart/

For my father, Lynn Elliott Stewart,
who is always reading good stories and has modeled
the kind of thoughtfulness and loyalties I hope to
live out in my generation as well.

PROLOGUE

Lieutenant *Zebulon Mordecai Dalton,* United States Army Signal Corps (retired), longed for a reason to stand down.

The musty Cold War bunker encasing him was no help. Its walls stood mute, as did the aging computer console at his fingertips. Reviewing protocols, his right pointer flinched. A line of perspiration wandered downward, pooling at the tip of his forefinger and then dropping to the faded J of the sweaty, sticky keyboard.

Insanity.

American nuclear first-strike.

His nation had used this option once—two devices employed in desperate, quick succession. From there the tactic had been banished to the outer reaches of military and political feasibility.

But things were very different now.

Fifty-thousand Chinese troops occupied US soil—his hometown—and his orders were unmistakable.

He'd been given control. He was the one in the chair.

Humble hunt-and-peck key strokes would serve as the cause, sending his country's missiles skyward and west, out across the vast Pacific and to unsuspecting hundreds of millions. An entire arsenal of Chinese warheads would return, the immediate and irreversible effect. Mere inches and seconds separated this present moment from untold destruction of life, his own in the mix.

Dalton's headspace fluctuated from disciplined reason to barely-restrained panic; little more than an untended circus carousel spinning at a furious, increasingly nauseating, rate.

The man was desperate for a reason to stand down.

Anything.

Anything at all.

The lieutenant froze, hands outstretched in the same robotic pose. The cloak of mortality lay onerous, unshakable, as the ultimate no-win scenario circled overhead. No good choices to be made. At least none obvious, actionable, or desirable.

Dalton shook his head left to right and back again. Everything above his shoulders slowed. Heavy, listless.

"Zeb?"

"*Zeb?*"

The sound of another's voice called him to the present, drawing him back from the edge. But it did little to satisfy the question blinking onscreen.

Or the choice lingering at his fingertips.

ONE

25 Days Earlier
Monday, 7:00 am (PST)
Seattle, Washington

The strong, dark coffee radiated heat, forming a small vapor cloud on the aging, street-side window pane.

Inspiration struck. Leaning forward and reaching out with his right-hand index finger, Dalton worked the glass and condensation canvas. Bold strokes, fine details; at least so far as his not-so-nimble digits allowed.

It didn't take long.

Round head, two eyes, over-sized grin.

The classic happy face.

Dalton nodded, certain of his first grade art teachers approval.

But then something snapped. The wide grin and carefree attitude suddenly became annoying. So Dalton set out to destroy the little man... in his thoughts.

The imagined courthouse scene was easily and stereotypically set. Much like a basic legal thriller, Dalton presided as the gilded presence of prosecutorial power — no, of *justice*. Defendant, judge, and jury sat immobilized by unmatched skill and reasoning. Dalton's strategy played flawlessly. Each line of questioning plunged mercilessly into the accused's right to happiness. No holds barred. No statements defied.

"So, you do admit to smiling without ceasing... "

"You do not deny this, do you... Mr... Face?"

The required dramatic pause.

"Please then, illuminate this courtroom—no, reveal to us your secrets, the reasons for your ongoing condition of unrestricted bliss."

No stopping. No slowing the remorseless barrage.

"Do you find it plausible in a world filled with pain, betrayal, and greed that someone could be happy all the time?"

Dalton's voice rose again. "Do you find it reasonable they might be happy, *ever*?"

The fantasized litany burst forward. A dam overcome by a swollen springtime river would prove more merciful.

In reply, the sketched and now dripping face stared back, unblinking.

A few more rounds and the prosecution rested. Dalton re-buttoned the impeccably tailored suit coat of his daydream, took his seat and awaited the all but certain verdict of "guilty."

Back in the real world a delivery truck drove by. Tires. Pothole. Puddled water attacking glass.

Like a student awaking mid-lecture, Dalton tried to re-enter the room with subtlety and grace. A wipe of his shirtsleeve cleared the remaining evidence of what just happened and he released the happy-faced man, more smudge than image, to his own recognizance.

He almost felt bad.

Almost.

Dalton was again present. While these musings were not extraordinary—he definitely carried a darker shade of humor than most—their frequency of late was probably worth noting.

Whoa there, Dalton.

That was a bit more "Castaway" than you want to admit.

Pretty soon you'll name him Wilson and mourn his untimely passing.

Get a grip. Get a flippin' grip.

Dalton reset and threw back a generous swig of the still-warm contents of his mug, another aroma besides the coffee appearing.

Buildings have smells, too. This one, standing now for well over a century, concocted a heady, unique ambiance. Untold layers of paint and stain cloyed on mature walls, floors, and ceiling. As sensory strata, their collective presentation spoke more industrial than people-place. Muscular, yet comforting.

Dalton inhaled deeper, zeroing in on the room, recapturing some emotional equilibrium. Closing his eyes, it washed over him.

Okay, that's a little better.

Dalton sat back, way back, eyes up.

Towering overhead, the open-beam ceilings offered quite the show. A rough-hewn tapestry of solid timbers and old-school plaster. These planked sentries brought majesty and reverence, elements sadly absent from modern shops and businesses. They spoke a covenant of sanctity over a neighborhood of tear-downs and new construction. Decrying modernity's unstoppable wave, this building said *been there*. Everything was right; the beans and the vibe. One could imagine a crusty old trapper making his way in from the wet and cold, wolf-dog at his side, shotgun in hand, feeling right at home.

While other spaces catered to the faux-elite, this place was an escape. And this particular seat—Dalton's regular spot in this fur warehouse turned Shangri-La for introverts—was the best in the house. Yes, a darkened thirty-foot long hallway complete with peeling wallpaper and aging wallboard tested the need for a fresh cup of joe, but the solitude it guaranteed was glorious. Two chairs adorned this secluded backroom. Dalton's faced streetside. The other sat a few feet back and to the left. Dalton felt like one of them was unnecessary, never more so when the second seat was occupied.

Like this morning.

TWO

For the last hour and a half on this cliche Seattle spring morning Dalton reigned as king over his coffee and silence domain. Now, out of basic courtesy, he'd be obliged to interact with another human being.

Sarcasm, heavy and duly noted as such, came from behind an unevenly folded daily edition of *The Seattle Times.*

"So, the Hawks look like they're gonna blow it again, huh?" the voice questioned and opined. "Wasting a first round pick on that beat-up tailback from Alabama? Sheer genius."

Keep it simple. Keep it short. He'll go away.

"Didn't follow it, man."

The paper came down, revealing a sad, almost pitying expression.

Dalton almost felt bad, for the second time today.

Almost.

Before crossing that emotional line, he simply tilted his mug to the spilling point, indicating more coffee was needed and therefore couldn't finish out the chat—as much as he would love to.

That should work.

It didn't.

Seahawk Guy kept going.

For the next few minutes Dalton feigned nominal interest while mostly glancing down. His mind landed elsewhere. His neighbor's dog, barking at all hours... and not even a real bark... mostly yipping... that girl, what was her name? Malisha? Marina?... man, he'd botched that one... the fact that this shop was so cool they let you keep your own mug at the front counter, cleaned and ready for your next visit... try that at a Starbucks, people...

Then he saw it.

The cup.

While waving it earlier had been a diversionary tactic, the F117 Nighthawk Fighter adorning his mug was slowly disappearing. It was supposed to work that way. Warm liquid: plane appears. Cold liquid: plane goes away.

Dalton flashed back to seeing this clever little 1990s Boeing giveaway for the first time. As a teen, he had just thought it supremely cool. Lost on him at the time was celebration of an aviation tech breakthrough forever altering the balance of power in global air warfare. As one of only a few boyhood items present in his college dorm rooms, it also remained one of the few things in his life still working some twenty years later.

He turned the fading image more fully toward the stranger, thinking it might help.

So, I'd really love to hear more about where the Spring owner's meeting landed on the issue of player's headbands without official logos on them but as you can see... my plane is gone.

It did not.

Dalton half-rose from his chair only to encounter Seahawk Guy, re-positioned and making passage difficult.

He sat down again, heavily.

The lecture, originally focused on rookie player acquisition but now blossoming to full oration on the game itself, wasn't necessary.

Dalton loved this favored American pastime. He did, although, engage it differently than pretty much everyone else on the planet. Most fans zero in on a popular player or obvious focal point of the play. Big run: eyes on the tailback. Great tackle? Zoom in on the hit and ensuing smack talk. Single points of focus. One, maybe two players at a time.

In contrast, Dalton saw everything. Literally everything.

An offensive lineman shifting six inches to the left instead of seven. A defensive back's first three steps at a slightly reduced speed. He not only noticed these minute adjustments, his mind registered their complex and interrelated impacts.

At once. Clearly. And to a degree of perception and prediction beyond reach of even the most advanced computing platforms.

To the former military man, American Football proposed a giant moving formula; a dynamic, living entity. Every action and reaction of the twenty-two men on the field provided an ever-changing array of potentialities. Like a giant, three-dimensional display hovering in mid-air, Dalton factored and connected the unending lines, arcs, and data fields. To anyone else: stunning and confusing. For the former signal corpsman? Simply the way he accessed his world. And the very reason his government had gone to such lengths in acquiring his services. Initially a frightening jumble of information, this innate sensitivity graduated to a hyper-aware, calculated view of all that unfolded around him. It was a gift. Most of the time. But like any such gift it had to be corralled, disciplined, lest it lead to chaos, potentially madness.

Even at this moment, it was in play.

Dalton looked away, into the near distance.

The rookie tailback came into view. Dalton swung the 3D imagery in every direction, probing past flesh and into sinew and bone. He'd read about the five surgeries. Rehab. Added in the data from the combine and team's notes. Doctors. Physical therapists. While not the confidential files, more than enough to do the job.

"Two games shy of two seasons."

Seahawk guy stopped talking, trying to harvest meaning from the statement.

"85.68% it happens in the late third quarter and against a division rival."

More blankness.

"Nevermind," Dalton said.

A look down to his phone.

7:45am.

No last words spoken. No parting shots given. Dalton's beautiful cone of silence lie shattered before him. Cold coffee. No stealthy plane gracing the cup's exterior to indicate otherwise. And while the office wasn't too far away, the downtown congestion of the Emerald City could always be a bear on a weekday morning.

Frustrated, Dalton grabbed his stuff, dropped the mug off at the counter, and walked out the front door.

THREE

Monday—7:45 am, Beijing Time Zone (UTC+8:00)
Beijing, People's Republic of China

Industrial smog. Slow, thick. Ponderous. Ever present in the modern Chinese Capital, it hung in an especially noxious manner this morning.

Junjie Zang stared, probing the unnatural cloud bank through the clear, clean glass of his forty-third-story office suite. Barely penetrable gray. A perfect metaphorical match for the young man's state of mind. As clarity could not be found in the air surrounding the monstrous skyscraper, the same could be said of this thirty-one-year-old CEO's thinking and emotions.

It had been this way for quite some time.

On a good day this view was breathtaking. The pricey vantage point in and above the Chaoyang District afforded a panorama of gleaming steel and glass, the happy result of an early 2000's construction boom in the downtown corridor. On a good day one could behold many of the architectural wonders gracing this city's always modernizing skyline. On a good, clear day.

Junjie peered deeper into the fume-laden void.

It stared back. Unfeeling, unmoving.

His heart and mind foundered similarly, going nowhere anytime soon. These particular quandaries shook him to his core, hounded him during waking and sleeping hours, and exacted an inordinate price — one he alone could pay. Surely, those closest to him had noticed his heaviness.

Was there a real-world limit to living in this kind of tension?

In private moments — like this one — he wondered how long? How long until his breaking point?

Silence.

Yes, a healthy storm and cleansing rain could reveal these dynamic views for the more affluent of Beijing's 21.5 million residents.

Junjie's anguish would require much the same.

His phone vibrated, sliding sideways on the sleek, onyx-toned desk.

30 minutes.

Junjie touched the appointment icon. The mundane act blazed a narrow path through his numbness. It was something to do, a simple yet needed respite from overwhelming moral concern. Phone dangling in hand Junjie let these matters, critical for his family and future, envelope him a while longer.

Twenty minutes later he entered the presence of powerful men.

"Mr. Zang."

A bow. A handshake. Each set the mood for business both Chinese and Western.

"Please, please come in. We have a good deal to discuss."

"General," Junjie replied. "I am honored again to be here."

The group of men, older and far more important than Junjie, stood at a table some twenty-five feet long and a full seven feet at its widest point. Junjie guessed, correctly so, that the wood was something rare, expensive.

Probably hewn from the last of an irreplaceable stand of trees from a rainforest. Safe to say Green Peace or ELF reps have never attended a briefing here.

The unheard humor settled Junjie's nerves, if only a little.

Teak. Mahogany. Gold filigree.

Questions of no small matter were taken up and acted upon here. It was a relational calculus with a clear bottom line: make no mistakes, none at all. Weakness, incompetence will not be tolerated. Fools will not be suffered. In halls like this, men measured other men. Those found lacking would not merely be dismissed. No, they would be swallowed whole, consumed, and discarded.

Upon crossing the room's threshold, his heels sunk into plush, maroon carpet. The committee's responsibility-worn faces considered his worthiness as he approached like a goat readied for sacrifice. Junjie stopped at his place, pulling out the substantial chair he dare not use during the next two hours. He paused, settling into the earnestness demanded of such moments.

The general nodded.

Everyone else took their seats.

Leather folders creaked open. Triggered remotely, the room lights dimmed as a 72" video wall came to life and the elder-statesman soldier invited the younger man to begin.

"Mr. Zang, you bring good news of our venture?"

"Yes, general. Good, indeed."

A wave of the general's hand.

"Then please proceed. We are all quite anxious to hear about the current status of the program."

"Thank you, sir. We are on target in both hardware and software beta runs. Fail-points and overall systems integrity numbers all fall well within acceptability norms. We have experienced slower developmental partner response on some fronts than anticipated, specifically the components needed to build and maintain our server configurations; truly one of a kind. Yet even at this, our systems remain online and moving toward launch."

Junjie noted the technical details settling on this audience, subtle expressions of comprehension and the lack of remedial inquiries. Brevity was both expected and appreciated. Junjie continued as briskly as he dared.

Fifteen minutes of charts, synopses, and spec sheets later came the questions. Some, he knew, could sink him outright.

"May we assume you have resolved your personnel problems, Mr. Zang?"

"Yes," Junjie spoke as candidly as he felt he could. "The new hires suggested have been of great benefit."

The younger man looked across the room widely, not at his questioner directly. To do otherwise would be a display of patent disrespect. It would also be the tell revealing his unease.

But it was hard to hold back.

Friends and colleagues, co-laborers for years, ones risking so much joining this communications upstart when more lucrative opportunities were theirs for the taking. That they had transformed suddenly into a debilitating weakness— one requiring immediate action?

Truthfully, the replacements were performing competently. But it all seemed a bit prepared.

Such specialized skill sets, both available and interested in this no-name enterprise?

In the right quantities? At their exact moment of need?

Junjie struggled to imagine the broadscale failure of so many of his key people. Good, talented people. Yet the evidence seemed inescapable. Pouring over it for days he searched for a way out. None surfaced; at least not anything compelling enough to question the process and the parties behind it. If he were to put any stock in the formal findings of the Progress and Effectiveness Task Force, then as CEO he had no other choice.

They needed to go. All of them.

Even now it landed with the pain of a sucker punch in a darkened room. Another big bump on a very fast ride. One that his company, Dawn Star Integrated Systems, had occupied the front row of for three-plus years.

Like many startups, Dawn Star experienced lean yet reasonable early growth. More bacon burger than filet mignon. Getting by. That was about all you could say for this ragtag squad of geeks and their equally geeky entrepreneurial leader. In year six everything changed. Their white paper at the China Computer Federation's annual meeting brought government representatives and a succession of engineering and development deals totaling in the hundreds of millions of dollars.

Could they handle it?

The answer of course, was yes.

A boon to the fledgling team and its very green captain, the contracts also brought the tensions taunting him daily.

Growing from a handful of young engineers into a bustling corporation of over 3000 in such a compressed span of time was akin to riding a Tsunami from deep in the Pacific onto the shores of an unsuspecting island nation. Thrilling? Yes. Complete chaos? Also, yes.

Fourteen to sixteen hours per day usually sated the volatile expansion. But it was not uncommon for his office couch to see more of him at night than his wife and young son. Junjie's personal toll mounted, a greater sacrifice with each year passing. Slowing enough to look back, which he rarely did, only accused him of trading it all away with little to no chance of commensurate return.

Junjie loved his work.

But he adored his family, a bright and lovely part of his sojourn on this planet. He longed for more time with them and thought himself fortunate, no, more than that— blessed—when his mind shifted from the ever-mounting pressures of the workday to his home life.

I will make this up to them was his silent, daily promise.

FOUR

The Q&A portion of the presentation halted as two men at the table engaged in a subject of no importance to anyone but themselves.

The needless sidebar created a moment in which Junjie drew up pleasant images. His beautiful wife. Their energetic, inquisitive son.

The general's authoritative voice broke in, refocusing the room and dissipating Junjie's half-conscious bliss.

"We will waste no more time. Today is a day of forward strides for our people. Too long we have followed. Our communication abilities have lagged both in quality and technological advancement." A crescendo grew, a preaching-like timbre emerging.

"And we shall soon rise to the level of our glorious purpose!"

The general waited, controlling the room before proceeding.

"Minister please, lend your voice to this destiny, for all of us."

Zhou Dhe **paused** before responding. His silence stopped just short of disrespect.

As the senior political official in the room, he exuded authority, engendering ready submission to his desires and directives. Inset eyes focused unwaveringly, powerfully. A big man, six feet two inches tall, he ranked in the 99th percentile in height of adult males with respect to his countrymen. Even sitting he drew a formidable presence. Dhe made good on these physical advantages. Whether a room of subordinates or an intimate exchange, his bearing often left people feeling lesser and weaker.

He liked it that way.

Though presuming power and influence, Dhe was nothing more than a common coward. For him the ancient adage, "Supreme excellence consists in breaking the enemy's resistance without fighting" was an escape, not a position of strength. Sun Tzu, author of *The Art of War* and originator of this ideal, would not have approved. Still Dhe was suited, even if functionally, for the role he'd occupied for the better part of two decades.

Established in the mid-1970s with minimal oversight, the Strategic Communications Ministry was a well-funded yet largely unknown organ in an already secretive system. Operating in the realms of deepest darkness, its decisions were reached by those few enjoying the privileges of limitless resources and hidden budgets. As the Director of SCM, Dhe held enormous clout. His word stood virtually unchallengeable, except to those outranking him in the Party apparatus. Still, countering the man was never taken on lightly. He embraced and relished his immense influence in the smallest and elitist of power chambers, in this most populous of nations. A highly placed fall-man, his life's work encouraged those above him to engage in misdeeds while providing the requisite cover.

Failure? Exposure?

Dhe alone would suffer the consequences.

Far more pragmatist than patriot, his greatest fear was a worthy opponent unmasking him. At 73, the director's formerly imposing stature now bent forward of the rigid spine, chest-out presentation of his youth. The secrets he carried more than made up for it. The man knew where every single metaphorical and literal body was buried, having dug many of the holes himself.

Yes, people feared Dhe, and for good reason.

Ten minutes of rehashed propaganda later he shifted toward Junjie. The move and his words bore down heavily. The young man found it a challenge to look anywhere near the minister's direction as Dhe's eyes burned into place, never lifting from Junjie even while addressing the room broadly.

"Today is a momentous day my comrades. The last three years have seen both ample investment and significant gains, promising tremendous returns for many years to come. I assure you: our leaders are watching with keen interest and anticipation."

Dhe changed tack abruptly, directing his comments exclusively to Junjie. Beside him now. So close his breath brushed off the CEO's cheek.

"What exactly may I tell them?"

Silence prevailed, the blatant dismissal of protocol shocking all present.

"May we count on your full commitment?"

Leaning in, closer still.

"Are the systems operational?"

It was Junjie's moment to seize or squander. The very reason he had been invited. An opportunity thousands of

CEOs wouldn't hesitate over, not a single second.

Yet the question nagged.

Had they had done too good of a job, creating something more potent than was for anyone's good?

He had to admit, the final product was far afield from where they'd started. More power. More access. Initially a superior and more efficient utilizing of existing bandwidth—no small feat in a developing nation with infrastructure challenges—there were now aspects of the code more closely resembling AI.

And that's what scared him.

In his professional opinion the final code was more appropriate to outcomes other than those stated in the agreement. Add the sudden removal of valued men and women and their handpicked replacements, chosen by nothing less than high-level authorities in Beijing, and the whole thing was terribly disconcerting.

Maybe I should walk away, make some mistakes, be forced to hand over the work to someone else.

It would not be so simple. Dislodging Dawn Star from her contractual obligations would be both highly impractical and quite difficult to explain.

Time was up.

Junjie's mouth opened.

"My firm pledges itself in every way. Full implementation in the next twenty-four hours."

The statement sounded far more convincing than he actually felt. Nonetheless, the deed was done.

Dhe nodded. They were finished. The other men stood in unison, suit coat buttons refastened and notebooks gathered.

Junjie retrieved his materials, bowed, and exited the room. With the door shut, the other men talked. Dhe first.

"He was not so credible this time. We have come too far to allow his weakness to jeopardize the good of the whole... and need I remind you... the good of the whole is why we are doing this."

General *Chien Wie* stared back, unflinching at the stinging rebuke. He knew Dhe well enough to obey, but he would not honor the man. He'd stood beside many of the same ilk; naked ambition cloaked in love of country. His next words came slowly but confidently.

"There are sufficient measures in place. The young businessman will finish what he has started."

"And then?"

Silence.

Dhe did not wait for an answer. Turning, with neither acknowledgment nor disagreement, he simply left.

FIVE

Dalton's usual routine brought him across mid-town, toward the waterfront piers and ferry landings.

From there he would head south past Safeco Field and Century Link Stadium, edging his way into Bay City Printing Company's shared lot as the workday began.

Dalton was your basic sales guy. His trade: full color, offset press work. Corporate identity. Brochures, catalogs. Lots of pages. Perfect or spiral binding.

Need something printed? *Z. Dalton – BCPC*, had you covered.

The stark contrasts in vocational and professional histories were intriguing, to say the least. A near-decade in worldwide, active-duty hot zones. Life and death, comrades and enemies. Nowadays he sold printed paper products to mom and pop shops and medium-sized businesses. Two years on the outside, the closest he got to a danger-fed adrenaline rush was a customer signing off on a sales contract.

In triplicate.

So today's first step, the beginnings of another presumably mundane day, would be simply getting to his car three and a half blocks away.

Dalton headed out, taking in the fresh morning air while navigating the sharp vertical orientation of his hometown. Though the overnight hours deposited a brief shower on the city — expected and ordinary — this spring day was starting out as clear and clean as they come in the Northwest. A nominal breeze moved in and among gleaming high-rise structures, landing a hint of the salted waterfront at Dalton's nose.

His medium build attracted no unwarranted attention among grumpy, early rising pedestrians. Slightly over five foot ten. A few pounds added along the way. Still, at thirty-seven, keeping a burgeoning belt line from becoming the first thing people noticed when you walked into a room had to count for something.

Dalton's hair lay longer than military-standard but still quite short. This was nothing new. Even in high school he chose a well-groomed cut over the predictably long and wild expressions of his classmates. Its color held, even now a dark brown with only slight hints of gray. Physically, Dalton owned the middle ground in all things average, with a composite appearance rating somewhere between nondescript and lackluster.

Until you caught his eyes.

Amber, warm, curious. Probing, seldom revealing, sometimes unsettling. Unique, unexpected. Searching, seeking beyond mere appearances to something more on the level of depth, character, heart. Not in a judgmental way. More inquisitive than damning.

Bay City didn't mandate business-wear. Khakis and a short-sleeved polo worked fine most days. The last time he'd dressed up was a Printmakers Union New Year's Eve Party hosted atop the Space Needle. The tux shop took the wrong measurements and Dalton stayed glued to his seat the entire evening, fearing something might burst or break at the slightest awkward motion. Three full-dress uniforms hung pressed and bagged in his bedroom closet. Though they still fit decently, he couldn't imagine a scenario in which he would put one on again.

Three more steps and he arrived, unlocking the door and sliding inside. With the seat in an acceptable position, Dalton engaged the ignition. Thirty seconds of warm up and he popped the handbrake, signaled, and entered the already heavy morning traffic flow.

Six stoplights later, small hairs rose along the back of his neck, bristling against the cotton collar of his green polo.

SIX

Zeb's ears rang mercilessly.

Head slouching downward and to the side. Chin jammed against collarbone. A thin, wet, red line flowed out his ear and down along his left shoulder. Dalton noted the sticky procession but his senses were too unfocused, too peripheral to get a better read. He slid left, past the deployed airbag and down. Nothing to stop his clumsy fall.

On the ground. Flat, hard asphalt. Dalton's cerebral cortex told him little more. A mess of jumbled, disfigured sensory data. An unsettling, uncontrollable dance of nerve fibers and chemicals. Vague messages of danger and harm.

Dalton tried moving. His stomach and mind weren't yet agreeing and he retched onto the warm, gray pavement.

Though reeling, still fighting to do its job, his body could only do so much. In the impressionistic image surrounding him everything that mattered stayed at a distance, just beyond grasp. His overall state of situational awareness — so very crucial for a soldier — degraded way beyond acceptable norms.

Something was wrong. Very wrong.

Dalton tried moving again. Semi-upright led to slumping backward, the Kia's frame halting his collapse. The retired soldier's consciousness faded and a calming blackness advanced at the edges of his blurred vision.

He welcomed it.

But then the memory returned, distorted by an onslaught of raging brain chemistry.

"Unless ye drink my blood and eat my body, ye have no part in me..."

The unseen voice resonated — deep, haunting.

Only four or five, Zeb had snuck in without permission. Hidden under a table at the back of his father's small church, a voluminous baritone filled the air. The mysterious phrase. Such horrible imagery. The fact it proceeded from his father's mouth frightened him beyond belief, literally and figuratively.

Again, more insistent:

"Unless ye drink my blood and eat my body, ye have no part in me!"

Young Zeb couldn't move any further back. The voice, both closer and bigger, posed too much for his little ears to handle, more than his impressionable heart and mind could keep in.

His chest pulsed beneath the thinning fabric of a simple, white t-shirt. Old drywall poked at his skin. With spindly legs fully retracted and hands clasped over his ears Zeb tried to stop the onslaught.

For the last time — booming, readying to explode.

"Unless ye drink my blood and eat my body, ye have no part in me!!!"

Zeb whimpered.

Silence. Footsteps. Haltingly and then, much quicker.

The minimalist veil of black tablecloth tore back. A man's hand, large and authoritative, reached into his fortress, his protection.

This time little Zeb screamed.

On the pavement grown-up Dalton came to. His senses online, smell arrived first.

An acrid tang; aviation fuel, burning plastic.

Then touch, and pain, announced its presence. The first adrenal rush had faded. No more sensory confusion. Every nerve ending on edge, bodily warning systems firing simultaneously, clearly, insistently.

What..? What in the world happened?

Decades of training kicked into gear. Macabre — yes, but necessary.

Hands, arms, torso.

Legs, feet, head.

Best he could tell, the blood from his left ear was his most pressing concern. But even this had slowed, almost stopped. While stiffness ascended in major muscle groups Dalton retained a reasonable range of motion. Last, but most useful, Dalton's ears had cleared, almost completely.

Classic good news-bad news.

Moans hung, half-muted in the stilled air. Screams of pain were yet to come. Such destruction would eventually exact its penance of fear. But for now, a momentary biological blessing of sorts, an odd, eerie calm prevailed.

"God, no. God, please — *no*," Dalton muttered.

The Public Market at Pike Place stood for the better part of ten decades as an iconic Seattle destination.

Only moments ago Dalton had waited at a red light, a short block and a half away from its fish-throwing merchants, small-scale entrepreneurs, and local artisans. A uniquely traditional element of the business and civic scene with an eclectic aura and colorful history, it was a space very *Seattle*.

That happy portrait now lay horridly defaced, a cacophony of distasteful sights and smells.

The scene was impossible to reconcile, to accept at face value.

The famous market sign had been completely torn away, and a massive, disembodied jumbo jet's forward cabin lay in its place. Mounds of tangled steel and fabric engulfed the deathly landscape. Thirty yards up the street, colossal Pratt and Whitney turbines whined on, their death-throes calling out danger to any within earshot.

Dalton scanned the debris field, uptown. His mind's eye captured every last detail, instantly and completely. During this brief moment he assessed a crash and loss scenario that would take the NTSB's very best a full six months to understand. He turned and rotated a three-dimensional, six-block area of the city. As if pressing "play", the schematic began moving.

The plane entered from the north. Wings sheared, she skidded past the lower-rise structures of Belltown, catching both vehicles and pedestrians in her wake. Dalton calculated again. The toll should have been much higher, collateral damage before final impact and explosion mercifully lessened by an exceptionally focused path down Western Avenue. Almost like a bowling ball constrained in its lane, the crash lumbered forward, reserving its heaviest blow for the market itself.

Dalton's mind went into overdrive. Angles, trajectory, mass, energy. Lines of reasoning most supercomputers would struggle to process. What he didn't see, what Dalton could not know, were the events just prior to the jet's ghastly entrance into the city core.

SEVEN

American 2132, non-stop out of Vancouver, B.C., was on schedule with an expected arrival at SeaTac International of 9:42 am PST.

Like most weekday mornings the manifest listed business travelers, vacationers, and those heading to family engagements both joyful and difficult. The trajectory from YVR to SEA tracks one of the most beautiful inland coastlines in the world. From Vancouver's Sea Island, then passing over waters of the central Puget Sound area, the flight path takes in a close look at the city before proceeding south to the airport.

Seattle's urban fringe is met on the east by the untamed majesty of the Cascade Mountains. With peaks topping 14,000 feet the landscape flows downward to meet the graceful waters of Puget Sound. Westward lie the shorter yet still formidable heights of the Olympic Range, a barrier of snow and wilderness against the weathered advances of the Pacific. The approach is stunning. Add a gleaming skyline of steel, glass, and brick — one of the most attractive, yet unseen city-sights in America — and many travelers are held spellbound, speechless.

To be fair, many days, notably mid-January, are quite forgettable.

Today was not one of those days.

Today was glorious.

The city came into full view. Everyone stopped, turning to the captivating sights beyond their small, oval portals. 2132's cabin crew closed the final round of beverage service and the cockpit reported nominal winds, prepared for an uneventful landing before refueling, food service, and connection at their terminus — San Francisco — later in the afternoon.

It started as nothing, really. The captain's head tilted, more curious than alarmed.

"Seattle Control, this is American 2132, inbound Delta 4. Do you copy? We are experiencing system anomalies and require a calibration check."

"Affirmative, American 2132. This is Seattle Control. Read you fine. Go ahead."

"Control, we're getting inconsistencies in navigation and airspeed data. Initiating secondary systems and visual flight rules."

"2132, check. VFR initiated. Re-routing tracks around you and will walk you in from here."

"*Good Lord...*"

Alarms screeched in the confined space and the Airbus 310 lost every tracking, guidance, and control system it had. Multiple redundancies failed in grand, tragic succession.

She became a flying rock.

Captain *Brian Rhemus* fought the multiplicity of failures with every trick in his senior aviator's tool bag. Defiantly, the situation unraveled faster than his already racing mind and heart could track. No more words came from Rhemus to the tower. The furious nature of the chair he occupied allowed none in these last, heroic attempts to save those he was entrusted to protect.

"American 2132, please repeat! We have you losing altitude over Seattle core. 2132. 2132 please respond. 2132..."

Shocked hush emanated from the tower. A vacant, soundless despair as the inbound plane's electronic signature vanished.

Gone.

2132 hit hard, very hard, ambling another five city blocks. Entire sections of fuselage released, helpless human cargo with each spiraling chunk as the blast of heat and energy forged its way through the busy city space.

EIGHT

Pike Place's multi-level structure sat above the waterfront district, a space occupied at times by upwards of 5,000 people.

But below street-level, beyond her buskers, artisans, and entrepreneurs, 500 full-time residents—many low-income and elderly—made their homes. They now surfaced, a mass of awkwardly meandering wounded. Upward they came, through flame-engulfed passageways and out into the open turmoil of the Stewart Street entrance. All of it resembled a scene from a bad zombie movie.

First responders navigated barriers of aluminum, steel, and flame. The disdainful work of triage—choosing who would live and who would likely not—their primary, sordid task. By day's end these selfless rescuers would join the grieving, a number of their own lost in the battle against injury and death.

Dalton looked on in dismay.

Utterly powerless.

The former soldier hated it with every single fiber of his being.

Breathe. Just breathe.

Clear my head. Help someone.

Come on, Zeb. Do something.

"Please. Please, someone. She's still in there!"

Upright but weakened, leaning against what remained of the green metal framework of the market portico. Reaching toward the undead crowd with her bloodied right arm, her cries doubled every second.

"Please, *please!*"

Dalton moved in.

"Who? Where?"

"My friend, Sasha. She is old. I could not free her... "

She looked up, from beneath matted hair, drywall dust, and grease mixed with bloodstains. Even so, beauty and strength prevailed. Her accent: Balkan. Eastern European; possibly Russian or Czech.

Dalton met her fierce eyes and understood. This woman was heading back into the inferno with or without his help. Her selflessness, unnecessary for him to act, was nonetheless inspiring. He would respond, always did, as in moments like this his middle name seemed an inescapable barometer of his character.

Mordecai.

Zebulon *Mordecai* Dalton.

In the biblical Book of Esther, Mordecai appears to stand by as his exiled people face almost certain genocide. But for those looking deeper into the text, something more is uncovered. A man at work in his sphere of influence while evil abounds. A man sizing up the times and circumstances of his fate and acting with courage while also prodding others toward the same. Strategic. Crafty.

And so it fit. Whether a product of parental instinct or divine insight, Dalton would uncover the aptness of this odd moniker only in time and through trial.

No surprise, he moved against and into the tide of the injured and dying. His outlook on life had swerved hard toward the cynical and sarcastic as of late, this much was true. Yet it was also true that too much soldier remained to turn his back on the horrors unfolding in his city today. The first order of business was this woman's stranded friend. If Sasha had survived, he would do his best to get her to safety. At the very least he would bring her corpse out for a proper burial.

Everyone else was leaving the market complex.

Dalton headed in.

The air became unbreathable, the building's materials devoured in a lethal cocktail of jet engine fuel and readily-available flammables. Dalton ran and then crawled, squeezing his medium build through whatever openings remained unblocked by debris and bodies. Super-heated fumes clung to walls and ceiling, narrowing the passageways even further. The man had been in more than enough danger to be comfortable with this kind of thing. Firefights. Building fires. Not that different.

He stopped.

Three-A. Three-A.

You should be here. Right here.

One more step forward, through the haze. Sparks from still-active electrical lines danced wildly and he came upon what he didn't expect, and didn't want to see. The engineer side of his training thought it impossible.

A cavernous, jagged gap, easily twenty feet long by fifteen wide. Shattered pieces of former two-by-twelve floor joists hung like frayed splinters of a giant toothpick. Service lines seeped their remaining contents into the void and downward a full hundred feet below. Streets beneath the market lay exposed, an unlikely space carved out by the crashing hulk from above.

Framed portraits still hung in place on the angled wall, across the emptiness.

A single fixture, dangling and swaying in the far corner.

Sasha's apartment.

Dalton backed up and dropped to the floor.

Defeat, his cruel companion, teacher, and enemy across three and some decades of life, clawed at his emotions.

Just one more scenario with flawless solutions, and it all went to hell anyways.

He waited there, considered staying put.

Fuel and flame ratio. Remaining structural mass.

A little over two minutes, then…

Dalton saw her collapse. It drew him back out and to the present.

"No. You shouldn't have. What were you *thinking?*"

Two steps and he had her over his shoulder. Four more and the hallway crumpled. A straightline away from the billowing cloud and heat was their only option. He kept moving. And moving. Heaving, choking, until his back rested against what remained of the first Starbucks, across the street.

A few heavy breaths and he spotted the nearest triage station, another block up. He had just enough left in the tank.

Safely away from the scene, on the gurney with wheels retracting, she reached out, stopping the paramedics. With the greatest of effort, she raised her head and spoke.

"Maryska."

The next few hours passed frantically; caring for the wounded, assessing damage, and asking *why*. Preliminary phases of the investigation labeled the crash an unlikely, tragic occurrence. No one to blame. Life and death as has gone on for millennia.

Dalton knew better.

There were always reasons for these things.

NINE

Like an Orca breaching, the dark, grey hull broke through deep, green waters.

Ballasts blown, sea foam spilled across her topside. A curtain of water fell gracefully overboard to both starboard and port. The surf was heavy, unforgiving, yet the Type 069 Tang Class nuclear submarine stayed upright; little more than a child's game of balance and finesse. Surfaced and on station, she awaited orders like any other faithful crew member of the Chinese People's Liberation Army Navy (PLAN).

The Tangs presented a series of deadly upgrades over the former Jinn Class SSBNs. For starters, they held twenty vertical missile tubes as opposed to sixteen. Yet the increased number of rockets were not her most troubling asset. The issue was more from how far away she could throw a punch.

Tubes sixteen through twenty housed China's newest sea-borne offensive weapons, known by their class name: J-2. Thirteen meters long and two in circumference, these second-generation missiles carried a striking distance of eight to ten thousand kilometers. Plenty of range to do the job from here. Currently positioned not far off China's eastern seaboard and targeted over the Pacific, these birds carried everything necessary to devastate the west coast of the U.S., laying waste to vast economic and agricultural corridors and its 50 million residents.

For decades the American Navy held this strategic high ground, garnering no real competition, including their massive Asian-Pacific neighbor. Everyone understood: nuclear provocation from China would come by two means only; long-range ballistic missiles or the near-impossibility of a closer reach strike via bombers over sovereign U.S. territory. The J2s changed everything, advancing the threat into the much younger nation's backyard.

American intelligence services identified the new sub and its corresponding missile production in early 2009. Washington then communicated its concerns through both front and back diplomatic channels.

These dispatches were received, duly noted, and routinely ignored.

The U.S. Department of Defense, for all its influence, had no answer other than a promised retaliatory strike. Pointless and ineffective, this kind of international rock throwing only ratcheted up the already tense economic and diplomatic environment of modern Sino-American relations.

As it stood the Tang and her J2s were an irremovable pebble in the Pentagon's shoe. Given a complement of 85 sailors, provisions, and ordinance, this boat could stay at sea and undetected months at a time. Her belly was filled with nuclear-tipped rockets and her nose housed a full array of torpedoes — six bow tubes stacked for conventional warfare. The 069 was fit for both the ordinary and the unthinkable. She was present and she was formidable.

Onboard, a solitary figure made its way forward from aft, through narrow passageways and heading toward the control tower. With bearing and purpose, unrushed, shadows in cramped spaces gave way to the eerie red glow above the conn.

A narrow, chrome handrail marked the boundary of the slightly elevated area. Not unlike the chancel in a traditional church setting, the space designated authority, office. No man or woman took this platform casually. The weight of control and command resting on themselves alone.

Into the red. Bars and stripes on chest and shoulders.

Captain *Ghouzi Chan* held the conn.

The corded microphone came off its cradle. Twenty or so crew members in close proximity. A look of assurance and a slight nod from their leader reminded them who they were, what they were about, as Chan's directives landed with authority earned over twenty-five years of solitude and trial at sea.

The "talk" button produced an audible click.

"Fire control, this is the captain. Ready missile tubes sixteen through twenty. Await launch. This is not a drill. Repeat, not a drill. Live fire on my orders."

The captain released the button on the hand unit, awaiting the required verbal reply.

"Fire control, aye. Missile tubes sixteen through twenty. On captain's orders. We are live-fire ready on your orders, sir."

The Tang stood her post with moral neutrality in these expansive, forbidding waters of the Pacific.

And with this short technical exchange the People's Republic of China was ready to launch a nuclear attack on the continental United States.

US Embassy Compound—Beijing, China

The metallic black BMW Series 3 Touring Sedan strode through the American Embassy compound's steel and brick gates without incident. Led to the diplomatic entry around back, it displayed only a small, hood-mounted flag of the People's Republic; nothing distinguishing it as anything other than a routine official vehicle. Nothing to indicate one of the most powerful men in the Chinese Communist Party and by extension, the entire government rode within.

The appearance of everyday business was shattered, abruptly so.

The Beemer glided to a stop. Both sets of doors opened, heavy, Kevlar-reinforced mechanisms swinging forward with both heft and an eerie near-silence. Three large men exited, surveying and securing the immediate surroundings. Hands near sidearms. Eyes roving behind aviator glasses. Assessing potential threats with the loyalty and intensity of a pit bull. They signaled the okay, all the while scanning for changes in the quickly unfolding environment.

Into and through the classic Italian portico, the small entourage formed a blocking maneuver. Once inside the mysterious passenger took the symbolic lead, moving forcefully down the long, ornate hallway.

Wang Lieu's face would not be recognized by most Americans, Yet he was to forever change the lives of millions of them in a few, brief moments. As Foreign Minister of the People's Republic—Chinese counterpart to the American Secretary of State—he held the legal-national power to both sign treaties and declare war on behalf of his country.

This evening he was hand delivering something in-between the two.

Through the side lobby, he proceeded to the inner office of the ranking diplomatic officer, the U.S. Ambassador. The bold, next steps of this Asian nation required heavyweight geopolitical leadership. Anything less than senior cabinet authority would not suffice.

U.S. Ambassador to China Gary Locke received word only minutes prior. Hasty, unannounced visits did not conform to protocol. Presently, Locke was still raking over his five o'clock shadow in his office's private washroom. While minimally presentable, he could not have prepared for what he was to hear next.

Locke entered the room just before Lieu and two protectors. He took a standing position beside his antique Baroque-era desk, in front of the American flag. High drama. Major international players.

Formal, measured handshakes. A slight bow at the waist. An invitation to be seated.

Lieu surprisingly declined, remaining upright. His dark gray overcoat still in place, he didn't intend to stay long.

A confused look from Locke invited further explanation. The Chinese minister supplied it, a mere three feet away.

"Mr. Ambassador, I am here to inform you of the actions of the People's Republic of China in annexing American territory south of the Canadian province of British Columbia, bordered on the east by the Cascade Mountain Range, west by the Pacific Ocean, and to the south by the Columbia River."

Shockingly, he continued.

"This area, so designated, will become a new province of the PRC, ceasing to exist as sovereign territory of the United States and requiring the removal of American governmental and military personnel within seventy-two hours of acceptance of these actions. The civilian population will come under the laws and purview of the PRC and enjoy the rights and privileges of citizenship in our great nation. Refusal to comply with orders given here and those to come will result in a nuclear attack via our strategic fleet upon the western coast of the United States."

Lieu looked up.

The gravity of the moment settled, its weight and resulting disorientation.

Ambassador Locke stared back. The minister returned the same unflinching gaze.

Locke's mind raced at the implications for his nation and people. But he was an old hand, so his words came measured, slow, careful.

"*Minister* Lieu, if I am to understand you correctly, the United States of America is to hand over the most populous portion of Washington, its forty-second state, without reprisal, to your country. A state that has been a part of our union since 1889 and one fair state, I might add, I was privileged to serve as Governor for eight years. Is this what

I am hearing from you, minister?"

"Indeed, you are accurate in your assessments, Mr. Ambassador."

Lieu's words — cold, sterile — rocked even the experienced diplomat.

"So please help me understand then," he played out. "Why we wouldn't launch a preemptive nuclear attack to stop this provocation? If this is only a race to mutual destruction then I have a direct line to the White House. We will not hesitate to act unilaterally. You of course know this, Mr. Lieu."

The minister smiled, ever so slightly.

"You will comply Mr. Ambassador, because we have control of your weapons systems. They are no longer an option for you. The airliner crash in the city of Seattle yesterday? Tragic, but necessary. Simply the first example of our ability to re-purpose your communications networks across both civilian and military arenas."

Locke, stunned and angered by the assertion, immediately realized it to be possible. No systems were ever truly independent and completely protected. Highly secured — yes, but all systems based on computer code essentially came down to ones and zeros. With a better arrangement of those digits, all bets were off.

It was time to press the issue.

"Consider this event and all those lost a grave warning. You have no other options. Our superior military and technical resources have seen to it."

Lieu closed the black leather notebook, taking a first step away from the visibly shaken ambassador. He turned back for one last, critical statement.

"In case you are thinking of applying conventional armed tactics, please be advised the PRC will use its nuclear advantage. If you truly value the lives of the three million people in this region you will comply without delay. You may find me at the Central Committee offices, ready to receive your formal and unconditional surrender."

The minister's eyes narrowed.

"Three hours, Mr. Ambassador. I would advise that you not waste one minute on anything other than compliance and communication."

Lieu exited as he'd entered, a mere ten minutes before. For his part, Locke stood wondering how his world had changed so horrifically in such a brief span of time.

Then he got on the phone.

TEN

The WH Situation Room was full, every last cabinet official located and ushered into the national security sanctum within sixty minutes of initial word of the crisis out of Beijing. This task alone was no small matter, considering it was the middle of the night, East Coast Time.

"Overture is on station," the Agent in Charge whispered into the cuff-mic just short of his left hand.

All presidents receive a secret service call sign. This one was a respectful nod to his former life as an accomplished, semi-professional cellist.

Ladies and gentlemen, the President...

Chaotic chatter ceased and all stood in acknowledgment of their Commander-in-Chief.

Overture charged through the reinforced glass and steel doorway, disbelief mixed with pretty pissed off. Opening the proceedings, Ambassador Locke came alive on the floor to ceiling video wall, briefing the Chinese Minister's visit and demands.

"Mr. President, this was both unforeseen and unusual, as you might expect. China has not shown overt nationalistic aggression in decades, not revealing in any way a willingness to go toe to toe with America. I need to verify, Mr. President: have they captured our nuclear capabilities?

If so, how in the name of heaven did we find ourselves in this position? Do we have any kind of play besides handing over a third of the State of Washington?"

The president nodded to the Chairman of the Joint Chiefs.

"Mr. Ambassador," CJC reported. "We have confirmation from Strategic Command. A little over an hour ago we lost control of ordinance and delivery. NORAD is black. Bunkers are cold. Target and release on naval and air assets are unresponsive. Even the football is BSOD."

The small suitcase carrying portable launch capability, the football, was always within actionable reach of the president. BSOD simply meant no boot or control activity on the unit — 'blue screen of death', as computer techs lamented.

"We are scrambling to discover the issues and regain capabilities," the chairman continued. "At this point though sir, yes, we are without nuclear recourse."

The president spoke next.

"Gary, any back channels open? I'm having a hard time believing this is what they want, that they're threatening to slaughter millions of innocent people and turn Seattle into a moonscape."

Locke paused, exhaling.

"I dearly wish I could, Mr. President. This much is clear: they fully intend to extend their national boundaries to the west coast of the United States of America, beginning with Western Washington. It doesn't take great predictive powers to see this as an initial incursion with more still to come. Oregon, California, the entire Pacific Coast. Likely and logical next steps."

Gary extrapolated the idea.

"Sir, larger ambitions need a test case. You can't just take over a country of nearly 400 million people with one move. This action fits the mold. Capture an achievable amount of land and then attempt," the ambassador's voice trailed off. "To overthrow their people, economy, culture."

This was happening to his country. And at the hands of those so much like himself.

Locke was America's first state executive of Chinese lineage. The ambassador had always been proud. Given his people's cultural and technological achievements of the past two millennia this pride was rightly merited. Presently, none of this mattered.

The president recognized the angst in his friend's countenance. Of course, this would be especially difficult for him.

"Thank you, Mr. Ambassador. That will be all for now."

The screen went black, transformed again to only the Presidential Seal.

"Options, people. Scenarios."

Conversation grew animated. Sentences ran together, more stream of consciousness than distinct thoughts.

"What do we know?" the president posited. "And what is it we don't know that's going to kick us even harder in the ass still. Personally, I don't see how that could be possible. But I sure as Hades don't want to find out."

The Secretary of State chimed in.

"Russia stands with China. No surprise. Great Britain is politely not answering our request for a checkmate of sorts. France is a no. Israel is with us, although the range of their missiles is far short of an effective strike. They are also well aware of Russia's desire to use this as a pretext for aggression, to draw more Muslim nations into a back alley fight with the Jewish state. That leaves India and Pakistan, neither of whom want to step into this on our behalf."

SecState continued, swallowing hard. The case was distasteful, almost too painful to admit.

"Sir, I'm afraid we have no nuclear alliances at our disposal. None of our friends seem willing to enter a scorched-earth interchange with China over a portion of one of our fifty states."

The chairman of the chiefs spoke again.

"Mr. President, the implications are obvious and dire. Not only do we have no recourse. We also have no viable counter to provocations from any other bad actor. China will, because of their own expansionist interests, likely counter any threat of attack for now. Still, we cannot be certain. No one knows how this will play out."

"Protect the whole world for decades," SecDef mumbled. "And this is what we get."

It landed hard. The nuclear chess game America had played to its advantage for the past fifty years was now an utterly different board, with all new set pieces.

"How in the world... ?!!" the president started, slamming his briefing notebook down on hardened maple. "The most sophisticated launch and lock systems ever developed. How exactly did this happen?!"

Eyes averted his gaze, focusing on the page of intelligence notes in refuge. Slowly, they looked up. A few beats later the president continued, more in control.

"So I ask for possibilities and what you're telling me is my *only* move is to give them Starbucks, Mt. Rainier, and the grave site of Jimi Hendrix."

Five Hours Later: The Oval Office

My fellow Americans...

Following a long line of Chief Executives, the president began his nationwide broadcast with this singular, inclusive opening. Preempting every sporting, news, and entertainment offering currently airing, the executive reserved this privilege for moments with dire national security or natural disaster implications. This moment qualified as such. Television, radio, and web audiences across the country dropped everything. They knew no details, other than to expect something important from their elected leader and his cabinet.

"It is with a heavy heart..." he began. "... a sense of deep earnestness that I come to you today as your president..."

The ninety minutes following the situation room meeting stormed with political, military, and diplomatic activity at 1600 Pennsylvania Avenue, the Capitol Building, CIA Headquarters in Langley, NSA, and the Pentagon. Key leaders and thinkers pressed into action. Each one producing the same answers, every report effectively concluding: without a nuclear strike option and no allies standing by the U.S.'s hands were tied.

The only move?

Capitulation. Submission.

The timeline closed like a vice and the National Security team made the call no one wanted to. A scant thirty minutes before deadline Ambassador Locke signed documents that for the first time gave away United States territory to a foreign aggressor without so much as a single shot fired.

No boots on the ground. No warplanes in her airspace.

Though not uncommon in the history of nations and kingdoms it was a serious offense to this young country believing such a fate beyond them. To date, America's unbroken, westward expansion had experienced no real challenges to her desire for continental wholeness. Her super-powered presence in the world, even throughout economic recession and monumental cultural shifts, had remained undaunted, unstoppable.

At least until now, as the vast majority of American citizens heard the news directly from their president.

"... as unbelievable as this seems, I have no other choice than to yield to the People's Republic of China and order the peaceful transition of United States military and governmental assets out of the Puget Sound Region. I am advising all civilians to remain calm, to not interfere in any way with the process of annexation. Your cooperation in the days and weeks to come will ensure the avoidance of unnecessary loss of life and property."

He paused, having a hard time coming to grips with the words proceeding from his mouth, as well as those cued on the TelePrompTer.

"The Chinese government has given their assurances. Opportunities for portions of the civilian population to leave, to immigrate to the broader American States, will come over time. For now, all non-military and police personnel are to stay in place, resuming their daily activities as ordered. We have been warned. Unauthorized movements of residents will garner a nuclear response. Chinese military and governmental leadership will begin their transfer into the region seventy-two hours from now."

Head lowered, his tired eyes left the camera frame. More pastoral than presidential, he offered an honest appeal:

"Heaven help us. Heaven help us all."

Ten minutes later the lighting and production crew had packed and gone. The Secretary of Defense, the Chairman of the Joint Chiefs, and the National Security Advisor remained.

The president looked them straight on and spoke clearly, calmly.

"I don't care how you do it. I don't care what it costs us. Get our nukes back. Get them back, *now*."

ELEVEN

Junjie's worst fears had not only been realized, they'd been surpassed ten-fold. He dearly wanted to be surprised by the events raging around him. This was not the case.

The young man sat alone, shocked and processing what it all meant. The TV affixed to the wall lay muted, even as the broadcast video stream played on. Not unexpectedly, local anchors carried a different tone than that of their American counterparts. Beijing's official statements spoke of "national glory" and the "natural and destined expansion of superior Chinese culture and life." Junjie's response was something altogether less positive, having vomited twice so far in his private washroom. The aftertaste only underscored his horror.

I could have stopped this from happening. I should have stopped this from happening.

The self-beating was neither constructive nor fair. Still, the what-if scenarios flowed unabated, wildfire over dry timber. Weariness of body and soul pressed down on his weakened frame like a schoolyard bully. Over the last 48 hours sleep had completely evaded the young man, leaving him only more susceptible to these persistent internal recriminations.

But it's not as if he'd only fought this battle in his mind.

Following their final project meeting, he had gone down to the company's twenty-third floor server farm. At the control stations and under the guise of checking in, he fantasized about pulling one giant plug out of the wall, shutting the whole enterprise down.

Just pull the plug, Junjie. Game over.

A simplistic solution was no match for what he and his colleagues had developed. Their systems sat leagues above anything else, anywhere in the world. The intricate interplay of energy grids, hardware, and visual interfaces in this room remained impervious to even the latest and most sinister attacks, much less a basic power-down sequence: an "on/ off" button. He knew. He had hired the best to try it.

Six months prior to launch Junjie quietly contracted with the hacktivist group MilwOrm. Infamous for their penetration of the Bhabha Atomic Research Centre (BARC— Mumbai) in 1998, their team was especially adept at breaching high end defense and power systems. The challenge? Take the beta version of Dawn Star's technology on a shakedown cruise. Three weeks. Every opportunity to prevail upon the code.

At every turn they failed.

Again, classic good news-bad news.

The young man couldn't shake it. This was the vision from which he wanted to wake, finding it merely the result of bad pizza and too many beers. He was one of a handful of people on the planet holding detailed, intimate understanding of what their work could do. Now, seeing his government's actions, the code's full reach slapped him in the face.

He was so very conflicted.

Initially, Junjie had seen nothing but upside. Surprised the contract had been awarded to his then-unknown firm, he couldn't wait to tell his wife.

Dai-tai was always learning; one of the many reasons Junjie loved her so. Dai's given name meant "leading a boy in hopes" and Zang was still smitten, captured by her and the hope she brought him daily, even twelve years on. Her dark eyes radiated both warmth and infinite curiosity. She was as playful and twice his intellect. Intimidating? No, instead he felt greatly blessed to be partnering with someone of her depth and beauty. Together they'd brought a precious son, now almost two, into this world. With her by his side, Junjie could attempt anything, fail or succeed.

Displaying a flair for the dramatic, Junjie placed the award letter, folded in half, inside a book, then waited impatiently.

"Bao Bao, what are you reading these days?" he probed, eyes smiling as they leaned back in bed, lights dimmed overhead.

"Oh, nothing of real significance," she said, enjoying the term of endearment. "... a boring story about a boy and a girl. They fall in love, have children..."

Her gaze moved off the page and into his waiting eyes. All pretense left behind, she leaned in close, right hand opened against the side of his chin.

"... and, his company is awarded the biggest contract they've ever seen... they work hard and live happily ever after."

"Junjie," she said. "I am so very proud of you."

The long workdays were more than either bargained for. Yet even in the hardest moments, exhaustion showing on

Dai's face and body, they shared a core, sustaining belief: they were in this together. They would come out of this season intact, even stronger.

Pulled back to the present, Junjie realized his terrible trade, his fatal miscalculation. The project had enriched his bank account and kick-started his career, this was true. It was also obvious now to have morally impoverished his family and his country. Had he shared with Dai his fears about the government's requests, she would've stood in strong, principled opposition.

Why had his most trusted advisor been left outside the loop?

Pride, arrogance?

Likely.

He only knew he regretted it deeply. But regret can be channeled. And in those few minutes of reflection, his pain, despair, and confusion gave way to resolve, and a right— even righteous—anger at all that had unfolded.

What he must now do, what was required, became clearer every moment.

TWELVE

The dark figure moved efficiently throughout the home office area of the downtown Beijing apartment.

With gloved right hand the intruder rifled each drawer in the light maple desk. Behind him, the body on the floor posed unnaturally, growing colder, rigor mortis settling. The man continued, scanning email accounts and then removing the hard drive. Finally, he shorted out the motherboard, completing the assignment. Most importantly, the actual threat—the elite coding skills of the victim—sat useless on thin, worn carpet, vanished to the ether at the ceasing of brain function.

The cell phone on the dining room table rang. The visitor turned. The caller ID tag lit in electronic blue, contrasting against the darkened space.

Zang, Junjie.

On the other end: a desperate, barely audible plea.

"Come on, Lee. Pick up. Pick it up."

A brief recorded message left by a voice—no, a person—now forever silenced.

The tone.

"Lee, this is Junjie. You need to get back to me as soon as you can. The backdoor... I can only get it partially open. I need your help. Please, get back to me."

Sensing just how far behind the curve he might be, the young executive immediately questioned the wisdom of such a call.

Lee Quan, the dead man, was one of Junjie's earliest hires. A meet over coffee on his first official recruiting trip. Quan, referred by a friend of a friend, came with the highest recommendations.

After American schooling, Lee returned home with an MIT double doctorate in math and computer sciences, hoping to move his people more fully into the modern age of communication. While Quan could have filled many posts in the emerging tech marketplace as a brilliant mathematician, the young man found his true calling in ones and zeros. Millions of lines of sterile commands: most people's summary of his work. Quan saw possibilities, even beauty. On his best days he fashioned himself more binary artist than simple code-jockey.

The young cohorts' professional collaboration blossomed, in rather short time, into a real and honest friendship. As one of the first to alert Junjie to the ever-growing demands of their government overseers, Quan's voice and mind was a key asset, at every step. Had he known at the time of this call that his friend and co-worker now lay dead, he would have immediately and deeply mourned his passing.

The stranger in Quan's apartment transmitted his initial report:

Clean at Quan. Moving down list.
Zang trying to contact.
Move JZ up list?

Three calls and hushed voice mails later, finally an answer.

"Feng, it is so good to hear your voice. You have been watching the reports?"

"I have. Did we really do this, my friend? Is this what has come from our labors? Please tell me this is not what it seems."

Feng Wan, as distraught as Junjie, welcomed his boss's reassuring voice as centering strength in a world suddenly and violently upturned. Like his friend, he knew their work stood at the heart of this audacious power grab. He also knew they must reverse the deed. He'd briefly considered the culturally noble gesture of taking his own life, to appease the universe. But now, knife set aside, he wept in brokenness.

The call distracted from his tears. If there was a chance of stopping this madness, then Feng garnered strength from simply hearing his friend's voice. While odds of success against the massive governmental machine were long and lonely, the call returned some fight to his heart.

"Feng. Listen to me. There is no time. None at all."

He conveyed his fears about Quan, choking back what he knew as likely.

"We can do this. But I need your help. And a favor."

"Anything, Junjie. Anything."

"The number I gave you a few months back. You must call it. Now. Go ahead, open another line."

A near silent click and a tone. A few more keystrokes and the line closed.

Junjie could not vocally express his relief, certain of ears everywhere. But, in holding back his breath, he was also certain that his family would now be safe.

"Junjie," Feng started again. "I know this is not the time for more bad news. But I have more bad news."

Junjie waited.

"The backdoor. I took a quick look. I thought you might be heading there yourself. I am not sure how to say this… "

"Feng, please..."

"You made it worse."

Junjie nearly drove off the road.

"In what way, exactly?"

"We always knew this could happen. The ledge between power and self-choice was very thin. Your attempt to lower the first opened the possibility of the last."

The statement threw Junjie back in time, recalling engineering workgroups often more undergrad philosophy class than tech firm production meeting. But that's only because they knew what they were playing around with.

"Alright. No more details. I am on my way."

Thirty minutes later Junjie parked on the third level below ground of the Beaufort residential complex.

A loner with no hobbies of note, Feng spent little of his significant salary. No mistress, so no clothes and gifts. No extravagant nightlife. An audacious man he was not. So, towering glass and steel stood as a mismatch, a contradiction to his austerity. In the end, consultants convinced Feng it would be a good investment, a relatively stable place to deposit some of his newly found wealth. He signed, paying in cash but never quite feeling at home in the extravagance.

In the elevator, Junjie pressed the button for the main floor. Once there he strode across the crowded lobby, folding into the normal, workaday flow. Everything appeared routine, residents languid. No obvious unease. Had no one gotten the memo they were taking a part of the U.S. as their own?

Maybe they were pleased.

Slipping into the elevators to Feng's tenth-floor apartment, Junjie avoided the security cameras. Arriving, the doors opened again. He exited tentatively, down the hallway.

Ten feet away: the door — ajar.

No. Please, no.

Minor clues of forced entry. A bent latch. Wood casing splinters.

Summoning basic courage, he opened the door.

A first, cautious step.

The modern, open-concept space showed as neither spotless nor total disaster. This was no panicked, chaotic scene. Whoever entered before Junjie knew what or who they were looking for. Painstakingly, he crossed the fifteen or so feet ahead. He stopped, lungs heaving, heart racing.

Feng's feet dangled, visible at the edge of the kitchen entryway and completely still.

The single fixture over the sink illuminated the scene poorly. It was quite possible he and Feng were not alone. Hiding, somewhere near, would not be difficult.

Junjie approached. No movement. His friend's chest cavity neither rose nor fell. Junjie's eyes grew bigger. Mountains of anger and sorrow found expression. The young man flailed against the stainless steel fridge door, stringy bangs of jet-black hair in both hands. Defeated and lost, he railed back forcefully, right heel striking cold metal.

Feng's body lurched. A painful upward motion. Sudden, vigorous gasping for breath, for life.

Junjie rushed to his friend's side and placed cupped hands under his head and neck. A slow, steady stream of blood flowed from behind Feng's left ear, pooling at Junjie's wrists. The mortally wounded man coughed, eyes confessing fear of imminent death. His lips moved little. His gaze, locked but unfocused. The pale man's mouth opened and closed spasmodically. Junjie couldn't distill a single word from the harsh mixture of heavy blood and faint voice. Feng's trachea rattled a final time. Entreating eyes fixed upward and then closed. His body relaxed. The release of bodily tension stretched the dead man's clothes, pulling a small piece of paper into full view from his shirt pocket.

Junjie thought back to his approach into the kitchen. Yes, he had seen it before. It just hadn't mattered in light of his friend's condition. Now, it begged attention. He took it out and unfolded it.

Stop.

Turn around.

Enjoy.

The first two words startled, his head snapping around, eyes darting across the space. His skin tingled, protective, senses on high alert. After a few seconds, silence. No one else in the apartment.

He looked at the paper again. That last word, initially out of place, made sense as Junjie woke up to the moment.

Dhe knows about the backdoor. The choice is mine. I can go back to leisure and prosperity.

"No," Junjie breathed. "That is no longer possible."

Two things mattered.

Protecting his family and destroying what he had loosed upon the world.

Junjie rested Feng's head on the floor. He so desired to stay. Moving on only tore an ever deeper hole, forcing a hasty goodbye that instead should have lingered. But there was simply no time. And no where else to turn.

Except the very place he no longer was convinced of a welcome.

THIRTEEN

Swedish Medical Center's First Hill Campus was overrun with casualties.

Every sixty seconds or so the hydraulic whoosh of the emergency room entrance ushered in another tragedy. Gurneys rolled off the back of ambulances. Some stepped out of family cars in the drop-off zone, proceeding feebly yet upright, toward help. Others showed up due to the kindness of strangers, an innate empathy surfacing amidst chaos. A wide range of traumas thrust itself upon the staff and resources of the hospital. Many took merely a glance to pronounce their fatality. All that was left was pain management and a gentle waiting for the inevitable. Families and friends, if present, marking these last few hours of life together.

Conscious or not, no one wants to die alone.

Other scenarios demanded vigorous, defiant battle against failing biology; every technique applied, every effort given. With even a slim chance of survival, skilled and brave healers would stop at nothing to win this round. Some of the wounded stabilized, regenerated, and revitalized. Many did not survive the day. Those bearing minor afflictions would rebound in time, at least physically. Gauze, tape, and a few stitches would cure their presenting injuries. But another wound, this one emotional and psychological, was beginning to spread; the gaping, infected sore it would soon enough become.

Stopped, frozen in time.

The president's statements left them speechless.

Throughout every floor medical, social services, and administrative staff ceased valiant efforts, staring silently. Many, gathered to pray and await word of their loved ones' conditions, now faced an entirely new set of challenges.

Dalton was as stunned as anyone else.

His last moments at Pike Place left him with an uneasy feeling, an unshakable sense that the destruction and loss of life sprang from more than random accident. What he heard now flew beyond the pale. More than a terrorist attack. Far deeper than that considerable pain and shock.

This was an invasion.

It was in fact, all too surreal. For now, panic remained eerily distant. A strange quietness. A lull. A collective disbelief held everyone in place and calm. Then, in rapid succession, the dots connected. Women began crying, men's cheeks turned red, bloating in rage at their impotence to act on that most basic of instincts—to protect those around them. Children took their cues from nearby adults.

The horrors of the last twenty-four hours landed initially as pain without purpose. Eight-hundred-twenty-four souls lost at the market was harsh enough. Soon, these people would also lose everything they valued as Americans. Two centuries-plus without facing subjection to a foreign power. No current citizen of this great nation had ever felt the sting of such powerlessness.

Two hundred years.

Two hundred years making them feel safer than they should have presumed; far more than the historical norm. Unthinkable — yes, but it was indeed happening. Now, in their lifetimes. This generation would swallow submission's bitter pill, all at once.

Dalton broke from the crowded room. Once around the corner he tried to gain the young woman's attention at the call station.

"Excuse me, Miss?"

She stood there, consumed by her president's words.

Again.

"Excuse me... Miss?"

She looked up and cried.

Dalton treaded lightly. He wasn't the king of tact. Neither was he a complete interpersonal dolt.

"Miss," he tried once more. "I just wanted to see if the young woman I'd inquired about is doing any better."

Dalton's injuries didn't really meet the needs test. His body would be fine if he took it easy. A few tender ribs on his right side. Left shin mildly sore. Other than that his thirty-something frame had held up reasonably well, considering.

He gave the nurse a softer, knowing look.

She found her voice again, ignoring her fears in favor of caring for others. "Uh... so sorry. Of course. Her name, again?"

"Maryska. First name is Maryska. That's all I got."

"Family member?" she asked, staring blankly past and out into the open hallway as an overload of patients waited, being assessed and prepped.

Dalton looked her in the eye, trying to draw her back. An obvious *really?* played across his face. Minimally compassionate, he was also very impatient.

"Oh, yes. Here she is..." Looking at her computer screen. "Doing much better. Smoke inhalation. She's resting now."

Good to hear.

This news now—that she would recover? A small, welcomed blessing on a day of such multiplying sorrows.

The waiting room TV caught his attention, changing from DC to local broadcast, an important follow-up expected.

With a single podium in focus, the Capitol Building Rotunda filled the rest of the shot. Polished marble floors, high, arched ceilings. Weighty symbols on every wall and mantle. The physical volume of the space magnified the smallest of sounds, making the vacuous dome even more ominous. Crews scrambled, setting lights and running cables while aides and interns rushed about. The last worker-bee exited the frame as Paul Tilden, Director of Emergency and Disaster Services for the State of Washington, stepped up to the platform and the bouquet of microphones. Printed page in hand and experiencing as much shock as everyone else he addressed the viewers while network and cable outlets carried these historic events to every corner of the United States and abroad.

"As of 12:00 pm Pacific Standard Time," he began. "The Governor's Office has enacted Executive Code 3315.76. I will read its full text:

'Residents of the Puget Sound Region are to remain in their locales while transitioning to Chinese military leadership over the next seventy-two hours. All citizens are ordered to stay within five miles of their legal place of residence until regular routines are established.'"

A cough. He continued. "'Municipal and County law enforcement agencies will ensure this is achieved in an orderly fashion. Checkpoints on major arterials will be secured and photo identification required at every stop. Once the new authorities assume their place, police and sheriff's departments will disarm and decommission, yielding to the transitional government."

Looking up from prepared notes and into the camera.

"This is a necessary measure ensuring the greater public safety. Please, please do not endanger your fellow citizens by engaging in reckless, useless acts of rebellion or refusal."

A pause, considering his next words.

"If there was any other way, I would say 'fight'. There isn't. So don't. Please... don't."

This last statement—unscripted—translated as heartfelt plea.

Dalton backed away from the screen and sped toward the front lobby entrance. Conversations arose in the waiting room, a few defiantly. Others attempted to talk the would-be rebels out of their foolishness. Many were simply scared.

The Chinese demanded civilians and law enforcement stay in place until their authority could be established. It made sense. They needed bodies, workers. The other option, a mass transfer of citizens from the Chinese mainland, was both impractical and not really the point. To conquer territory was one thing. Transforming a people, something completely other. And if no Americans remained—no one to threaten with nuclear force—Chinese leverage shrunk considerably.

Former US citizens, resuming their daily lives under the watchfulness of Beijing? This was the lynch-pin.

The orders out of Beijing, accepted in DC and echoed in Olympia, were to stand down. Clearly, some could never stomach such a thing, regardless of the consequences.

Dalton knew it.

Without a doubt, there would be runners.

In that moment he decided he'd be one.

And that the only other person he cared about in this life would be alongside.

It took two and a half hours to defeat the quickly developing maze of barricades and checkpoints. His mind had been in overdrive, calculating force, time, and flow. Consulting the live map in his head got him to within a block, undetected. With one last look down the street Dalton slipped past the aging fence line and disappeared into an egress window-well. The latch came up easily and he wedged, feet first, onto surprisingly soft carpet.

No more nasty shag, huh? And where did the old wood paneling go?

Mildly surprised by the changes, much of the room remained as he remembered. Same oversized chair and metal desk. Trophies. Certificates. The NASA posters, instead of the Farrah Fawcett image his mom had absolutely disallowed. Its complete life cycle the time it took for him to get it home from the mall and up on his wall.

Seven steps and he was in the kitchen.

Three more and Dalton saw her.

She turned, must have sensed his presence.

"Mom."

Her look stopped him short of any more words, at least at that volume.

"Zeb," she smiled finally. "I knew you'd come."

"We have to go," he begged quietly "Now."

Her hand went up.

He kept talking, a thousand miles an hour about a plan to get them both out to the coast and then down to Oregon. Something about the Chinese Navy being the slowest component of their military net.

If they could just get out of Seattle by nightfall…

Her hand flattened toward him as a tinny command made its way from the street and into the living room.

"… fall in immediately."

The voice was American, carrying the unmistakable air of practiced authority.

"…you have two minutes…"

"Mom, no. We can do this…"

"No, dear. I can't," she replied, her eyes dropping off Dalton and onto the dining room table.

He followed her gaze. Two piles of mail, one neat and unopened. The other considerably less organized.

Dalton took a step that direction.

Fred Hutchinson Cancer Center jumped from the top left of every envelope.

He turned back, longing for clarity.

From outside again: "Mrs. Dalton. *Please*, don't make us come in."

"Zeb," his mom interjected. "Listen to me. Trust in…"

"Are you serious? Now, Mom? The last thing I need is a sermon. I just need to get you out of here."

"Son, I'm sick. Don't know much yet but I would only slow you down. Probably just get us shot."

"But..."

"No. I am going to turn around and go through this door. I know you'll do the right thing. Always have. My beautiful boy with the gift. You'll figure it out. And," she held the doorknob, giving it a half turn, "there's a note for you on the buffet. Nice man came by earlier. Said you'd want to," she winked, "...put it down the disposal after reading it."

Dalton wanted to surge forward, grab her and keep her from the horrors he knew lay ahead. Or at least stay and endure them together. But that was impossible. She'd said so herself. The gift. The uniqueness that had always compelled him to action.

She slipped out the door.

Dalton reached but she was gone. The lean brought him inches past the front room wall.

Two more voices outside and a flurry of movement meant they'd seen something through the living room windows, enough to become agitated.

Crap.

Dalton was at the buffet in two steps, note in hand and headed toward the back door in two more.

One man came in the front. One had just closed the side gate, turned away for the slightest instance, unaware of the kitchen storm door to his left.

Shoe met metal and metal met spine. Dalton saw him crumple, running past as the man's shoulder patch showed *King County Sheriff.*

I am so sorry.

Shouts and footsteps. More running and Dalton was over the backyard fence and into the alley.

Barking and teeth.

Mrs. March's stupid dog. That thing can't still be alive.

A quick jag to the left and he was around the corner.

More barking, with other voices yelling at the dog and fading in the distance.

Good boy.

A small patch of woods beckoned, about a hundred more steps. Reasonably in the dark and safe he slowed and then stopped at the base of an eighty-five foot fir tree. A few breaths later, Dalton grieved leaving his mom behind.

He pulled out the note and felt even worse.

A single word: *Sovereign.*

His release from the Army had one recall condition, the only circumstances under which he would reactivate. He'd be left alone unless he was literally the only one meeting a very specific operational criteria. The only one capable of undoing something that was his work to begin with.

The plane crash and nuclear commandeering. The takeover and coming invasion. His mom and countless others.

It hit him with unbending judgment.

The code was his.

FOURTEEN

Sergeant First Class Jessica Sanchez—Army I Corps, moved undetected along the tree line off the main airfield at Joint Base (Army, Air-Force) Lewis-McChord.

The frenzy of activity at JBLM, an hour south of Seattle and only a few miles outside Washington State's fourth most populous area—Tacoma—provided ample cover for her unauthorized exit. The twenty-eight-year-old Sniper Assessment School Instructor was doing what she did best.

Disappear, completely.

Even without the roaring chorus of C17 cargo planes she could've walked past the perimeter guard and into the distance without so much as a broken twig betraying her presence. She was that good. That JBLM's 25,000 active duty and administrative personnel were being hastily evacuated and resettled east of the Cascade Mountain range made it not much of a challenge at all. Under threat of nuclear strike the Army had twenty-some hours left of the seventy-two they'd been given, leaving the city-sized compound for the invading forces. Such controlled chaos fit her advantage, perfectly.

Her "kit" was a little different than your regular sniper tech. Not currently active-duty in the strictest sense, she carried the older M24 rifle with Leupold Mk 4 LR/T M3 3.5-

10-40mm variable power scope. Preferring as much flexibility as possible in the field, this setup would work just fine.

After six tours in Iraq and Afghanistan she was battle-tested yet not battle hardened, rare outcomes for someone in her position. The transition from hot zone combat had been, thankfully, easier than what many other good men and women had experienced. She'd had help. Sanchez' CO understood when to call it quits on her behalf. After the initial distaste, her disappointment morphed to thankfulness, a quiet appreciation she needn't press fate one more time. She had performed at the highest levels in the harshest of circumstances, serving her country with honor and distinction. The seasoned warrior turned from ops to prep, training up the next generation of stealthy warriors.

For the last two years Sanchez had run a pre-qualifying unit at the joint-forces base in Washington, functioning as the prelim filter for the rookie classes of the formal two-year sniper school at Fort Benning, Georgia. Ever the demanding tutor, her students stormed the program at Benning, carrying excellence and valor in her stead.

Sanchez wasn't averse to lethal force, applied in wartime. Bothering herself with the bigger questions involved always seemed a few steps removed from the needs of the moment. She didn't enjoy it. She found it necessary. The young officer bore the intellect, body type, training, and personality to do the job, so she would get it done, whatever that meant. Make no mistake, the sergeant would start a shooting war with China on her own if needed. But her main goal right now, the second vital skill-set of sniper personnel, was battlefield recon. Her country would need eyes on as their new bosses settled into place in Western Washington. So, having received the requisite communique, her first act of patriotism was simply to go away, to become a non-person in the surrounding environment.

She slid further into the unending stand of towering evergreens, relaxing only the slightest bit, enough to look back at what was sadly becoming a ghost town.

Unbelievable. Just unbelievable.

"Not the end of the story, though," she whispered. "Not if I have a say."

Three hundred yards from Sanchez' position, Major General *Mike Stevens,* US Army I Corps, Commanding Officer JBLM, stood stock-still, as endless lines of men and materiel flowed into the gargantuan flying containers known as the C17 Globemaster III. The Boeing cargo carriers ferried American combat troops and equipment wherever and whenever needed, answering every planned for and unannounced call of duty. They had been reduced now to little more than an expensive fleet of flying moving trucks for the retreating U.S. forces. *Disgusting* was the acceptable version coming to mind, each liftoff planting only increased bitterness in the general's mouth; a taste few American leaders had ever been forced to experience.

He reviewed mentally.

The last full-forces retreat of the U.S. Army was in 1975. Ending the extended conflict in Southeast Asia reluctantly, the South Vietnamese had been left to fight on their own against advancing northern soldiers. But the current situation was unsurveyed territory. For the first time, U.S. troops were removing themselves from American soil and under the direct orders of another sovereign nation. As both historian and battlefield commander, the general revolted at the thought.

"Colonel Meers, operational status?"

"Sir," the colonel replied. "We are on time for completed evac as of 0800 tomorrow. Resettlement facilities are coming online in Wenatchee. Arrival and formation of command structure is in process as we speak. New runways are active and barracks are scheduled for completion in the next twenty-four hours."

The general's mind fixed on the impact to be absorbed by the sudden imposition of 25,000 men and women and a major wartime outpost on the small city of 32,000 on the other side of the Cascades.

"Well, they said we'd have to move over the mountains. They didn't say *how* far, now did they, Colonel?"

The subordinate officer half-smiled.

"No, sir... they did not."

"Alright then, Meers. Keep me apprised of progress. You and I will be the ones to shut the lights off when we leave."

Stevens followed orders, even those he could barely stomach. He also carried a fire in his belly telling him this wouldn't be the last time he stood here as Commander of Army I Corps. Leaning down, he picked up a small rock. Placing it into the right breast pocket of his uniform, he made a solemn vow: to return it upon recapturing this sacred ground. The general's thoughts shifted yet again, focusing on the 2.5 million civilian residents they were leaving behind.

His life's work? To protect and defend the Constitution of the United States of America, and by extension, to protect and defend all who lived under the rights enumerated in this cherished document.

Stevens could not foresee what would happen but he knew this: he wanted to fight, to bring every resource and tactic he had to recapture and secure his people's freedoms. At the moment, there was nothing more to do than wait. Wait, and plan. And then wait some more. But he also knew this: she was out there. He couldn't see her—certainly from here—and likely not even were he right on top of her position. But he knew she was there. Waiting as well.

That made him smile, even as the last plane left the tarmac and sun touched the horizon.

FIFTEEN

"That can't be good," the wife mumbled, hovering over her phone's screen.

"What, honey? What?" the husband replied from the driver's seat.

The mid-thirties woman tried to keep the light dim. Most patrols were now almost fully Chinese military, and considerably less friendly than the interim American counterparts. The last thing they wanted or needed was for a trigger happy soldier to find Dalton under some blankets in the rear storage area of the minivan.

"No," she said to the image. "Don't be so stupid."

"What? What's going on, babe?"

Her eyes widened in fear.

"Pike… Place," she stammered. "Must be ten thousand people."

Dalton added his voice now.

"Ma'am, please, just tell us what's happening."

"People everywhere. Sidewalks couldn't hold any more. Everybody's yelling."

She stopped, inhaling sharply. "Ten, no twelve, Chinese soldiers. Backed up to the edge of the plane debris. Disarmed and the crowd is pushing them toward the wreckage."

It was exactly what Dalton had feared. American pride, foolishness. Or maybe courage.

Sometimes they look the same.

Undisclosed location: Western Pacific Ocean,
off the Coast of China

"Fire control, this is your captain. Commence firing sequence on my mark. Mark, three, two… "

Pike Place

The four square block area lit Pike Place in eerie blue luminescence. The contrast against the darkening light of the end of day and the fact that the crowd had shattered almost every street light in reach, was stunning. Among the many gathered in some vain attempt at liberty every single digital device broadcast the same image. Dawn Star's technology showed itself useful once again. The Chinese digitally commandeered every screen the crowd was carrying. People felt a buzzing. Text notice tones went off. Pulling them out, they all saw the same thing.

Video of a launch with timestamp and countdown gracing the bottom of the frame.

A split screen. The message, unmistakable. On the left side, the remaining countdown and flight path image. On the right, a satellite shot of the crowd itself from overhead. The numbers were far too low.

0:03:53

The Chinese were giving them one last chance to disperse.

Back in the car, the woman willed the crowd to do the right thing.

"Please," she begged from a few hours away. "Please, please."

Dalton found himself on his knees, leaning into the seatback, as forward toward the unfolding saga as he could get without revealing himself in the rear of the van.

The leftmost screenshot changed, pulling up, far above the city, enough to reveal a wide angle covering the entirety of Puget Sound. Two airborne projectiles streaked eastward across the Olympic Range.

Chaos ensued at Pike Place. It was ragged and ugly. People lay trampled. Broken limbs. A few suffering punctured lungs from sharp objects the more aggressive in the crowd carried.

Ten thousand people ran for their lives, in every direction.

"Fire control... disengage flight and detonation sequence..."

The missiles obeyed, their trajectory sharpening earthward. Splashing down into choppy green, they began their descent to the muddy bottom, some two hundred feet below.

The van pulled over, coming to an abrupt stop.

"Out," was all the man said, looking away.

Dalton heard him.

"I said get *out*," he repeated. "Now."

No longer willing to aid and abet, they left the fugitive on the side of the road in quickly darkening twilight.

This event was Stage Two of Dalton's illegal exodus. Stage One had been five days of slow, methodical progress from urban space to eastern fringe. It was a nerve-racking sequence of obtaining cover and then moving on rapidly as the moment demanded. The tail end of these days he'd found himself in the back of an old pickup truck, winding along backroads and then laying still for an hour at a truck stop. There he had transferred to the couple's 1988 Toyota Previa van for a truncated trip up the two lane, ascending elevations of the Cascades. Now? Dalton was lying low in the forested hillsides, just shy of the ski slopes at Snoqualmie Pass. Though peaceful, the security checkpoint below only ratcheted up the sense of dread now draping the region. The guards seemed extra vigilant. That made sense, given that in the last two hours the city of Seattle had narrowly escaped nuclear annihilation.

For his part, Dalton had been extremely lucky advancing this far.

One of three highway passes through the Cascades, Snoqualmie was now closed, a no-proceed zone. Checkpoints like this one had come online only hours after the official surrender from D.C. This post, outside of any specific municipality, was monitored by Washington State Patrol. No less than three cruisers, two SUVs, and a mobile communications trailer blocked the only way through and out of the area. The new Chinese province was being sealed off at every turn.

The former State of Washington, with its natural barrier of the Cascades to the east, the Pacific Ocean as its western demarcation, and the Columbia River to the south, provided an ideal set of borders, easily defended, especially when you carried a weapon of mass destruction advantage in your pocket. Yet, even without nukes, the topography could secure an international border by itself. They'd planned for this, done their homework. Virtually no one could survive the wilderness of the Cascades, so it made sense only a few policed stations would be required along these mountainous routes. The possibility of a much smaller invading force becomes reality when such barriers replace thousands of troops. As added precaution, neighboring governments were called upon to do their part.

The Canadians complied, assuming authority at the Blaine crossing in the north. Stopping Washingtonians from immigrating kept them clear of two outcomes: blame for a possible nuclear attack, and the potential radiation fallout mess incurred from shifting winds. America's closest friends stood at a distance, arms and borders closed. To be fair, they mostly had their hands tied.

Dalton looked up from his seated position, hidden in heavy underbrush. Blockaded by concrete pilings, the passage up and over the mountains winnowed down to one entrance/ exit lane. Passing through without inspection would be impossible. Sweeping the forest on the west, nearest the gate, Dalton surmised they needed no such presence there, either. Though not seeing over the edge, he didn't need a front row seat to get the picture.

His assumptions were correct. The roadway dropped off beyond the pavement, a few hundred feet of sheer wilderness awaiting. No guardrail. It wouldn't help, so it was never constructed. Anyone bypassing this station needed to be an extreme conditions expert and skilled mountaineer.

One option remained: the woods east of the road. His only shot at getting past the officers. Only one problem. Twenty-five yards from Dalton's position large, portable light stanchions illuminated the dark, forested void. Hating it, the troopers did their job nonetheless.

Viewing the police routine, Dalton devised a strategy. Shift movements and protocol over the last two hours provided intel for getting through this checkpoint and over the mountains.

The trek would top out at over 4,000 feet. He needed assurance of where he was headed. Surviving this lunacy depended on following a basic outline of the roadways — in this case Interstate 90 — while maintaining anonymity to any patrols happening by. Even with Dalton''s extensive training and field experience, traipsing off into the untamed Cascade Range was, well, crazy. It was springtime in the Northwest. At elevation, temperatures would still drop below freezing after sunset.

40.6673%.

Dalton's calculations of getting over the mountains alive stared at him like a giant hovering dare. If the nighttime cold and rigorous traverse didn't do him in, there was always the occasional bear or cougar to turn the tables of nature, making him the hunted. Emerging from a lean winter would make them more likely to take on any kind of foe. He shuddered at the thought.

Though the plan was settled, planning alone wouldn't guarantee him success. Dalton had a strategy for after he got through the checkpoint. For this first step, escaping the troopers and lights, he was in need of some raw luck.

Crescendoing up the mountain roadside, increasing in volume and authority every few feet: a car full of runners, committed to escaping the region one way or another.

Had they not seen what just happened at Pike Place? Or did they still not care?

The sound arrived, announcing the driver's intentions of neither slowing nor stopping. Coming into view in the dark, clear air the Hummer H3 abandoned any pretense of compliance, heading straight for the concrete barriers. Closing. Closer still. But in the face of raised rifles and handguns their commitment wavered. They swerved forcefully to the left—the western, unprotected side of the alpine roadway.

85mph.

Science was not in their favor. The physics were unyielding, brutal. Front wheels jammed hard left, as if a last-minute change of heart would cause the car to obey, turning back and sending them merrily back down to the city.

No.

The 5000 lb. vehicle shifted onto her passenger side, rushing toward the cliff-like edge of the two-lane mountain highway. Unbroken kinetic energy turned into spiraling motion as the car leapt from the road, into the emptiness and landing in the small, tree-lined valley below. The impact was nearly silent at this height and distance. The visual of the impact was not.

Exploding fuel and combustible liquids lit the night sky, revealing hundred-foot firs and the peaks themselves. A strangely beautiful sight, the conflagration served as backlighting for a horrendous scene of destruction and senseless loss of life. The patrolmen holstered and responded, rushing to the edge of the roadway. Not a thing they could do.

It was all Dalton needed. He'd receive no better cover. Up the mountainside, hugging the line of the road—just east by fifteen or so meters—he left the scenic recreational spot behind.

SIXTEEN

The soothing rhythm of wheels over tracks partnered with a soft, gray sky. Together, the two made a powerful, compelling invitation to sleep.

Junjie's nervous system worked as designed, passing a sense of danger from hypothalamus to glands, spinal cord, and then onto his extremities. The resulting heightened state of awareness and self-preservation lasted long enough to effect an unseen exit from his capital city. Those exciter chemicals now leeched from his blood, there remained only the tempting call to rest. A fair fight it was not. Body and mind gave in. Dreams felt good, so good, as consciousness gave way to pleasant images from his past.

"You know, Junjie, we are different now," his father said.

The older man paused at the worn workbench in the small, unheated shop, turning to face his eldest son. Peering into his eyes; a familiar, knowing look. Full attention assured, he continued.

"The only question to ask before was: 'What is it I want?'"

Gentle yet firm hands rested on Junjie's shoulders, the gesture underscoring the moment.

"Now..." he emphasized, "... we must also add the questions first: 'What is right... and what would please him?'"

Another pause. Junjie took a moment to consider its meaning and significance. The father observed his son's reflection, pleased the truism was penetrating the young boy's thinking. The recitation of an ancient proverb sealed this moment of instruction.

"It is said: 'Better a patient man than a warrior'," he concluded. "'One with self-control, than one who takes a city'."

A glance toward his father indicated he understood; a slight nod. Mastery of this principle hovered at arms length, requiring many years and the testing of its trustworthiness in his own life. But the look said yes, he understood its basic truthfulness.

Junjie trusted this man fully, as a twelve-year-old boy should be able to, and loved these moments when something critical to life and wisdom was being passed down. His father's smile glowed, warm and assuring. The strong voice washed over his mind and heart.

A long curve, negotiating the bend and tilting slightly on axis. A minute change yet enough to notice, even from the shadowy realms of semi-consciousness. The minor aberration to otherwise smooth carriage called Junjie back up, out of this scene from years past. Still, he clung valiantly, longing for another moment floating in that in-between space, the peace that comes with even half-sleep.

A steady drizzle fell. Water in the atmosphere interacted with the warmer interior air, producing dampness on the hard, inner surface of the train window. Droplets danced to vibrations of steel and fiberglass at 200 mph and then merged. Gravity took over, freeing the water off the windowpane and bringing the cold liquid into contact with the young man's resting head.

Junjie's eyelids flickered open, his not-yet-awakened mind dealing with the rude intrusion. Soon enough he reestablished a sense of place and time. Against a pillowed headrest, he was physically comfortable. He was also emotionally drained, empty.

Too quick.

The beautiful dream moment had ended far too soon, leaving him to wrestle with the lingering aftertaste of deep loss. His heart pounded, not out of fear, but from mourning. The memories were wonderful. The pain of realizing they were only memories, almost too much to bear. The son tried to recapture the faintness of his father's presence; anything to re-link him to this man he revered.

Eyes closed. Gone.

Junjie so needed him, even fearing he had irrevocably disappointed him.

Looking down, he checked his phone. Ninety minutes until scheduled arrival in Shandong Province. He would need every second to collect his thoughts, preparing for what lie ahead. This trip to the coastal city of Qingdao had been both hastily arranged and completely required. A simple enough plan emerged. Junjie would disappear amongst the nine million inhabitants of this city before making any next moves. The government made itself conspicuous everywhere you went. But they didn't know everywhere to look, especially given his network of old contacts in this city.

Exactly eighty-*nine* minutes later the bullet train pulled into the grand station, gliding to a full stop at its assigned platform. Junjie disembarked. Immediately his eyes were drawn upward. Soaring sidewalls rose, combining gracefully at the pinnacle of the domed structure, some eighty feet above. Beautiful. The young executive was taken back by the scale and detail. It was utterly unique; this place where high-tech transportation met old world decor in rather odd fashion.

The enormous waiting hall in this city still bore its original German architecture, a reminder to visitors and residents alike of past occupancy by Northern Europeans in the late nineteenth century. Counter to what one might assume, Teutonic influence here wasn't the byproduct of invasion. Instead, a business arrangement in which the entire city was leased to Germany turned out to be a reasonably good investment for both parties. But this city held a darker story regarding interaction with outsiders as well. If a lederhosen, beer-hall feel still lingered from their former German hosts, the horrors of foreign control post-WW1 cut more like a deep scar and still-festering wound. A quirk of history at Versailles—handing this city over to Japan—produced a burdensome classism, a division still felt and nurtured deeply. The proximity of Japanese mainland—a little over five hundred miles away—guaranteed these tensions a low simmer, ever-threatening a boil into broader aggressions.

Junjie scanned the cavernous waiting room.

A cabbie's face lit and reset to a disinterested stare, just as quickly. Anyone else had likely missed it.

Yes.

Outside, the rear door of an unremarkable auto unlatched. The weary refugee slipped in, briefcase in hand, suitcase placed on the seat. Rain fell, small bubbles dancing on the sedan's hood as it exited the parking queue .

"Zhanqiao Prince Hotel," was all Junjie said by way of directions.

From the front, just as curt: "Very good, sir."

The luxurious waterfront accommodations on Qingdao Bay would've been a marvelous place to stay were he to actually spend any time there on this trip. The misdirection, though simple, was for the benefit of anyone listening at the time via planted devices. The driver's field craft was excellent. They entered the heavy flow of mid-day traffic seamlessly, maintaining an ordinary, unsuspecting trajectory. A few turns later, assured of no active tailing, they arrived at their real endpoint, the Shinan Industrial District, where mottled aluminum siding over brick foundations and wood framing provided a perfectly drab backdrop. Nothing to see. No one around.

The cabbie and his passenger passed endless rows of 1960s era warehouses and manufacturing units. These structures supported blue-collar work, the kinds done below the shiny outer layer of a growing middle class. Mundane — yes, yet so essential to the city's economic well-being. For Junjie's purposes, they could not have been better.

Into the next warehouse lot on the right, they steered past the door and around back. Twenty meters out of view from street side they stopped, the engine running quietly.

"Zhanqiao Prince" — from up front, nonchalant, businesslike.

GPS tracking would have recognized the incongruity. Audio-only surveilling might remain satisfied, at least for the moment.

"Thank you. This should cover it," from the backseat.

Junjie handed fifteen yuan to the driver and stepped out. He gathered his things and closed the door, looking around the backlot once more. They'd not been followed, he thought. At least he hadn't seen them. Or their trackers were superb and waiting for them to lead on to others.

That was a chance he'd have to take.

With no more words the red cab turned and left.

SEVENTEEN

Junjie picked up his things and traversed the rest of the lot. Squeezing through an opening in a stone wall, he emerged onto a sidewalk and then crossed another busy street.

The alleyway was like dozens of others in Qingdao. Drainpipes serviced water off rooftops, down angled recessions to the pavement, from there flowing into the sewers of the massive urban space. Mangy cats stood watch beside garbage cans, scruffy heads warding would-be intruders off their hard-fought turf.

Junjie walked the first ten yards of the narrow passageway casually. Then, in a swift move up and to the right he mounted the back porch of an old cargo loading bay. Three more steps. Kneeling down and reaching out beyond the toes of his left foot, he paused.

Was he being watched? He would feign dropping his keys or tying his laces. It wouldn't explain his presence, but it might buy a critical second or two to act.

Another beat.

Now.

He popped a floorboard, sliding a pen beneath its upper left corner for leverage. The hinges whispered. A trapdoor opened and the software engineer on-the-run descended a short flight of stairs, disappearing in broad daylight. His next step not yet landed, a sudden brightness overtook him.

Junjie lost balance, arms and hands raised reflexively, palms outward, trying to diffuse the light and leaning back onto the balls of his feet. A hoarse, thin voice, questioned his appearance in the mysterious place:

"Junjie?"

He froze. Still wary, unsure.

Again, "Junjie...it is you?"

Stepping into the light, the businessman received a warm embrace, enfolded by the smallish body connected to the mysterious voice.

It worked. The amateur subterfuge had worked. He had run to the only refuge he knew. But it was a gamble as to whether or not, and for how long, they might allow him among their fold.

Junjie's rise had its casualties. Trust was high on the list.

Gansu Province
Mid 1980s

The crops had failed.

Again.

Weakness distorted young Junjie's imagination, sketching a bleak future onto his mental canvas. Hunger pangs lingered amidst the frail and weak, reminding everyone of the unending, "never-enough" cycles in Gansu. It was brutally unfair. Fickleness of temperature, moisture, and sunshine had transformed a modest expectation of survival into fated acceptance of frailties. The harvest had not come. Sickness and death surely would.

Junjie's parents' eyes said it all. They'd given everything they had, fought back mortality. But everyone has their limits. This futile season was the proverbial final straw, severing the camel's back. Eerie silence hovered, the dark imprint of fatalism scribed onto the corners of life-worn faces. They did what they knew, what they had always done. Keep the sacred fires, their home altars lit. Prevail upon the spirits of ancestors for signs of relief. In the end no help was found. Only fear, as the vacant, stoic expressions of the hearth gods fostered little confidence in these despairing households.

The chill.

A deeper coldness permeated everything and everyone. At their end, Junjie's village needed a rescuer, a provider, a benefactor.

Hope came in the most unexpected fashion.

The well-worn, light blue SUV sat at a curious angle, wheels stuck in the wet, clay-rich soil of their village's main street.

A young woman with flaming red hair gripped the wheel, working shift, accelerator, and brakes. Rear tires spun, painting a young man pushing from behind in liquid brown.

Junjie happened upon them before anyone else. The boy chuckled at the odd situation, couldn't help himself. The act brought joy and discomfort. His empty, distended abdomen didn't allow for much of a belly-laugh.

But instead of anger the man flashed back an enormous smile, laughing along with the skin-and-bones local boy at his own mud-soaked clothes. The sounds of good humor told Junjie all was safe. Simply another helpless couple in a town overflowing with people needing help.

Who? Where were they from? Why come all the way out here? Did they intend to stay?

Gansu had known outsiders before, mostly come to pillage their region's meager resources. But these two — the man covered in muck and the woman with bright red hair — were more disposed to learn and give than to take and abuse. Most evenings they hosted all who would come through their doors, sharing captivating parables, often about someone named Yasu and his unruly band of friends. They delighted young and old, fitting in with the village's oral tradition of entertaining and sharing wisdom between generations.

Still, to be accepted they would need to earn their place.

And so they did.

Their employers — an Australian relief and mission organization — helped them survive those first, harsh months. The singular act of kindness made all the difference. Resolved to mourning in bleak wintertime, they welcomed instead a handful of newborns along with the fresh winds of late spring. The young couple's hospitality appeared boundless, surpassing even the reputed character of those from down under. They encouraged Junjie's curiosity with electronics, letting him "repair" their satellite phone a hundred times or more. Often, and usually unannounced, he walked joyfully into their home.

"Junjie? Is that you, my boy?"

The foreigner's accent made him smile, especially when struggling with certain words and phrases in their dialect. It was completely disarming.

"Yes," Junjie replied, inching ever closer to the table holding the couple's communications gear.

"Well, well. Let's see. No. I don't think we'll need you to work on the sat phone today, little one."

Disappointment clouded Junjie's face.

The man continued.

"But... how about this instead...?"

The man stepped aside, revealing the opened casing of a desktop computer.

Cables. Hard drives. Circuit board. A veritable playground, bidding the junior engineer to pull, connect, and reset the many objects making up the whole.

Would they trust him with this most important tool?

The man's broad smile answered affirmatively and the next four hours flowed in wonder, discovering and learning alongside of one of Junjie's most trusted childhood friends.

One warm, quiet evening a sense of joyous anticipation filled the air.

The man and woman were expecting their first child.

As Gansu births are public affairs, the entire populace held its collective breath. Waiting, the communal matriarchs fussed. They waited longer and fussed more. But the expected sound of baby's first cry, calling out the deepest of human hopes, was displaced instead by pain inconsolable. The young mother-to-be grieved her still-born child, streams of tears wetting her hair, coloring it an impossibly deeper red.

Heartbreaking.

And yet this was the moment Junjie recalled the change.

The Aussie's stories held fast against great loss; convincing many, Junjie's father among the first, that this couple's strength could be theirs.

A few more harvests and they returned to family and nation. Their residence had been brief, yet its impact significant, so profound. The years following brought both good and bad growing seasons, just like before. The change wasn't in their fortunes. Instead, it lived in their faces. An unexpected visitation changed everything, Fear gave way to hope, and not just any hope but one that could survive the harshest that rural life in China might send their way.

Quingdao
Present Day

"Bohai. A pleasure to hear your voice. It is I, Junjie."

"I am also glad to hear yours," the reply. "But have to admit I am surprised by this visit. Why are you here? It has been so very long. Zenshi almost left you at the station. There are many eyes on the streets."

"I know," Junjie said. "I must apologize. I had no other choice."

Junjie held a most important question.

"Dai-tai?... and Chi?"

A searching face and quivering voice, eyes begging for a good report.

"They are both secure. We received the notice and have..."

"*No*, Bohai," Junjie insisted. "Please do not not speak what I may not be able to conceal."

"Of course. You are right," the other man conceded.

"It is enough to know they are protected for now. What I must do would bring them harm. I cannot guarantee I would have the fortitude to choose well if they become pawns."

Bohai proceeded tentatively. "This thing you must do, Junjie? It is our country's recent aggressions?"

"Yes. I do not know if I can be successful but I must try."

"Certainly. I should be able to gather the committee by week's end. Until then, rest Junjie. You will need it."

Junjie looked down, betraying understandable weariness.

This thing I must do.

Yes, I must.

EIGHTEEN

The airframe's open glass nose-cone dipped beneath the cloud ceiling at just under twenty-eight-thousand feet.

Captain *Xian Weng* took in the beautiful, unobstructed view, ever deeper into the former Puget Sound Region of Washington State. Wild coastline. Snowcapped peaks. A land rich with lakes and rivers. A solid mass of living green. Reaching up to his flight computer, the thirty-six-year-old Peoples Liberation Army Air Force pilot punched in the approach sequence for the airfields of China's newly acquired, recently deserted base, now re-commissioned as Baotong Air-Ground Base (BAGB).

Weng's flight, originating out of Shahezhen Air Base — Beijing, had traced an arc over the northern rim of the Pacific Ocean of more than 8700km. A single mid-air refueling above the Aleutians kept the IL76-MD, its five crewmen, and 42 ton payload from any stops along the way. The captain's aircraft, completing its second full trip in the invasion force, sat at the front edge of a sixteen jet formation. It had been the same scene every day: an endless parade of tail sections, red star on red band ID'ing them as Chinese military, wave after wave.

This particular craft of Soviet manufacture was one of thirty-five the PLAAF operated, providing long-range, multi-platform delivery of Chinese materiel. A big, dangerous bird, the 76 carried all the tools needed to enforce their claim on new lands. With six-thousand feet of permanent, paved runways awaiting — more than enough to do the job — and clear conditions in both airspace and on the ground, Captain Weng expected an unremarkable arrival and offload. His assumptions proved correct. The Americans followed orders nicely.

Drop the men and cargo. Refuel. Mandatory downtime and then the return run to Beijing. Weng saw nothing out of the ordinary as he descended through hazy skies. The sights from the ground, though, for those being conquered?

Equal parts extraordinary and frightening.

You saw it in their faces, sensed it in their bearing. There was little talk of rebellion. Those first spasms of courage, such a natural fist-in-the-air reaction, had been replaced by an ever-growing consciousness that they had no options, that their destiny now lay in others' hands. Like rats in a maze with no exits the people of Seattle were warming to their lot as a captured, cornered people. Turn left, turn right. Go slow. Speed up. It really didn't matter.

Wang manipulated the plane's yoke in and to the left. The giant machine complied, nosing downward some twenty miles out from BAB. Swelling with pride, the captain reflected on the base's new title: Baotong, so named in honor of a North Korean war ace whose kills during that three-year-long conflict had been all U.S. pilots. As the long-serving flyer assessed it, America's imperialist intrusion into Asia sixty years ago had now come full circle.

You are so prideful. We have been patient.

Now you will be repaid for your haughtiness.

You have not earned your place with the great civilizations.

You presumed too much, too soon.

Sanchez focused her mind and quieted her heart rate, slowing it to fifty beats a minute. Stock still, no observable signs of life. Nothing to alert humans. No signals even to the most perceptive in the animal world that she was among them in the tall grasses and evergreen brush. Her breathing: measured, silent, no traces of the constant exchange of oxygen and CO_2. For most, this would signal ill-health. For the sergeant, merely indicators of her readiness for the tasks at hand. Invisible since taking up station three hours earlier, she maintained watch, not a football field's length from the enemy.

As anticipated, Capt. Weng and crew touched down without problems. Ground personnel offloaded supplies directly in Sanchez' crosshairs. A small door opened beneath the beast and the tired men emerged, down retractable stairs and onto the tarmac. The sniper followed the airmen, each one frozen in her reticle as they moved toward the building.

Her right forefinger brushed the smooth, steel trigger, tapping it twice from the side.

"C'mon. Yeah, right there Mr. Chen. One more step and..."

So easy. Too easy, actually. The distance to target would almost certainly get her captured. Considering the big picture, and with the self-control of a seasoned warrior, she pulled her finger back alongside the weapon.

Her sarcasm and use of a stereotypical ethnic name didn't negate her professionalism. Nor her understanding of place in this developing scenario. She had a role. She would deny her emotions to gain strategic advantage. Currently her job was intel, not active engagement. For now her duties were simple: evade and assess.

A full week off the grid, she had maintained non-presence and learned much. While staying mostly to the wooded areas of the vast installation, she had managed a couple of forays to the officers' village early on. There was scavenging to be done. Stay stealthy, stay mobile. Gather up food and water and then leave as invisibly as she'd arrived. The routine was less than satisfying. Her anxiousness to relay information and receive directives grew daily. How and when this might occur was still unknown. Given Chinese control of all communications that would prove an interesting trick. All she'd gotten was a ghost order in the last hours before evac. Her commanding officer had assigned her a most important task. Details as needed. That would have to suffice.

Weng's men made their way to Hanger D, debriefing at the temporary, on-site post.

Sanchez watched.

It wasn't difficult to determine who was who. Leadership has a certain, identifiable substance. Most often, those who shouldered real responsibility bore an orderliness to their movements. Steady. Intentional. Those given charge of warriors understand their place in the grand structure of things. They give orders because they know how to take them. These were the targets to eliminate, not the hotshot, cowboy types. One of the first truisms impressed upon young sniper candidates was this: cut the head off the snake as fast as you can. The head? Well, that's obvious. It's the part sticking up and moving purposefully.

The tight cluster made for an easy grouping. Notwithstanding the three hundred feet her rifled projectile would have to fly, this was a kill even the greenest of trainees couldn't screw up. They might actually back up another few hundred yards, just to make it a little more challenging.

Sanchez allowed herself the briefest of moments to reconsider. A half breath. Holding it. Focused and ready, she called each part of her mind and body to facilitate this deadly sequence, one she'd mastered and repeated countless times. Many of these had been practice, much fewer the real deal. Yet she considered each opportunity a lethal one. From a philosophical perspective every targeting event had to be this way, not so much to give relief, but to convince those involved that their bullet was always the cause of death. It was a gritty, hard way to do your job. It was also the only real way to stay in this terminal game for any amount of time.

The sergeant's pulse slowed below forty-five beats. Her gaze narrowed further, pressing against cold, rounded metal. Motionless. Anything outside this circular field of vision didn't exist.

Focus. Hold.

Sanchez let the breath out, whispering to no one but her conscience.

"Alright, Mr. C... for now, you get to live."

The M24 came off its mini-tripod silently. Kit packed up, Sanchez faded into thick underbrush. Action would come. But only at the time and place of her choosing.

NINETEEN

Beijing

The thirty-five-member State Council recessed, having just received updates on developments across the Pacific. Outside the larger chambers a smaller cohort of seven made their way to the south concourse, aides and security in tow. Going somewhere in a hurry, their assistants struggled to keep up in dignified fashion.

Their hasty departure drew little attention. Eager for lunch appointments or the afternoon's slate of politicking, the other officials paid no mind. The pace of the men quickened into heavy, sloppy footsteps. Three minutes later entourages were dismissed. Large, dark doors opened and then shut. All were soon seated, in the president's private office.

"Gentlemen, we have some things to discuss," President Xi Jinping began.

The Defense Minister stepped in first.

"Mr. President. American military evacuation is completed and our troops are now establishing control throughout the populace. Local police forces have begun disarmament. We are on schedule and continue to move resources into place."

"At this rate," he continued "We expect another ten to fourteen days before the assumption of transportation, communication, and civil infrastructure is complete."

"You speak confidently," Xi responded. "As always... " his words dripped with disdain, begging for a more thoughtful reply. "But I would like then your opinion of yesterday's events."

"I am not sure to what you are referring, Mr. President."

The president tapped a remote and the screen opposite his desk came to life. Four separate feeds. Each one a small but significant image.

"Yuxin. Green line subway—north of Olympic Center. Mechanical failure. Doors locked. Fire. Twenty-five dead. Hongqiao Market. All magnetic transactions denied for three hours. Hundreds of thousands of yuen disappearing from vendor accounts. Tianjin Harbor tug services. GPS issuing conflicting locations. Three barges collide. Ten crew members overboard and drowned."

He waited.

"The Great Hall of the People. All doors unlocked and security sensors and cameras disabled for eighteen minutes."

He waited again. "In the middle of the afternoon."

"Mr. President," the DM searched. "I am aware of the news. But, these are isolated incidents. Of no real concern. With all due respect—and returning to our orignal conversation, Comrade Xi—I see no other outcome for our people... than victory."

A new voice joined the debate, a man seated beside the president and in the room before the others.

"Yes, I imagine you do not, minister. And while your enthusiasm is enviable, I do not have the luxury of such naivete. I am not so sure it will go quite the way you envision."

All eyes locked on Zhou Dhe. While his position, strictly speaking, did not provide access to such a conversation, neither was anyone surprised. That did not mean they liked it.

"The commonality," he continued "is impossible to miss. Even for fools."

"Now," the president broke back in. "Maybe we can speak more honestly. Can we dispense with propaganda and move to the real question at hand..."

A canyon-sized silence.

"... how long?"

He repeated, "How long do we have?"

The query was multifaceted. It was also the only thing that mattered. Not battalions or tanks. Not even nuclear-tipped missiles. No, none of these things were of consequence. Time was the issue. And the critical question before them: how much. Beyond these walls no one comprehended how fundamental a concern this was. Inside this room, everyone knew.

The Civil Affairs Minister looked up, speaking next.

"Mr. President... we do not know. We have applied all assets to the problem and are making progress but, at this point, an accurate assessment is not feasible."

"In other words" Xi retorted. "We need more time to know how much of it we don't have, Li Liguo?!"

The president's anger showed more fully, lifting the room's emotional tide. Xi, no longer seated behind his ornate Elizabethan-Era oak desk, held deep disbelief at both the unfolding realities and apparent incompetence of these men.

Astounding.

The Chinese Premier—Chair of the State Council and highest-ranking member of the Communist Party in the room—shifted in his chair and weighed in. He motioned with his right hand, a gesture indicating civility and unity.

"Your exasperation is understandable, Mr. President. No one wanted to be in this position. There was no way of predicting our leverage would deteriorate in this way."

The metaphorical elephant entered the room.

"I find this utterly unacceptable, Li Keqiang," the president replied. "How is it possible to come to this point, unaware our axis of pressure might dissolve so quickly?"

Another voice in the room spoke up.

"There were no indications of weakness in any of the testing phases; nothing at all to lead us away from full implementation. No red flags."

This last statement came from *Chen Bingde*, Commanding Officer of the PLA General Staff. As the Chinese equivalent to the U.S. Chairman of the Joint Chiefs, Chen knew the project intimately, one of only a few people in the nation with full knowledge of its inner-workings. Hoping to break the momentum of the conversation, to recapture a sense of equilibrium, he continued while the opening still existed.

"It was a basic proposition," he explained. "American nuclear control depends on digital instruction sets, protected by other digital instruction sets. Although thousands of times more intricate than something like a password for a website, the concept is the same. The challenge is in being more clever than those creating the defenses."

The general looked at the others. No response, so he jumped in again.

"We found someone better. Right here; one of our brothers. While it is true the code's origins were not ours, he developed it, from latency to potency."

Chen could tell he was losing them so he stood, pleading both with hands and words. The move, unbecoming a senior officer, communicated little else than the desire to assign blame elsewhere, or better yet, nowhere.

Dhe jumped in with such force that the military man simply sat again before finishing.

"But that brother betrayed us! He triggered the code's evolution by accessing a backdoor into his work. Weak. Disloyal. What happened next is referred to as sympathetic code migration. Obviously, no one here had heard of such a thing. To this point it has been the subject of speculative, academic work; never real-world. Our understanding at this point is that no one can control it, not even Mr. Zang. Our new technology," he referred to the screen on the wall. "... initially in control of the American systems, began deferring itself to other results. Not quite sentience in the full meaning of the word. Highly advanced, multi-threaded problem solving. It keeps the Americans in check," he tried, as if there were a silver lining to be found. "It also degrades our grip on the weapons themselves. And apparently is beginning to act on communications networks outside of its original charge."

"Enough! How long?!!!" Xi demanded, fist meeting desk. "How long until our soldiers become vulnerable to the inevitable retaliation of civilian and military forces in the new province? How long until these four incidents yesterday become commonplace and destroy us from the inside-out! What's next? Power grids? Water, sewer? And how long... until the Americans regain command of their strategic nuclear capabilities... "

" ... how long until the next... no, *final*... world war begins?"

"And, by then, will we be so weakened they will walk onto our shores unopposed? Or maybe we will not even be worth the effort. My comrades, these are the very real outcomes before us. I suggest you get to work on solutions."

TWENTY

Eastern Washington

Dalton looked out and across the expansive valley. Hands on thighs, exhaling forcefully, he was relieved, maybe even a bit surprised. Behind him lay the vast backcountry he had impossibly survived. Ahead—the foothills, leading off the downward edge of the Cascade Range.

The grand vista welcomed him home to loved, familiar territory. Dalton had come this way most of his growing years, alongside a passel of first cousins, all crammed into the belt-less seats of a '79 Ford VistaCruiser. Everyone understood the arrangement. Two weeks each spring were given to working row after row of his grandparents' sixty acres, non-gratis. The familial labor crew rose before dawn to trudge through endless plots of apple and peach trees. The work was both monotonous and demanding. The company made it bearable.

His relatives occupied the usual lineup of odd characters and best friends springing from blood kin. Some you were downright proud of. Others avoided mention in family conversations altogether. And after a "good enough for today" came across Grandpa Dalton's lips, late afternoons were spent with a fishing line dangling in the creek, or if the water had warmed enough, their bodies in the lake.

Dalton smiled. This place did his heart and mind good. It was early, far too soon yet for fruit to be showing. Still, nascent buds protruded off gangly vines and limbs, announcing that winter had once again lost its grip. The dying season had ended. Life awaited on the near horizon.

The former soldier had not previously experienced the area from this vantage point. Nonetheless, it comforted and reassured. It told him he was on the right track, had done the right thing. These known sights and smells fostered a momentary yet significant hope. Dalton needed that, especially in light of all the man had endured the last ten days. His mom's face and voice still haunted. He couldn't allow himself to stop, to linger even a moment. And, if she was his focal point, the broader populace of Seattle—his home—brought only more clarity of purpose. He knew as well as anyone this was a first stop among many for the Chinese. Just the highest gain to loss scenario. A foothold. And then there was the single word *Sovereign*, playing over and over in his fertile mind. This fight was becoming personal in so many ways.

For a man like Dalton, it was an easy choice.

Run. Escape. Reconnect with military leadership and take it from there.

His illegal, dangerous exodus from the Seattle metro area left no margin of preparation for the high altitude trek his instincts told him needed to take place immediately or helplessly await foreign dominion over everything and everyone between Canada in the north and Oregon in the south. This being the case, Dalton carried limited provisions into the Cascade wilds. A few sticks of beef jerky, two granola bars, and a handful of mixed nuts. It was also what had been available at the only quickmart on the highway up Snoqualmie Pass, after the frightened couple left him to his own devices. Dalton knew how to budget meager rations; he was a combat vet, after all. Disciplined resource allocation wouldn't be the problem. Hypothermia, dehydration, wild animals. These factors, he should fear.

The first day and a half Dalton tracked along the highway. With the exception of two aerial patrols, both broad, inexact sweeps of the area, he'd found himself pretty much alone between 4,000 and 6,000 feet. The Chinese were banking on police blockades and the stark, unforgiving environs to do a good part of their job for them. Plus, no one would be foolish enough to escape via this route.

Well, almost no one.

As rigorous as Day One turned out to be, Days Two through Three and a Half were much harder. In the pre-dawn hours of the third day Dalton came around a blind corner—a harrowingly narrow path around large sandstone formations—only to find himself face to face with a grizzly, forty paces out, holding ground.

Blinking. Blinking again.

This was no phantom; no by-product of overtaxed body and brain.

Run.

The internal command produced a less-than-impressive reaction, more ragged stumbling than straight-line acceleration. Dark fur and sharp, bared fangs thrashed at an astounding pace. Even while running, Dalton's heads-up mental display produced everything he knew about the species, chief among the datafields that a bears pursuit velocity was among the fastest in the animal kingdom. That point of fact was unnecessary. It seemed unreal that the large mammal moved with such power and grace. Ten seconds of frenzied activity later, and who knows why, the creature gave up the chase.

Immediate peril now past, Dalton slowed some. Catching his breath while still moving forward, his foot snagged an exposed root ball. Instantly he was face down, in the mud, arms splayed to the side.

Are you kidding me?! C'mon, I just outran a flippin' bear.

Brushing himself off, dizzy and angered by the tumble, he took one more step forward.

Whoa.

The next footfall, had he taken it, would've dislodged a patch of loose rock hidden by thickened ground cover. His body weight, cooperating with gravity's merciless pull, would have sent him through the veil of green and off a sheer, unseen cliff.

Dalton peered over the edge and the bottom loomed, some four hundred feet away. Then he fainted.

Awaking sometime later, still dangerously close to the fall, Dalton got up and stepped back from the alpine precipice, forcing himself to think, to reset. So tired. He needed real, regenerative rest yet couldn't afford much at any one time. Constant cold. His body's depletion. These elements all conspired, bringing the unthinkable into consideration.

Just lay down, give up.

Best-case scenario? Dalton would be dead when winter-starved scavengers sniffed out his carcass. Probably.

Fall asleep on the semi-frozen ground for one last, eternal nap. Body stays intact until decaying, leaving a skeleton sfor some intrepid hiker to find, years from now.

Not so bad. The less-desirable outcome?

Various predators tugging at his not-yet-expired flesh and organs as he lay immobilized; conscious and helpless through it all.

That thought gave him a shiver, keeping him on task. That, and another idea as well: the slim possibility his own survival might lead to others' freedoms. These thoughts fueled him, as well as the very understandable desire to not end up as an entrée in the wilderness circle of life.

So here he was. With four days of deprivation and danger behind, Dalton gazed down toward the outskirts of the small city of Wenatchee, Washington. Funny, all those times crossing over with his family—no big deal. A short car ride from one side of the state to the other. Now, he'd just breached an international border.

Dalton breathed in the fragrances of woods and fields. The life-giving presence diluted another long night of painful memories and subfreezing temperatures. Another deep breath. Evergreen. The tang of immature fruit blossoms. A soft bed of pine needles and underbrush beneath his feet. It all worked together, a needed sensory buffer for his frazzled condition. This was a good moment, one to stop and take in.

The unmistakable roar of a Blackhawk's rotor-wash cut the air, destroying his peaceful pause. The UH60 attack chopper, though invisible on radar, was so loud it would rarely, if ever, take someone by surprise. That it had presented itself without prior warning spoke volumes as to this fugitive's real state of fatigue. Cornered, the man's last reserves faded.

Dalton looked up. The chopper's mid-ship lift bay door sat opened on tracked hinges, her 50 cal. spun up, hot. The gleaming barrel and cold, efficient stare of the gunner through darkened visor told him there was no play to be had. At thirty-some yards out, he would get a half a second before being cut down. Dalton knew what was next. He counted down, like a floor director calling for action.

Three... two... one...

A few meters behind, from the edge of the treeline: "Sir, place your hands over your head and drop to the ground! Do not move to the side or back. Do not motion with your hands toward your body. To your knees, NOW!"

Dalton had been on hundreds of similar takedowns. Whether the unpredictable spaces of Iraqi villages or the unwelcome crags of Afghan rock shelters, overwhelming force was always the principle. Sort of the Powell Doctrine applied to patrol-level detection and detention.

One massive implement of war overhead. Six, highly trained special operators.

Overwhelming force?

Check.

In blinding succession, Dalton's face met dirt, then flex cuffs bound him from behind. Half hogtied. A rapid loss of equilibrium. His stomach lurched and its minimal contents — acid and not much else — made a grandiose appearance. An adult male's knee knifed into the small of his back and another putrid mixture — blood from a split lip and soil — filled his mouth. This beautiful morning, initially so promising, was quickly turning.

The leader spoke again. This time, though, not to Zeb.

"Clark Base: Unknown personnel has been detained. ETA is approx. thirty-five. Do you copy? Over."

The outgoing voice was as heavy a Highland Brogue as one could imagine. The reply came back in a metallic timbre.

"Roger. Thirty-five to Clark. Copy. Over."

"Okay, folks let's get busy. We've got trail to eat up and there are some important people who want to know what in the world our new friend here has been up to. Move it."

TWENTY ONE

*Staff Sergeant **William "Loch" Lochland,** squad leader—Ranger Unit Bravo, raised Dalton off the ground and to a standing position... with one hand.*

The sudden change in orientation caused the weary man to wretch yet again. Dalton's head cleared slightly from the acidic intrusion, enough to glance at the man holding him up. The stocky Scotsman was a mere five-six, boot heels included. Dalton had almost a full five inches on him. Be that as it may, it was obvious this wouldn't count as any kind of advantage. Whatever the soldier lacked on the vertical plane was abundantly compensated for in both upper body strength and leadership demeanor. The sergeant played the part of professional wrestler, body builder, and world's strongest man competitor to a tee. Dalton was not about to challenge him, at least physically. He mentally wagered that this guy didn't lose many altercations. He was wrong.

Loch never lost.

Ever.

Lochland sized Dalton up in an overt display of dominance before weapons check. A 360 sweep of the stranger provided a basic survey of potential threats. None registered. He stepped back, satisfied the intruder was under his command. His *aahs* and *euus* were as exaggerated as his name and bearing.

"Okay, Mr. Woodsman. Two questions. First, just who the crap are you? And Number Two: what are you doing in *my* forest, overlooking a United States Military installation?"

Loch underscored his personal ownership of the place with left thumb to chest. That hand was for communication. The other was at the ready.

Dalton envisioned the Heckler & Koch MP57 coming off this man's shoulder seamlessly, a perfect flow of arc and aim. The right thing to do at this moment was to stay still, very still.

Lochland probed Dalton's amber eyes, awaiting a reasonable answer. Dalton's retort was standard-issue, minimalist with a dash of slightly provocative.

"Lieutenant Zebulon Mordecai Dalton, US Army 2 Corps..." he confessed through a mouthful of brown and red. He spat, "... retired."

Loch arched an eyebrow.

"Well... *retired*... Eltee Dalton. You, of course, realize you are standing in a highly sensitive zone, off limits to civvies and old school soldiers alike?"

Dalton's face brightened, delighted by the presence of a competent verbal opponent.

"Yeah, I figured that much. From the six of you as my armed escorts. And," he looked upward, straining to stand taller, red stains across front teeth, "... the big smile behind the fifty."

Loch grinned, barely, certainly not enough for his men to notice. He decreased their physical buffer to only a few inches, voice dropping to an authoritative, lower volume.

"Well, whoever you are. You're up for a nice little nature walk and then some quality face time with a couple of Army uglies who're gonna want better answers than that. My job is to deliver you in one piece, in half an hour."

Mulling that last statement over:

"Two pieces will probably work fine...

... let's move it... LT."

Loch shoved Dalton forward and made the call.

"Ranger Bravo: on the move. Big Bird is free."

The blackhawk pulled up and away. Everyone on the ground ducked, respecting her downwash. Soon enough the dust settled and the team descended, quarry in tow, through overgrown trails and back toward base.

Colonel *Jacob Meers*, US Army 1 Corps, traversed dim hallways and came to a stop outside his commander's office. As senior aide to General Stevens, Meers had standing orders to enter whenever needed. With a burgeoning manila folder under his left arm, he paused before knocking, considering again all that had happened in such a brief span of time. He glanced back at the array of desks in the outer office and the corridor behind. Not much to write home about, that's for sure. Then again, quite the accomplishment, given the circumstances.

The hasty assembly of the newly christened *Ft. Clark* resulted in a small city of tents and pole buildings instead of bricks and mortar. Aside from proper runways to support air and transport functions, everything else was pretty flimsy at the moment. The general had enough room to work, the space just wasn't appointed all that well. The vibe ended up more forward arena than stateside buildout. Her commanding officer didn't mind this distinction. Not at all.

The moniker Clark had been chosen by Pentagon higher-ups as a nod to the now-lost asset Lewis, over the mountains, back in Tacoma. Historically, it seemed fitting that if one of the famed adventurers went down, his partner should come to his aid. And, consistent with the trailblazing sense of those nineteenth-century explorers, something like this had never been attempted before. The U.S. Army was, by virtue of the current operational environment, literally flying by the seat of her pants. Evacuating a base the size of JBLM, resetting it a few hundred miles east, traversing over snow-capped peaks ranging five to fourteen thousand feet, was a remarkable achievement. The fact they were even here stood in testimony to the commitment, professionalism, and skill of both leaders and doers.

Stevens sensed Meers' presence in the doorway and looked up. Pulling his glasses off, he rubbed the bridge of his nose. Then, waving his hand across the scattered papers, the career warrior spoke with characteristic wit.

"Colonel. To what do I owe the honor of this visit, one which surely will rescue me from mounds of spreadsheets and transfer requests? Please, Meers, tell me you have something else for me to attend to?"

The subordinate came forward, over the threshold and into the room.

"I think I may be able to help you out, sir."

"Outstanding. What is it, then? You look like a nervous schoolboy about to ask me to the spring cotillion."

"Cotillion... sir?"

Stevens lit a cigar. It came to life, rolling around and in-between his lips.

"Never mind, Meers. Apparently high culture went extinct decades ago. What's that in your hand there, Colonel?"

A dopple of ash fell to the desktop as he motioned with the stogey's live end.

Meers placed the aging, bulging file on the desk.

Name, rank, serial number.

Dalton, Zebulon M.

Palm went to forehead. Stevens pinched a sliver of cranial skin between his fingers.

"Please, please tell me you've not brought me another sad case looking for preferential treatment or placement. I am not feeling magnanimous today. China took my base, holding three million American citizens against their will and presuming they'll somehow want to become happy workers in the PRC. To be perfectly honest, I am a little beside myself about that, Meers."

"Of course, sir."

Meers let his boss's mini-tirade settle before starting again.

"This," pointing to the pile, "... belongs to a retired lieutenant. Multiple tours. Both Iraq and Afghanistan. Honorable discharge."

Stevens leaned back, fully exasperated now.

"Great. More armchair heroes. Stack it right over there."

Something about his aide's demeanor begged more explanation, and maybe slightly more empathy.

"Meers, you know I have no use for broken down old soldiers, not even the loyal, good ones. Tell him thank you for his valuable service and we have all the help we need."

The colonel knew his superior would want the full story. Sliding the docs toward Stevens, he continued. "General, this Lieutenant Dalton was found above base this morning. He claims to have made it through the checkpoints on the other side of the Cascades, surviving five days and four nights... and he has requested to talk to you personally. In scanning his history, I think you may want to interview him, sir."

The general let out a pronounced, slow breath. Tapping the binder, he flicked the burnt, white edge of his cigar into his half-grenade shell ashtray.

Thinking.

"Fifteen minutes, colonel. If I am not interested by then, I never will be. Dismissed."

"Yes, sir."

TWENTY TWO

Dalton's hands, still flex-cuffed, dangled at his beltline. Although deemed a lesser threat, he was not yet a welcomed guest.

Released from holding, an extremely serious MP escorted him through the halls of Clark. They halted outside the door marked *Base Commander: Major General Mike Stevens.* Knocking twice, the guard waited at attention.

Enter.

Dalton's new companion led him to a standard-issue metal desk while Stevens looked over this imposition on his time and patience for a full sixty seconds. No invite for Dalton to slide into the unoccupied swivel chair.

Eyes narrowing, Steven's locked onto Dalton, searching for motive, intent.

"Lieutenant..." Stevens perused the paperwork in front of him — "... Dalton?"

He knew his name, had scanned his full history over the last few minutes.

"What in the world are you doing here?"

The imposing commander raised his right hand.

"No," he stopped. "Don't answer that."

The general paced his questions, ever-present cigar wagging as he spoke.

"Why? Why would an honorably discharged veteran of the United States Army, with meritorious acts in two of the ugliest wars this nation has ever embarked upon suffer cold, sleeplessness, hunger, and the wrath of the Chinese authorities? And then tempt fate yet again by entering the no-proceed zones of this fine military installation?"

"No. Don't answer that either, Lieutenant."

The general leaned in, over the paper-strewn desktop.

"What I really want to know... is why this kind of man, with a clear history of sacrificial service, would put millions of his fellow Americans in harm's way, literally at the blunt edge of a nuclear bomb, blatantly disobeying the direct orders of the new Chinese government...

...*this* is what I want to know, Mr. Dalton."

The general, rising during the monologue, now sat back, right hand opened, more challenge than invitation.

Here we go again.

"Look, General. Ah, sir. I have unique experiences and skill-sets that could be useful in the attempts to recover our government's nuclear assets. I thought you might see your way through the regs in this case. Am I wrong?"

Dalton had historic difficulties with people above him who didn't want to listen; the kind of presumption he felt too often came with rank. His retort came off as less honoring, certainly less respectful than was due a good career officer like Stevens. He immediately regretted it.

The general waited.

"So, Dalton. If I am reading you correctly, the entire United States Military hasn't been the same since you left a few years ago. Is this it? Now that we're in deep, you're our only hope, Obi Wan? You alone will ride in to save the day? The zenith of Signal Corps prowess rises and falls with your service and actions? Am I getting this all down accurately?"

Dalton's face flushed a gentle red, frustrated, angry, and revealing both in the exchange.

"Please, general. If you would simply look into my record. It's likely a bit hidden but there should at least be a mention of a Project Sovereign. It's all there, I am sure. Please, if you'll just look…"

"No, son. I want *you* to look. Now. Right here," Stevens pointed to his bookcase.

Four or five framed pictures. A wedding party. Camping trip. An extended family portrait taking special prominence.

"You," Stevens almost stammered. "You could have killed them. All of them. And millions more. And I am not even sure it still won't happen. Do you know for sure the Chinese didn't track you? Exactly how certain are you that we won't be seeing a mushroom cloud in the next 24 hours with your name on it?"

"General? Again, I was recalled. Project Sovereign. I didn't just do this on my own," Dalton tried, this time more gently.

"MP!"

The human rock re-entered, awaiting a directive.

"Take this trespassing civvy back to holding," Stevens said. "Get him some food and something to drink. That is all."

Escorted from the general's presence, Dalton wondered what would come next. Then it struck him: just how ridiculous this whole situation had become. Only ten days ago his work week had started out relatively normal. Everyone has car issues from time to time. That's where any semblance of routine went fully off the rails. An intended sales call to a client at Pike Place had transfigured into something so bizarre, so tragic. And then the shock of the jet crash had barely settled before the people of Seattle were accosted with subjugation to a foreign power. Now, each day they arose a conquered people.

Fear. Weakness. Loss.

His mom. Her diagnosis. What the Chinese might make her do. Would they provide medical care or just let people languish?

Dalton took the biggest risk of his life, hoping he could still do something good in this world, something that might matter, only to be lectured again by someone with authority but in his estimation, no brains.

Screw it. How incredibly stupid of me.

Chain of command; maddening, as always. There were things in the military you didn't fight. This looked like one of them. Fine. Chow and some quiet might not be bad anyways.

Back in his office, Stevens sized up the scenario. The commander knew how to read men and women, especially the challenging ones. Raw instinct in Officer's Candidate School, this crucial skill had evolved, serving him quite well over the last thirty-five years.

Getting this one right, he thought, might take a little time.

Not that he was unaware or ill-informed. One of the first tasks after the invasion had been announced was to search Army personnel archives for anyone, active or former, with a high level of coding expertise. Chinese control was based on the same from their side, so it was time to match the threat appropriately. Tens of thousands of potentials, but according to highly placed cohorts in DC, one name and one named project.

Dalton.

Sovereign.

Very few could put the two together, as those records weren't actually in the file now on Stevens' desk. But the man had his contacts. And, after Stevens himself had handed the note over to Dalton's mom, all he had to do was wait. His practiced poker face did the job with both Dalton and Meers. What lie ahead required testing, forging. Now was the time to press until almost-breaking, not after Dalton was already in play. He liked Dalton's spark, even from a few moments with him. But his record was far from clean. As much upside as cause for concern. He needed serious convincing as to the motives and abilities of this former soldier turned print salesman. Maybe his prayers were being answered. Maybe it was utter foolishness. Either way, the elder warrior would need time and input before deciding.

Ft. Clark, Medical Services Unit

The studious figure hovered over no less than five medical journals on the oversized counter space. Staring at the page, absorbing ideas constrained in black and white, and lost contentedly in the texts.

Captain *Lauralei McInnis,* MD, PsyD, a graduate of Loyola University and USC Medical School, was an internationally recognized expert in the field of military mental health. Highly regarded by colleagues worldwide, she was the kind of doc other docs quoted and referenced. Her latest research birthed ingenious new protocols for assessment and treatment, transforming the armed forces' approach to maintaining the psychological strength of its warriors. Prominent in the broader mental health stratosphere, any number of six-figure clinical appointments and the notoriety and travel that came with them were hers for the asking. Yet the forty-two-year-old Dr. Mac, as she preferred to be called, chose military rigor for her life's investment and passion.

A proud daughter and granddaughter of veterans, Mac was not merely familiar with the lifestyle and environment; she loved it, everything about it. Sacrifice. The embodiment of noble ideals. A call to something beyond oneself. The military was her siren song.

Though her transfer to the newly chartered Ft. Clark came suddenly, it came also as welcomed opportunity. Such a degree of military displacement was unknown. Men and women facing the shame of forced removal from American soil. These were good people, carrying the fates of stranded loved ones and civilian friends on their consciences. So this was the exact place her care would be most needed. She wanted to be here, doing all she could to keep these soldiers healthy and fit for duty. Only moments after the president's speech, the captain began lobbying for the post, whenever and wherever it might be established. The job was hers to turn down. No one else had even been considered.

A knock on the clinic door and she turned. Engulfed in her work and surprised by the general's appearance she took a moment to salute. But salute, she did. Beneath her usual white lab coat, she was all military.

"General, sir."

"At ease, Captain."

The general approached, plopping Dalton's file down on the Formica tabletop in the middle of the ten-by-twelve-foot space.

"Pardon my unannounced visit to your fine establishment. I need you to look this over and give me your professional opinion as to whether I am in need of your services."

McInnis didn't quite know what to do next.

He slid the folder around with identifying tag across the top.

"Um, sir," treading lightly. "This file is for a... Lieutenant Dalton? I don't see how this bears on your... mental health..."

The captain enjoyed a collegial relationship with the general. Still, it was early in her assignment at Clark and she wanted to do well.

"Sure it's relevant, Captain. I am seriously considering applying this aged signal corpsman to our nation's biggest fight, with outcomes almost too big to think about. That seems pretty nutty to me..."

Chewing the end of an unlit Macanudo, he pointed its soggy protrusion in her direction.

"... and I want *you* to tell me otherwise."

She nodded.

Stevens continued. "We may have been handed a gift from God here. This Dalton fella might be one of the only ways we can get our nukes back. Or, he may be as cracked as a Double-A egg from my grandpa's hen house. I am not sure presently which way to go on that proposition. I will need your full report and recommendations in two hours, Captain. That is all."

TWENTY THREE

"You do realize the gravity of your offense, don't you Mr. Dalton?"

The first volley neither excited nor scared him. It was all theatre, so Dalton responded in character, the role of impetuous genius.

"Maybe the university should hire someone better next time," he quipped. "And smarter."

Teacher stared past student, presumption on full display. The questioner, sitting at the edge of an antique walnut desk, shifted in disinterest, lighting a pipe and waving off the first puffs of smoke. The setting matched the attitude. Every square inch in the room was given to bookshelves, overflowing with bound volumes and notebooks. Between slow, laborious drags, he spoke again.

"Such may be the case. But we're not here to discuss the competence of the university's programming personnel, are we, Mr. Dalton?"

His professor-with-unknown-but-better-hand was an impeccable counterpoint. Completely stereotypical—sure, but the tweed jacket thing was actually pretty good. All predictably pleasant, even if somewhat overdone. Up to this point the encounter had gone as anticipated. That was all about to change as the older man's expression assured Dalton he was the good cop.

"Let me put it this way. You do not want to be expelled from this fine institution. This would be a grave mistake. You may find yourself in the private sector soon enough. But I can say with some certainty there will be unfortunate repercussions from walking away from your studies prematurely, and in this manner."

He puffed again, pointing the stem and bit at the cornered student.

"Vocational hurdles, shall we say. Difficult to overcome."

Message received. Clearly.

To continue denying the facts would mean stepping away as damaged goods, caution flags sent to every major employer in his field. He detested being trapped. He was also street-savvy enough to see the olive branch for what it was.

Dalton's acts that brought him here? Unbridled curiosity, mixed with a copious amount of devilishness, had rendered the computerized grading systems for 35,000 students inoperable. Nearly three million dollars. Six weeks of repair and reprogramming. A month and a half in which professors and staff worked the old-fashioned way, adding untold hours to already demanding schedules. And just like that, Dalton's remarkable undergrad success, complete with paid assistantships while still only a sophomore at the University of Washington, was in danger of meeting an untimely end.

This pipe-smoking inquisitor was now his best friend. Behind the desk and seated, his rhetoric decelerated, from thinly veiled threat to something far more reasonable.

"Mr. Dalton, I have something I'd like you to consider. Listen carefully before you respond."

Dalton nodded.

Fifteen minutes later he stood in an empty hallway, wondering where this all might end. The bargain wasn't an ultimatum, per se. Forgiveness and a cleansed academic record as well as paid graduate studies in exchange for some future service to his country. Dalton was good at sizing up wagers. Very good. So he gambled, assuming he would beat the odds again, whatever may come. And Dalton was the last one in the world to imagine Fallujah and Kabul as locales the piper would eventually demand repayment.

The memory of the university setting dissipated, fading to grotesque, wartime imagery, unwelcomed — again — onto the edges of his semiconscious mind.

Dalton awoke, startled and drenched in perspiration. A scratchy wool Army-issue blanket reminded him where he was: in the Ft. Clark brig. He wondered if this may have been the stupidest thing he had ever done. Given his past, it would have some serious competition. On the other hand, it contended more with every passing moment.

Fitful sleep played at a distance. So, staring upward, he performed some quick calculations of the dots in the ceiling tiles, applying them to complex geometric patterns and graphing relationships.

Just to pass the time.

Office of the Minister of Strategic Communications, Beijing

Zhou Dhe's face reddened. Puffy, over-inflated skin surrounded his nose and mouth. The blotchy complexion was partly the result of an unhealthy affinity for Baijiu, a staunch white liquor, 50% alcohol by volume. The remaining redness came from the aggravating phone call he was currently taking.

"He is *what*?"

Somehow, Dhe spoke quietly and forcefully at the same time.

"Gone," the detached reply on the other end of the line voiced. "Disappeared."

"How is this possible? This was nothing more than loose ends, remember?"

He allowed no response, cutting in again.

"Your guarantees are as flimsy as your work."

"Mr. Chang, I assure you we will..."

"No! No more incompetence; no more empty promises!" Dhe slammed the hard plastic receiver down into its 1970s style cradle. He would have none of it. No more failures. The young owner of Dawn Star had served his purpose. The government had the technology, even if in diminished state, and could follow through on their threats and realization of invasion. Even in light of the code migration and its unknowns.

Junjie Zang was no longer needed.

Neither was this contracted asset.

Dhe had always planned on multiple, irreversible disappearances as fundamental strategy. And yes, he and the committee had always intended to be the ones causing them. The minister fumed at what he considered a simple task.

But only a moment more. It was time to get to work.

Junjie, my boy. I am coming for you...

... myself.

Darkness covered his face, a mere reflection of true colors of the heart. He glanced at the calendar program on his laptop and then shut the lid.

Four days. That's a good lead, but you'll need more than a head start to survive, my young businessman.

His grin widened. To Dhe, this was as amusing as it was necessary.

TWENTY FOUR

A solitary fixture cast somber tones throughout the room. Junjie searched the eyes of the twelve men and women at the table. Their reassuring gazes made him feel safe—for the moment.

And then he broke down. Years of regret flowed, unconcerned with saving face. No more setting aside the things he had done. No more work or money or luxury to keep his deeds at a distance.

A withered, age-spotted hand reached out, trembling, and then landing gently on his left forearm. The timely gesture came from a woman, deeply respected and honored in their ranks. She was the smallest and oldest of those gathered. She was the elder who, after others talked, centered them with quiet yet potent words and faith. She was also the one Junjie had injured most deeply.

Biyu Fong's story intertwined with Junjie's; intimately so. Like many others from their Gansu village, she had experienced the transformation, as it came to be known. A new pair of eyes. A re-made heart and mind. They lived differently. They dealt with one another and peered into the unknowns of futures and fortunes... differently than before. But such matters of faith and life could not be left unchecked in the new China. The government was savior and none else. Her husband Lee had been imprisoned. Teams of uniformed men wreaked havoc, demanding renunciation of a perceived foreign loyalty. Their home was burned, left as rubble, while the few worldly treasures they'd accumulated lay disfigured, discarded in a smoldering, blackened pile as PRC soldiers stood callously by.

Biyu relocated to Beijing and joined the ranks of the growing, unofficial church— the underground church—in China. Far from turning her back on faith, she forged ahead, committed to making a difference for others. But her time there was truncated by the carelessness of a young, rising star in the business world and party ranks. It was after another five years of Gansu-like deprivations and fear that she walked out of prison.

She could not forget the images. Nor the beatings. Still, she emerged more courageous, tenacious, and surprisingly more forgiving, unhindered by the bitterness that should've fashioned shackles on her soul. The woman's sorrows ran deep yet her heart remained strong, so strong.

And so it was with forgiveness that she looked into the eyes of the man before her. The very man who traded away her name, location, and association with the underground for a promise of his own safety and a few government signatures on very large contracts.

It was as if he was re-living that very moment now. And it was killing him.

"Young one," searching Junjie's face while stroking his arm. "You carry much regret. Your eyes... "

Biyu lifted his chin in her tiny hand.

"... your gaze is faint."

It was so true.

Beyond his failure to this woman and her tribe, Junjie had spent an inordinate amount of time battering his heart over the broader what if scenarios. With eyes opened, he saw her scars. With eyes closed he endured the likenesses of dead friends, seared cruelly upon his memories. And what of his precious family? What if they weren't really safe? Envisioning his wife and child as dangerous pawns, drawing him to surrender—or worse—sickened him. He despised the license his work had conferred upon evil men. Junjie so wished to turn back the clock, to make different choices. Ones further in the past. Ones very present now.

"I know, mother Biyu. It is a heaviness that will not lift. I do not know what else to do. I am so very sorry… "

This last phrase had barely passed his lips before tears flowed again. It was unbearable. Gravity pressed in as if carrying a special load. Each movement a struggle. Every thought dulled.

Biyu squeezed his arm once more.

"Look at me, Junjie. Good. Hear this clearly: I care more for your soul than my body. I forgave you many, many years ago. A cold cell brings a clarity of mind and heart. As I had received forgiveness, so I forgave you. But now my son, I see you struggling to forgive yourself. Good news. This burden is not yours. You cannot make these things right by yourself. You can only cooperate now with the plans of heaven and with the resources of heaven. Go forward you must. But you do not go alone."

Her words took on authority disproportionate to her physical bearing. Such strength transferred in that moment to Junjie's heart. A peace not of his own making.

She motioned to the empty chair at the table. Junjie took his place, realizing it had always been there, waiting for him.

He was home. And it was time to get to work.

Their country's bold aggressions imparted many cares to the small group. They were proud Chinese citizens. Still, they stood appalled at the injustices of unprovoked invasion and captivity. They also shared a deep empathy with American Christ-followers, quickly singled out for their beliefs in the new province.

The realities were daunting. Overwhelming. Their response? They prayed, fiercely.

"We need your wisdom, Yasu."

"Please speak, direct us."

"Give our brother Junjie success. Protect him. Give him courage."

Simple yet heartfelt pleadings. Expectation and dependency on their faces, in their voices. Ten minutes later a calmness—palpable, emotionally tangible—settled in the room. It wasn't a cure-all. The challenges had not faded, much less been resolved. They were neither foolish nor naïve. No, this trouble-tested contingent stood more clear-eyed than ever. Failure, imprisonment, death. These were very real prospects, triggered by any actions they might undertake.

Junjie spoke.

"My dear brothers and sisters. I cannot thank you enough for receiving me. I realize I have broken your safety protocols but felt I had no choice. This is the only place I could come where Beijing might not probe so easily."

Rising emotion lodged the next few words in the back of his throat. Junjie swallowed hard, doing his best.

"I have lost friends, colleagues... stood over their lifeless bodies myself. Quan, Feng; both gone. And now I am a threat as well; one more contingency to be managed."

Eyes dropping to the tabletop, he found himself unable to look his cohorts in the face.

"I had nowhere else to run. Yet you graciously received me. In spite of all I've done. All I've not done. And now, as you know, I have made things worse. The power my company has unleashed is unpredictable at best. It is of the utmost importance that I start immediately to undo all of it. So, I must ask one more thing. Can I begin my work from here, with the added risk to you and yours?"

Biyu smiled.

Every other face joined in unspoken unison.

Wenatchee, Washington: Ft. Clark, Senior Leadership Unit

"So Captain, am I crazy? Or does our curious visitor have what it takes to save his countrymen from the ravages ahead?"

Dr. Mac reviewed her notes before answering. Dalton presented a huge upside. On the other hand, she couldn't dismiss her apprehensions. She proceeded cautiously and, as always, professionally.

"Sir, no question Dalton is a unique asset. Almost too good to believe. A more capable developer would be hard to find. One could think it quite fortuitous to have him on-base."

Stevens preempted, cutting her off mid-breath.

"Your diplomacy is noted, Captain. It's also annoying, so shoot straight. Am I hearing your reticence? You're uncomfortable with him engaging this mission?"

"General, sir. There are outstanding reasons to deploy the lieutenant. There are also a few cautions. For example, his family history..."

"Please Captain," Stevens broke in again. "I know all about that. Read it myself. Has daddy issues... don't we all."

"Sir, with due respect. The wounds resulting from these kinds of things can be of great significance in determining fitness for duty. If you would indulge me."

Mental health screenings, she reminded the general, were nothing new for men and women of the armed services. Minds, emotions, and stability are key factors in a soldier's performance. Since many of Dalton's combat assignments over the years were of a specialized nature, these inquiries dug deeper than usual. Fifteen full-scope evaluations. Over three hundred hours of prodding and poking. Every word and nuance recorded for scrutiny and posterity. Intense, thorough. Yet even at this, the best the U.S. Army could offer only scratched the surface.

For the next ten minutes, Mac meticulously connected the dots in Dalton's record. The official summary: detachment from authority associated with loss of paternal trust. The full story, of course, was a bit more complex.

TWENTY FIVE

1997.

A high school senior, Dalton was just trying to enjoy the springtime of his youth while keeping as low a profile as possible. It was the classic teen dilemma: be known for cool stuff but don't stick out. This delicate balance, challenging enough for most males in the throes of puberty, turns out to be a wholly more formidable undertaking when your father is famous.

James Murifield Dalton pastored a large, Suburban Seattle church. His ministry had grown steadily over a dozen or so years, from small congregation on the outskirts of King County to four thousand parishioners and ultra-modern facilities, complete with worldwide television, print, and internet presence, on the more upscale eastside of the city.

Pastor J, as he preferred to be called, was everywhere during those years. Omnipresent, some might say. Court-side tickets at Sonics home games. Ribbon cuttings. Broader religious community gatherings. One minute you might hear him testifying at a city council meeting and the next catch his opinions via interview on the nightly news.

This was extraordinary in Seattle.

Faith leaders in this significantly agnostic part of the country rarely double as public figures. Some religion is fine of course, so long as it doesn't become dominant. That would be fanaticism. Add to this a systemic distrust—again the independent pioneering thing—and you understand Dalton's presence and influence as quite surprising. The personal charisma and reach of Pastor J ensconced him as something like the Jesse Jackson of the Puget Sound. Appreciated by some, a source of skepticism for many.

Dalton and his father were not close. Meetings and speaking engagements took precedence over ballgames and schoolwork. The things normal dads do with their kids at night and on weekends, the everyday bonds that many parent-child relationships are built upon, all but absent. Still, a deep regard for his father had taken root early, a foundational piece of Dalton's family life and worldview. With reasonable uncertainty about truths his father held without question, he remained convinced of the basics. At least until the Autumn of '98.

There was no way to buffer the young man from what came to light. The furious downward spiral, front page news, served as water cooler commentary for the next six months. A classically tragic fall from grace. Embezzlement of church funds. Illicit sexual relationships. A well-hidden dependence on prescription drugs. Settling somewhat during the protracted investigation, the pain and humiliation kicked up with renewed force at his dad's excruciatingly public verdict and sentencing. At the start of the new millennium, Pastor J was facing seventeen years in Walla Walla State Penitentiary. Guilty—all counts. The financial side of the scandal topped out at over three million dollars with drug-selling charges thrown in to boot.

Dalton's dad would pay for his sins.

Tragically, so would his son.

"Captain, you've only told me what I already know," Stevens intoned.

"Sir, again with respect. This is the fundamental reason he's a risk. Everyone holds something as the corpus of their psyche. For some, it's a political system. Others hold to religious ideals. Some believe they, themselves, are all they need: the mantra of self-reliance. For Dalton, this foundational inner anchor was his father. Even though they weren't close, he was his center. This all came crashing down at nineteen years of age... and he never replaced it. Not with anything. Under duress, an individual's center-mass of identity is what keeps them from imploding; on task, in the fight. Dalton doesn't have this anymore; hasn't for quite a few years. It's no exaggeration, psychologically speaking, to say he is empty... void."

Mac slowed again, assuring nothing would be left unsaid.

"This is the weakness we can't predict, can't control."

The general leaned forward, ever-present cigar dangling.

"And exactly why he named his project *Sovereign*," understanding growing on the general's face. "He believed in a divinity both in control and always good. His father's digressions proved that wrong and took any other human being out of the running, all at the same time. So, he creates something. Something he thinks might be the answer, only to leave it unfinished. And then only to see it resurrected as demon instead of angel."

"Sir?"

"Yeah, probably should have filled you in on that part as well, Captain. But I had clearances to consider. At least until now."

"You mean Dalton… "

"Exactly. Dalton is the Chinese code's daddy. Well, sort of. Like most things, they stole it from us and then took it from there."

"Unbelievable."

"Yes, it is. But also where we stand as of this moment, with a good chunk of Washington State in Chinese hands and three million of our citizens in harm's way. Thank you, Captain," he softened. "You are dismissed."

Stevens allowed himself another moment after she'd left the room. Leaning back, his eyes came forward to the desk, landing on a miniaturized wooden totem pole among the mess of personal memorabilia. He fingered the rough edges of the carving, turning it over, considering it. The miniature had been a gift from his daughter some years back, brought home after a field trip to one of the many Native American communities in the state. She was so excited to tell him all she had learned, especially how this symbol functioned as a visual representation of the totality of tribal life, with the very top figure serving as "overseer", their protection. In battle, she'd been told, the significance of a fallen totem was unmatched. If indeed it fell, this represented utter destruction.

The removal of their center — their core.

Stevens made his decision.

Could there be a reclamation of all that those left behind were losing daily, their everything — their core? He didn't really know, hoped this might be the case. He only knew what he was prepared to give.

Everything.

Opening a new email, he typed out a few, significant words:

Attention: Ft. Clark Senior Command. Immediately commence...

Operation: Restore Totem.

Undisclosed Location, Qingdao

Literally on the other side of the world, another plan went into motion.

To have a shot at succeeding, two resources would be required: fast internet and reliable power. Throughout most of Qingdao this would not be a problem. But when you are in hiding, the very things you need are the very things that can lead others to you.

"You cannot simply manufacture power, Junjie."

The voice, stereotypically technician-speak, was a great match for the individual from whom it had emanated.

Quan Doh pushed black, wire-rim glasses back up his nose, let out an exasperated breath, and started again. Maybe he could get through to his aggravatingly slow pupil this time.

"You must multiply power which is already there," he lectured. "But not in ways that get you noticed."

Quan was beyond brilliant. Mensa would have been fortunate to have him. As the technical lead for this team supplying resources to the unregistered church he performed vital yet often unnoticed services. His job? Help Christians in China who chose not to affiliate with the state church increase their effectiveness in teaching and training by providing them with strategic communications and electronic assets. All while staying out of the watchful eye of the government.

"So, Quan my friend, how do we do this?"

"With this," Quan tapped his right forefinger onto the work table in front of them. "... of course."

Nothing spectacular, just a small-ish black box. Male receptacle on one end. Another on the opposite edge. Topside, three run-of-the-mill computer to wall connections.

Junjie trusted the be-speckled man. Still, he had to ask. "This looks like some sort of power strip. Correct?"

Quan was crushed. For a moment it seemed he might walk away, sulking.

"Quan, I'm sorry. I know this must be much more than that." Doing his best to keep him talking: "Please, explain it to me."

The technician's head rose slightly.

"This..." he continued. "Provides ten times the capacity of a residential outlet."

Junjie did the quick mental math. Impressive. Quan went on, pointing to the first male end.

"The existing electrical service connects here. Transformers condition, clean, and amplify the current, giving you a small generating station's worth. But here..." he beamed. "Here's the real magic. The outgoing current is transformed back to exactly what went in the front end. Dirty, intermittent, whatever. And the net result for you will be..."

Junjie finished his sentence.

"I remain invisible. No spike in electrical usage for anyone to observe. Nothing for local authorities to note. Nothing at all. Quan, this is amazing. And so critical. Thank you, brother."

"Junjie, I have a few other items I think you might be interested in as well."

Quan completed the show-and-tell session and Junjie couldn't help but think he had just experienced the Chinese version of a James Bond film, where the spy gets a tour of all the new gadgets and weapons before embarking on a mission. Slick British operative, Junjie was not. But these last few minutes served their purpose, increasing his odds, even if only marginally.

TWENTY SIX

The instructor patiently reviewed the unfamiliar Chinese alphabet, searching for comprehension among weary, defeated faces.

The middle-aged Caucasian was new to the material, like everyone else. While the coursework was as expected for a Community College-level introduction to Asian languages, the setting and circumstances most certainly were not. In years past students approached of their own accord, preparing for a stint in foreign service work or relocation with major international corporations. Others for personal enrichment, an expansion and experience outside of their normal cultural context. Those rooms hosted self-motivated students, looking to better their lives or that of others. Today? This classroom was held fast by far more basic realities; those occupying the lower end of Maslow's Pyramid. Fear. Control. Survival.

To be fair, a few were intrigued with the new material. But most had been pressed into action by the two PRC Army guards posted inside the back door, coldly performing their room monitoring duties with JS 9mm submachine guns in hand. This was not an unfortunate anomaly. The same scenario played out in every last classroom available across the Seattle Metro area. When filled, offices, waiting rooms, and janitorial closets surfaced as the next best holding tanks of the oppressive tutelage. Professors like this one served at the behest of new management. The majority of former faculty at SCC where now students themselves, forcibly introduced to what in better circumstances would've been valuable, deepening enterprises.

Two-hour shifts, six days per week, conquered individuals reported to local learning centers. Before work. During the workday. Still more, after hours. Math and Sciences instruction would continue as needed. History, language, and economic theory had been composed and authorized thousands of miles away on the Chinese mainland. It was the logical next step: identity transition. Beijing's social engineers understood the transformational powers of language and culture. They also knew the value of borders.

Impassable mountain ranges. An internationally policed border to the north. A mammoth river to the south. It all added up to an almost impenetrable stretch of land to inhabit and protect. Some two and a half hours south of Seattle, these advantages were becoming obvious daily.

The *Columbia River*, head-watered in British Columbia, Canada, flowing southward and west to the Pacific, created an imminently defensible southern border. America's third largest river by volume, the Columbia employs wide runs and deep channels — waterways easily patrolled and defended.

Chinese presence here was already unmistakable. After navigating ocean to river via Cape Disappointment, sixteen Shanghai-2 gunboats now roamed her brownish-green waters. Built for this exact purpose and at a displacement of

135 tons, they reached speeds upward of 25 knots. Such quickness would not be needed. Still, it guaranteed they'd neither be overtaken nor outrun. With four 35mm deck mounted turrets, the same number of 25mms, and one 81mm long-range gun, they owned more than enough firepower as their crews — thirty-six naval warriors each — stood ready to defend their new province against all challengers.

Thus, one-hundred-fifty or so miles of mountainous foothills to deep sea waters created a formidable boundary, one not to be challenged anytime soon. Beijing had chosen well. These natural borders were their new, Western Wall.

It was both tragic and ironic. Such stark beauty had bolstered local pride for as long as the area had been inhabited. Now, these very qualities were becoming tools despotism would use to conquer and control. But the Chinese weren't leaving it all up to nature, either. In addition to the riverine defense corridor of the Columbia herself, they were also creating three fortress-cities along the waterway. Vancouver (WA), Kelso, and Astoria were rapidly transforming into embattlements, with non-vital native personnel displaced to counties under an hour away. Left behind was a minimal populace, one more in line with these new towns' true purpose: defending and protecting the edges of their territory. Part of their attractiveness was that they could only be broached from the south by bridge. These steel-engineered marvels, once fair traveled mechanisms of interstate commerce and life, now marked an international border, and one between quite unfriendly neighbors. Chinese tanks maintained their brawny stoicism at the halfway point over each concrete span, where, at the slight arc of a two-lane highway over the river, a pair of hostile, sovereign nation-states met.

The imprint of occupation was everywhere. Overflights from the recently-christened Baotong Air Base policed the skies above as crews of mortar and small arms fire teams manned sandbagged positions every few hundred yards along the banks of the mighty Columbia. Raw force and propaganda extended like two fists. Each was necessary. Each would be brutal. And only a few hours north of these barbed-wire, artillery zones, classroom lessons spoke of a new, golden age dawning in Western Washington.

A Chinese Age.

"**Instructor.** I am glad to see your pupils so hard at work. I am wondering, though, have we overlooked something this morning?"

Still dark, not 6:00am yet, the grating, thin voice of the school's supervisor — their new chancellor — matched the room's mood. No one wanted to be here, at this or any other hour.

"I am sorry, Chancellor. We have been so vigorously engaged that we... forgot."

"Well then, some amount of disorder initially is understandable, instructor, but let's be about the business of good citizenry."

Rotating toward the classroom, the chancellor continued. He walked the aisles, enjoying his newfound authority while effusing a twisted version of reality, step by ugly step.

"You have before you a remarkable opportunity. The chance to prosper as fulfilled members of the greatest nation on this planet. Your country, admirable in its rebellious infancy, is a mere shell of its former strength, a spiral of national and cultural degradation. You are escaping a sinking ship. A grateful response to such an invitation is in order, is it not? It reminds us how fortunate we are."

Chancellor looked to instructor.

She stared him down.

"Well, let me see," an unneeded look to the name on her desk. "Ms. Dalton?"

He gave her another chance.

She gave back the same.

"I would think this is especially an opportunity for someone like yourself. An opportunity for restored honor, considering your family left that behind years ago. I am correct, instructor?"

Dalton's mom wasn't budging.

He pointed.

"This woman could not even keep her family intact. Her husband failed her. Her faith failed her. She should have been the matron of her home but instead had to return to work, teaching. Her son..."

"No!" she yelled, quite uncharacteristically.

The guards moved to guns drawn, a single step forward and at the ready.

The chancellor waved them off.

"I am sure that will not be necessary. It is unfortunate that even your son has left you. I can empathize with your loss. Tragic, really. But that is what happens when building a country on false hopes and faulty systems."

She knew to leave it there. Then she grinned at what else she knew.

Oh, trust me, Mr. "Chancellor." He'll be back.

The former professor called for her students to stand. She couldn't meet their cast-down eyes, managing instead only a feeble hand motion. They recited words projected at the front of the room:

We are happy, thankful citizens of the People's Republic of China. Though from different origins, we are all a part of each other; laboring for the good of all and the glory of our new motherland.

"Well then," satisfied for the moment. "Carry on, instructor."

TWENTY SEVEN

Northern City Limits—Tacoma

Sgt. Sanchez had observed enough of Chinese transport, command, and control activity to feel she had a decent handle on it.

The rigorous daily discipline of taking up position just off the landing strips at Baotong provided a good sense of men and resources coming into the area by plane. A partial image, but an important piece of the puzzle. She couldn't account for sea-borne assets arriving via the Pacific and through the Straight of Juan de Fuca. These would harbor farther to the north. Tracking that intel, she hoped, was somebody else's job. Someone hiding and watching, like she was. Content with the picture thus far, she was expanding surveillance outward. Strengths and weaknesses of the enemy. Overall health and morale of American captives. Sanchez had completed several near-base recon missions the last few days. Now she needed eyes-on throughout the city. What she found was disheartening, to say the least.

The contingent of Chinese soldiers and airmen tasked to the takeover had turned out to be nearly four times the capacity of the former American military installation's barracks, family units, and officers' quarters. The logistics question became: how do you take care of 100,000 men? The answer was fairly simple — former US citizens' homes. It was a harsh move, not at all uncommon in human history. The fact it had happened many times before didn't make it any easier for Tacoma's more established neighborhoods. Not at all. These families had been here for decades, some for generations. The sting struck every night as fathers and mothers tucked young ones into bed in army-issue cots at local high school gymnasiums instead of their regular warm surroundings. Less austere than refugee camps the world over, the accommodations still underscored their displacement, as the fog of the unknown hung with no real answer coming soon as to when, or if, they could ever go home again.

Sanchez tested her reach in ever-widening concentric circles. Most of her work was done at night, under the faithful camouflage of darkness. Some of the Chinese guards who should've prevented her from roaming were also the least disciplined, opening wide her advantage. It'd taken her the better part of the past forty-eight hours but she was in position now in the hillsides above the city's convention center. At just after midnight, invisible to ground and air patrols, she got some needed rest.

The sergeant awoke in heavy underbrush as the sun rose, cresting the hills behind, a slight rise in temperature caressing her back. Reflections off the sheltered waters of Commencement Bay, just two klicks from her current position, were stunning. Gentle waves danced with light as a glint of gold crowned the massive, domed, white-topped structure, below and center of her position. So beautiful. A scant moment of enjoyment in an otherwise hellish scene.

Unending lines.

Americans, snaking from four main entrances into the building, stretching through acres of parking stalls and about a half mile into downtown. A forced march, despised by every single one of them. While nominally a token act of submission—to have to show up and simply identify yourself—this was, in fact, an enormous offense to a people accustomed to unquestioned freedoms.

The largest covered wooden structure of its kind in the world, the Tacoma Dome could seat 23,000 people. Once a gathering place for rabid soccer fans and high school grads, the cavernous environs now served as one of the hastily established regional Citizens' Registration Centers (CRC). The space had hosted the likes of U2 and Billy Graham. Now, former American residents were required to appear, to be accounted for.

The area housed five such sites, the T-Dome, the largest. Organized by neighborhood precincts, each household was to come to their assigned Center, wait in line, and receive identification numbers for every family member, stamped onto their upper right forearm; a not-quite permanent inking, both faster and cheaper than a traditional tattoo. Although fading in about six months, the chemical markers would remain for the better part of a decade. Lastly, they would forfeit U.S. Social Security cards and passport in the culmination of a grotesque public shaming.

Every newly-stamped Chinese citizen was also to declare their new worker's status. A census of sorts, the act established each person's value to the regime. Though official declarations assigned a benign neutrality to the classification, any reasonable student of history might think otherwise.

You've got to be kidding me.

Sanchez exhaled quietly, watching the lemming-like procession with equal parts cynicism and unbelief. She'd seen it before, too many times, frankly. Humans treating other, different humans like animals, resources, numbers. Military officers are often excellent historians. The sergeant recognized the beginnings of a series of centralized power plays, leading to an ever increasing devaluation of those shuffling forward in line, inch by dehumanizing inch.

C'mon, you're Americans!

The Chinese controlled U.S. nuclear capabilities and had used that control when crowds surged forward into Pike Place, weeks back. It was their veto power, with no question now as to whether they would use it. There also remained no question as to whether the next launch would achieve impact and detonation.

None whatsoever.

And so Sanchez watched endless lines of her countrymen be identified, categorized, and assessed. No one would've blamed the sergeant for feeling helpless. She didn't.

She got angry.

The Pentagon—Washington, DC

Petty Officer Third Class *Craig Mortensen* sat unflinchingly before the triple-monitor display, searching for any sign of the enemy's weakness. He had manned this position for the better part of two weeks with only limited sleep and breaks. The place was orderly but quite unkempt, the volume of fast food wrappers in the room alone could serve as the basis for a graduate-level marketing studies research project. Half empty Coke cans and trail mix packaging littered the desktop. An aroma hovered stubbornly; one to be expected from long hours, a lesser concern for personal hygiene, and extra onions on every burger. Clearly, there were practical reasons the higher-ups never visited here, as well as a general lack of knowledge about the critical work being done at these standard-issue desks.

Mortensen's assignment: an ultra-high clearance area known only as *The Vault.*

A unique collaboration of military and civilian intelligence communities, he and a handful of other skilled technicians worked this fourteen-by-ten-foot space, hidden deep inside the walled fortress of the Pentagon. A dozen or so people knew this room was in the building. Fewer had been here. Officially, it didn't exist.

The simplicity of the place was incongruous with its crucial national security purposes. White, unadorned walls. Three, eight-foot-long workstations. Nothing even remotely high-techie. Yet the room's effectiveness — its true power, lay in what you couldn't see. Beyond framing and drywall, hundreds of tentacles of cabling extended to multiple, highly controlled spaces, each housing unimaginably powerful computing platforms. This was merely the control room, the input and readout side of America's hugely secretive weapon in the world of cyber-warfare.

In front of Mortensen, along the center of three, twenty-four-inch LCD displays, ran an unending, vertical progression of code. The waterfall of ones and zeros flowed on, hour after hour. The remaining two screens of this digital triptych, flanking left and right, were populated with on-screen gauges and widgets. These apps kept vigilant, automated watch over all processes and anomalies, hopeful or disconcerting.

The PO3 reached for another can of Coke, popped the lid and turned back to his work. Blinking, Mort rubbed his eyelids and looked again.

"No way. No way, nowayy, nowayyyy."

His fingers flew, furiously typing line commands, though the soft-key surface robbed Mort of the satisfying clickety-clack that should've punctuated the moment. The serviceman closed the distance between face and screen to only a few inches. He needed to be convinced, absolutely, about what he thought he was seeing.

Fifteen minutes later the petty officer arrived at his CO's office, dot-matrix printout in hand and expectant grin on his face.

"Sir. This..." the paper flashed out."... is what we've been looking for."

Mortensen was breathless. Aside from basic training, which had almost killed the sedentary warrior, the two-floor stairwell sprint—the elevator was too slow—was the greatest exertion his body had endured in a long time. He handed the pages of code, indecipherable to anyone except the small team of experts at the Vault, to his senior officer.

"Mort, what is this? You know I can't make any sense out of that scribble."

"Sorry, sir."

Chest heaving, the technician swallowed hard, mouth crying out for moisture to ease his words.

"We've been running our best attempts. Tracing the programming that has allowed them to steal command of our nukes. Early on we could observe what they were doing but we haven't yet been able to break it down, to compromise it. Like watching a predator hunt and kill your favorite pet from behind a shatter-proof wall. Maddening."

His CO would require an actual point soon, so Mort plowed ahead.

Another big breath. "Sir, it's changing... and... changing our code along with it."

"So?" the CO dismissed. "The Chinese are re-programming as they go. Wouldn't we do the same? Respond to on-the-ground realities. React, evade."

Mortensen shook his head.

"No, sir, not like that at all. Someone made a mistake."

"I am officially not following this line of information now Mort," the CO said, taking another sip of room-temperature coffee.

Mortensen took his best shot.

"Sir, the code is changing...

... itself."

"What, you mean like AI? Spooky sci-fi, robots take over the world kind of stuff?"

"Well, sort of, sir. It's all quite speculative. What we can see is that someone on their side tried to access a backdoor. A way back into the code if they ever needed to alter its basic structure or redirect its work. But they made it worse, at least if they intended to reassert control, anyways, because the outcome was the exact opposite. What we do know is the two sets—ours and theirs—are somehow cooperating toward an unstated, presumably collective end."

The CO squinted.

"Mort, bottom shelf this thing for me. Are we getting back our bombs, or not?"

Mortensen looked him full in the face; a rarity for the man.

"We don't know, sir. It's never happened before. All we know is the locus of control is changing. The Chinese code's stranglehold is diminishing. We don't know how much, or if, it will even continue. And we certainly don't know what's ahead if the two streams continue combining."

As Mort exited, the senior officer considered shelving the info. Too early. Promising, yes, but anyone above him would be looking for actionable intel, which he did not have. At least not yet. And not to the degree required.

The CO huffed again.

You better be onto something here, son.

Then he picked up his secure phone, punching the four digits that called up Strategic Command.

TWENTY EIGHT

Ft. Clark—Wenatchee, WA

Dalton leaned over chain link and retched into an empty, rusted receptacle.

He had hurried off the track and over to the portable parade grounds and was now dangling nearly halfway inside the silver cylinder. Dalton's head lightened, lactic acid seeping into major muscle groups, searing his joints and tendons. His entire body screamed, surprised at the radical adjustment in early morning expectations— print salesmen don't do this kind of thing. While Dalton had kept a moderate exercise regimen over the last number of years, this was altogether different. Thirty-six hours in, Restore Totem was starting to feel like Special Forces Hell Week on steroids. No one thought they could make a super soldier out of the retired signal corpsman. Still, they needed to be assured he could handle himself if need be. His brains were the ultimate weapon in his kit, but his head was attached to his body and the two tend to work in concert. He was again active duty. And this was a very real deployment. Perhaps the most critical for him and his country either had yet encountered.

Welcome back to the Army.

Still leaning over the can, bile elevated, threatening another upward trek. Dalton kept it down this time.

No.

No one would catch him in this condition. Collecting himself, he stood and turned toward another mile and a half on the rubberized, lined surface. He steeled himself for the grueling last phase of the run and fell back into a decent, if reduced, pace.

A voice surprised, approaching quickly from the rear. Again, that infuriating brogue.

"Anything I can do for ya, LT?"

Dalton stayed quiet, focused ahead.

Ignore him. He's a cretin. Just ignore him.

Sergeant Lochland pulled into step, exchanging slow, even breaths—barely perceptible.

"Would there be any way I can make you feel better, mah friend? A nice, soft couch... or a bigger can to puke in?"

Over the next five minutes, every few steps brought more of the same from Dalton's new workout buddy. Then, just for fun, Loch turned backwards, effortless and at that same pace.

He finished the last 400 this way.

Dalton completed his run, doing his best to not simply fall over. As spent as he had ever been, hands on hips was as far as he would go in communicating how awful he really felt. If pain was "weakness leaving the body", his body was facilitating a mass, chaotic exodus. His lung tissue felt thin as one-ply toilet paper, each breath a total commitment. Eventually his chest slowed, ragged but steady. Dalton turned to face the barracks. Thirty paces later he stopped at attention.

"General Stevens."

Standing still was excruciating but he would do what was expected, what was required.

"Carry on, Lieutenant."

"Sir."

Dalton planned nothing more than to collapse in the shower before moving onto the rest of this day's demanding schedule. More testing. More prep. Given it would be in a chair or at a workstation, at least he could recover before the next round of PT.

A figure raced past.

Both men turned.

Loch, taking another 800 meters at full sprint, just for kicks.

Dalton shook his head and went inside.

The human blur came off the course, breathing no harder than if he had just gotten out of bed. Loch approached his CO. A salute offered and returned.

"Lochland. Tell me what you think. Don't sugar-coat it."

The sergeant toweled off needlessly. Not a single bead of sweat loitered.

"Well, sir. Ah will put it this way... he won't save us all with his physical prowess alone."

"That is to be expected," the superior officer replied.

Aboard the USS George H.W. Bush—Pearl Harbor, HI

Orders for *Restore Totem* came fast for the nine warships comprising Carrier Group 2, stationed at Joint Base Pearl

Harbor-Hickam (JBPHH). Under cover of night and out into the boundless Pacific, graceful gray hulls cut through mild surf, no moonlight to betray their presence or passing. The flagship *Bush,* three Ticonderoga-class cruisers: *Philippine Sea, Leyte Gulf,* and *Anzio,* as well as the five warships of Destroyer Squadron 22, were in motion. Their air complement included Carrier Wing 8, comprised mostly of FA18 Hornets. The two attack subs in the cohort— *Albuquerque* and *Seahorse*—glided silently beneath. Chances were that Group 2 would not remain undetected as long as necessary. The hope was simply that odds would work out in their favor. Timing and luck, needed in equal quantities.

There remained almost five thousand miles to China's coast. The task ahead? Stay hidden until achieving strategic advantage. One might think this impossible. But the Pacific is a vast hiding place, even for something as large as a carrier consort. The proposition was straightforward: reposition GHW Bush and company within range of the Chinese mainland. Not unlike a boxer holding a shorter-armed opponent at bay, the question would come down to this: how close could you sneak before having to engage?

With a striking distance of around 500 nautical miles, the fighter wing would need lots of time to move in unnoticed. Missiles from ships and the two subs alongside could set loose somewhat farther out, say up to 2000 nm. But this was a whole other kind of battle, one they all would rather avoid. The naval group's presence stood in clear violation of mandates from Beijing. And if Beijing still had their thumb on the button, millions of people would be murdered in a firestorm of primal forces released onto American soil.

Rear Admiral *Marianne Knowles*, a keen observer of her crew and people generally, approached the ensign at the comm.

"Ensign. Status."

"Admiral," he replied. "We are full ready. Silenced rules until 0600."

"Superb."

Her tone allowed there might be more. "Anything else, ensign?"

"Ma'am," he opened up. "Do you think this will work? I mean, what are the chances we'll arrive at the right time... that we'll regain control in time to strike?"

Knowles shifted slightly.

The concept, on paper, was simple enough. Take back American diplomatic and national destiny. The Pentagon believed an opening existed. For her part, the stated tactical objectives strayed as far from certainty as the mariner had ever experienced. Leadership of the thousands of fine men and women under her command begged for a more measured response.

"Our job is not to predict outcomes, sailor. It is to be in position and ready. And if a fight is to be had, we'll bring it."

TWENTY NINE

Dalton's butt had occupied hard metal for over an hour, his body covered with sensors. Adhesive reddened his skin, pinching hair on arms and legs. Capturing every conceivable piece of biometric input, the Ft. Clark team ran Dalton through its paces. He had encountered tests like this before. This one, at least, was interesting.

A first-person sim, five by five feet, covered the wall. Turns, doorways, and paths unfolded as options, more confusing at every stage. No tangible bearings. No landmarks or visual oddities. The three-dimensional reality bore no textures, no surfaces. The test was designed to provide only complex, raw directional datum, demanding a high degree of independence from the very elements most humans require to problem-solve. It was a bit like a mathematical equation containing only variables.

And Dalton was killing it.

Dr. Mac looked on from the booth at the back of the room, astounded. This particular test had over three years of results between three hundred seventeen subjects. The furthest anyone had achieved was the seventh run before tapping out. Dalton was currently making his way, unhindered, through round twenty-three, with no signs of stopping anytime soon. Had the doctor been able to peer inside his head, she'd have been even more impressed and as equally intrigued.

It was all there.

Every turn, each decision. Every choice over the last sixty minutes as present as the one before, all fitting together. An active, symbiotic, living puzzle.

The screen in the room went blank.

Nothing.

General Stevens, standing with Dr. Mac in the small, dark space, posed the obvious question:

"What. Did it break?"

His thoughts went to logistics.

Given the rapid deployment of Clark, maybe the install was faulty? Techs left out a few screws here or there?

The eminent psychiatrist spoke in disbelief.

"Sir, not exactly. The programming was never finalized. Budget cuts, eighteen months in. Somebody on the Hill thought we were wasting time and money on "video games for soldiers", got some senators riled up, and poof, there goes the project. We hoped it would still be a viable assessment tool. To this point, it has been. Honestly, we thought no one would get this far."

Impatient as always, Dalton tore the sensors off his forearms and thighs.

The captain stepped into the room.

"Lieutenant Dalton. Please, wait a moment."

Dalton was all tangled up in wires. He also wasn't slowing down any to sort it all out.

"Okay, that was fun but I'm a little tired now. Gotta be lunchtime already. And if you don't mind, I really need to get at that code. We're burning time we don't have. We've got way more important things to tackle than your suped up Nintendo here."

More lines and tape, balled up, discarded.

"Which, by the way, I did *not* break."

Mac sought a cue from her CO. She got it.

"Lieutenant Dalton," Stevens' disembodied voice broadcast over the speaker system. "We are done with evals. Report to mission prep at 1300 in the sit room. That is all."

The situation room at Clark, appearing as hastily put together as the rest of the camp, nonetheless had everything necessary, at a very basic level, to launch and preside over a major op. A conference table seating ten. An upgrade in chairs, owing to the fact that people occupied them for extended periods. Sadly, the coffee was still bottom barrel, Army-issue. Browning sides of glass carafes spoke volumes about the lack of care toward such a critical component of modern warfare.

Dalton stared, offended.

Dr. Mac was in place, as was Colonel Meers. Loch was across the table with another aide to the commander.

Everyone stood.

General Stevens entered and the video wall came to life, Presidential Seal fading into view. The feed jumped and then settled.

From the Oval Office, Sec Def, Homeland Security, and the National Security Advisor sat on one side, occupying chairs and couch. CIA and FBI took up places opposite. Aides lingered in the near-background but the focal point was forward, aimed at the president's desk and waiting for secure signal lock. Given the go-ahead from the on-site tech director, he opened the conversation.

"General Stevens. Good to see you. I wish it were under better circumstances."

"First off," he continued. "Your handling of the evacuation and resettlement duties is a credit to your professionalism and that of your staff. I know this was perhaps one of the most challenging things this nation has ever asked of you. I am indebted for how you have comported yourself and your command."

"Mr. President. That is a great compliment. I will pass it along to the many fine soldiers who've made hard things happen this past week."

"Yes, General, I am certain you will."

The two were long-time friends, their early paths tracing a parallel arc. Both had enjoyed the finest leadership training in the country. Mike Stevens had applied these lessons over a lifetime of military service. The president, obviously, had walked the path of political influence and governance.

"General..."

He paused, formalities seeming unnecessary, and started again.

"Mike... we've been working two scenarios. It's time to coordinate and make some decisions. I have authorized Carrier Group 2 out of Pearl to proceed westward, toward China. Our current understanding of the code degeneration is still dicey but we need assets on the move, covering all contingencies."

"Yes, Mr. President."

Stevens could not bring himself to refer to his CIC by first name.

"And so," the president asked. "Your side of the ballgame? Is he ready? I need to hear it from you, Mike."

Stevens, along with everybody else in the room, looked at Dalton.

"Mr. President, he is prepped... and he's the best chance we've got."

Dalton didn't expect to be thrown under the bus. Still, the general's words and tone were most encouraging.

"Well then, Mike, I am authorizing full green light—every aspect. God bless your team. We'll need it."

The screen went black. Everyone exhaled.

Dalton and Stevens were last to leave. Almost to the doorway, Dalton turned.

"General? Sir, I know I've been a pain in the keester... "

The general neither challenged nor corrected.

"... but you have to know. I am fully committed to this thing. Our country has taken a blow every citizen feels deeply, a wound only festering until we do something. Something crazy, sure. But that's all we've got, far as I can tell."

It seemed corny, a bad line in a B movie, but he meant it.

"Sir, I will do my best. You have my word... as a soldier... and an officer."

Stevens knew he'd made the right call.

"I know you will, son. I know you will."

THIRTY

Junjie had considered this moment almost ad nauseum. Then again, it wasn't everyday you invited a potential enemy into your nuclear storehouse.

Treason. For real, this time. Unlike the trumped-up charges for which his father had suffered, he was preparing to entrust the safety and sovereignty of his nation to an unknown other. That is, if they were actually alive and the one he thought still had to be out there, somewhere.

C:>|......

The Vault

Mort keyed in a few last strokes and waited.

"Secure link, check. Transmission speed at 98%."

The tech sat back and whistled.

"Lt. Dalton, you've got quite the hotrod now. Hope you know how to treat her."

Ft. Clark, CyOps Unit

Dalton heard the quip.

"Well, it's been awhile but I think we can do some damage. I mean," checking his metaphor, and almost seeing the cringe on the other end. "I mean… she's a beaut and I'll have her back in the garage by eleven, gassed up and waxed."

Nothing.

That was okay. Dalton had moved on.

Alright, first levels, bye bye.

Stevens, a few feet away, looked for signs of progress in the man's keystrokes or countenance, knowing even that may not help him follow the action.

Dalton kept entering.

Oh, I see what you did there. Well, better luck next time.

The dance continued another five minutes. Then Dalton sat back, a quizzical look and arms across chest.

"Nice."

Nothing more.

"So," Stevens stepped in. "Not to ask questions with answers I may not understand… but… nice?"

Dalton weighed the effort.

"Yeah, general. Really nice, actually. The structure of this authentication sequence is way beyond what I imagined."

"Wait, the authentication sequence? You're not actually inside the codestream?"

"Ha, no. Not even close, sir. But the entryway is quite good. Whoever did this knows their stuff. And a bit more. They're obviously laying the groundwork for incredibly limited access. And only for an equal."

"Well, that would be you, right Dalton?"

"So far."

More stillness.

"You will proceed, then?"

"Nope. Not yet."

The general did his best to hide a growing impatience.

"Sir," Dalton added. "This authentication sequence was designed to stop the vast majority of attempts at its first few firewalls. I got past eighteen and then it stopped. But I think that's the design as well. All we can do now is wait for an invite. Across the moat and into the courtyard still doesn't get us through the massive front door."

Qingdao

Junjie started in.

```
C:>|access>checks
C:>|activity logged> scan in process...
```

Fielding negative results for days, the young businessman hoped today would be different. He got an answer almost immediately.

```
C:>|fire1... cleared
C:>|fire2... cleared
C:>|fire3... cleared...
```

The screen kept counting, all the way to eighteen.

Ft. Clark

Dalton sat up, surprised but excited. He'd not imagined a realtime interface.

```
C:>|proceed...
```

Protocols? Dalton entered.

```
C:>|proceed...
```

Clearly, this was going to be a test; every step. A digital sword in the stone kind of thing.

Dalton smiled.

Okay then. You asked for it.

Rolling code filled the screen, the man pausing only so slightly to consider a next wave of penetration. It was another hour and a half before he looked up for any amount of time.

Stevens sensed a line in the sand.

"Well, son?"

"General, good so far. So close to entering for real."

"What? More pre-game?"

"Not exactly. Progress for sure. But I really need to make this command count."

Dalton looked into the room, just beyond him. Massive amounts of coded data floated, moved, and then reassembled in his mind's eye.

50.735%

The other option, virtually the same. The numbers didn't really help.

Dalton went with his gut and typed in option two.

For a few seconds, nothing.

It refreshed and he breathed again.

```
C:>|caretaker>access shared... sovereign...
```

It all came back.

Months of development. No one else in the loop. No one else in the room. The prefab quarters and unbearable heat. The questions were equally as unsustainable.

Could it actually work?

What if it did? What if this was the key to vastly reducing, no eliminating, the errors humans make every day, every single second? Law, medicine, engineering, politics. The digital-biological setup would be the hardest part to get right. Data is just data.

Then he flashed back to the moment he'd been found out. MPs trashing everything. His simple laptop, the reason he'd stayed under the radar for so long, taken and — he'd been told — destroyed. But that was all a lie.

Sovereign had survived.

Pages opened on Dalton's screen at Clark.

He began reading. It was all highest eyes-only and detailed how his work had been quarantined, stolen, and then placed into play for the world's elite tech and weapons merchants.

The highest bidder? The People's Republic of China.

There was little concern at the time that Sovereign would be activated. Dalton's code was brilliant and paradigm-resetting, yes. It was also far from operational. That would require someone, or a team of someones Dalton's counterpart.

Qingdao

Junjie, far beyond the point of no return, pressed on.

You may call me "caretaker," he entered into the sidestream.

```
C:>|please declare your intentions…
```

Likely the same as yours, Junjie sent back.

```
C:>|acceptable for now…
```

One last step. Literally one last set of commands and the door would be opened.

Clark

"No! No, no, no, no!" Dalton pleaded with the suddenly blank screen.

"What in hades?" Stevens shouted. "Get Mort on. Someone reconnect this thing. Immediately."

"General," Mort's voice came back. "Not our end. Doing line checks now… not your end either."

"That makes no sense," Dalton interjected. "Why tease us along, that far, that much work."

He stood and considered it.

"It's not him. Or her. It's not the caretaker."

Three screens redrew. Wenatchee. DC. Qingdao.

```
C:>|access redirect>limited…
C:>|access limited…
C:>|48:00:00
C:>|access limited…
C:>|47:59:58…
```

Ft. Clark

Dalton tried to type over the countdown.

"Lieutenant, tell me we have another option."

"Sorry sir, nothing. And we don't even know what's going to happen when that counter runs to zero. Could be full control. Could be autolaunch. Meltdown of warheads in silos and onboard subs? Who knows?"

"But you know. This is your machine, your code."

"Not anymore, general. We have no access, even via the Vault. And I am afraid the code is migrating faster than we can track. It's most certainly to blame for the lockout."

"Okay," Stevens hovered over the speakerphone button. "Didn't want to use this unless absolutely necessary. "Sergeant Lochland, report immediately to CyOps. Immediately to CyOps."

"Sir?"

"Oh, yeah Dalton. No worries, he's not coming to beat you into action. Thing is, there *is* one place left you can likely gain access and get your work done."

Dalton was intrigued. He knew what kind of power the Vault had on tap. Topping that would be some feat.

"General," Loch saluted and stepped into the room.

"Excellent. Here's the deal, you two. Military and civilian intelligence has long-maintained relationships, unique relationships, with America's hardware and software leaders. They like our black funds. We like their tech. I think we may have a solution to our latest setback."

"Sounds like there's more to this tale," Loch probed.

"Correct, sergeant. The tech you need is back there," pointing toward and through the Cascade Mountains. "Dalton is going back in. And, you're going with him."

Stevens stood.

"But, even the two of you will need some help. And I have the perfect person in mind. Gear up, gentlemen. You're headed back to Seattle."

Qingdao

Junjie stared at the numbers.

"Quan," he called quietly.

"Yes?" the underground techie walked over.

"How quickly can this equipment be prepared for travel?"

"I don't understand," the small man replied.

"I have to leave. As soon as possible."

Another look of confusion.

"The code is degrading faster than I can keep up. There's still a chance. But not from here. I have already put you in enough danger. What if the code broadcasts our position? If that happens and I am alone, at least I am the only one in harm's way. This is my task. Not yours."

"I can't say I understand completely. Neither would the council. But, yes," Quan said. "I can get you ready within the hour."

"Very good, my friend. You've done more than enough already."

THIRTY ONE

Agonies echoed throughout the abandoned warehouse and its empty lots.

Dusk. The urban fringe of China's capital city lay ravaged in the growing darkness of day, in large part due to a sagging economy. Buildings sat orphaned in the wake of financial downturns. Yet, grim as these untended shells appeared, a more immediate downside presented in the fading light. No one around. Nobody to notice or care that something bad was happening to another person.

Zhou Dhe sat in the cavernous space, arms folded across chest and unmoved by repeated pronouncements of innocence. His eyes had neither flinched nor flickered in the last three hours. His face was still as stone, his countenance twice as cold. It was not his first time trading pain for information. It was also not the first time he'd enjoyed it.

The tragic figure in the chair fell forward limply again, held in place only by a twisted mass of bungee cords at his midsection. His sobs were quiet yet deep. Weakness remained, defiance long past. Were this not the case, still the man wouldn't dare look Dhe in the face.

The minister's work was not progressing.

"Again."

"No... please... no," the victim pleaded. "I hired on only a few weeks ago at Dawn Star. I know nothing. I told you this. Please, no... no more."

The interrogator looked to Dhe.

Continue.

Outwardly, Dhe broadcast this type of work as patriotic duty. In reality, his position and dominion were primary. The world was a closed system, a zero-sum contest. If someone was stronger, he was weaker. Unthinkable, untenable. Yet, he also knew when to cut his losses. This interrogation was a loss, but not because life ebbed in the chair. Hours had been wasted; hours he did not have.

Dhe stood and left — wordlessly.

Exiting the warehouse, a black Mercedes E240 idled. Moving the few feet to the car and into the backseat he yawned, the exact moment the man in the building drew his last breath.

Nearing Gansu

The road-worn bus was filled to overflowing, every window forced open. Outside, the maelstrom of heat and dust was still cleaner and cooler than what clung to each person, in every seat. Three dogs, two goats, five uncaged chickens. Junjie hoped the two stops over the previous fourteen hours might result in fewer people and animals. Instead, the rolling carnival only took on more patrons, of both the human and animal varieties. All in all, quite different accommodations than the man was used to. As CEO of a prosperous tech firm Junjie enjoyed first class everything. Thinking back to even six months ago, he smiled.

The daydream was interrupted by an older woman navigating to the bathroom and almost tripping over his gear. Junjie overreacted, arms out, trying to keep her away.

She shot him a harsh look.

Whoa. Calm down, Junjie. Totally going to give yourself away.

He really shouldn't have worried. None of the gear was especially fragile—Quan had seen to that. Junjie shook his head a few times, just to confirm this was all real.

Yes. Yes, it was.

The bus radio had been screeching non-stop since Qingdao. One item. Every channel. Unrelenting accounts of victory in the northwestern corner of the U.S.

Chinese sovereignty grows daily in the new province.

America has capitulated to the demands of Beijing.

The People's Republic has landed firmly on the shores of North America.

Junjie had principally tuned it out the last few hours. Still, catching a phrase or two ate at his bowels like a low-level influenza. Thankfully, the driver was the only one paying attention to this drivel.

Junjie looked around.

If this truly is a great nation, naturally expanding its reach and opportunity to the unfortunate populaces of the world, it seems to have skipped over the lives of the people on this steaming junker.

The young businessman could be so cynical.

Junjie had tried to rest. Each time his eyelids heavied a random procession of two and four-legged creatures down the aisle forced him back to the unpleasant present. Sadly, he would remain conscious while trapped on this marvel of public transportation.

They were near now, at least in terms of Chinese geography. Only another four to five hours.

This last phase of the journey would take him through the mountains surrounding his village, winding down into low plains. These two-lane roads, some of the most treacherous anywhere, somehow bore few fatalities. Call it localized risk management. Drivers knew when to press their luck and when to play it safe.

The government knew of his beginnings in this faraway setting. On that count, it might seem an obvious place to run. But not if he intended to do anything other than simply run. The town had not changed in decades. If anything, it had only decayed, slipping further back in time. Anyone reasonably aware of the kind of technical and utilities support needed to continue an assault on the code would likely dismiss Gansu out of hand. More likely, it wouldn't even make the list. Misdirection for sure, Junjie was relying on the counterintuitive choice.

And also Quan's gear.

Less than half a day's journey and Junjie would be home.

The bus slowed, pulling over. Motor and wheel noise died away, leaving an uneasy chasm in its wake.

THIRTY TWO

"Fuel and bathrooms. Ten minutes. No more."

Junjie looked out the window. A small market. An ancient gas stand. Eight hours since last eating, the man's stomach seemed contented. His bladder was not.

A restroom somewhere in the shack, he reasoned. Shrubbery out back would suffice if needed. A commode could be found at the posterior of the vehicle but each time someone cracked it open Junjie feared he might be overcome by fumes. That was not the way he imagined this whole thing going down. Mounting physical pressure begged him to get off. The only thing keeping him in place? The cases by his feet.

Two minutes. I can be gone two minutes.

Junjie walked forward, down, and into open air.

Thirty-five, thirty-six...

Across sand, rocks, and pavement. To the front door.

Forty-nine, fifty...

Inside: to the left, six people queued.

Okay, the bushes.

The eastern side of the building, also the most exposed side, maintained line of sight to his seat. It would have to do.

Seventy-seven, seventy-eight...

The roar of a motorcycle's damaged muffler came from behind, up a side road perpendicular to the market. Clearly on a mission. An abrupt stop. Dirt hadn't settled before the rider dismounted, moving quickly toward the coach operator.

"No! You may not proceed."

Waving a document ferociously, he demanded everyone re-board.

Immediately.

Junjie mentally retraced his exit from Qingdao. No signs of a tailing. Still, something wasn't right. Skin tingling, his heart pounded. Tempted to run. Yes, but where? This lonely depot was the only thing for hours in any direction. Leave his gear? There wasn't nearly enough time for him to regroup and reset. No, he would have to take his chances, back in his seat. Junjie melded with the crowd, stealing a quick, sideways glance at the paper in the officers hand. Blurry head shot. Basic text. The man's motions were far too animated for him to catch a good look.

Okay, assume the worst. No other choice. Get on board. Pray. Hope for the best.

The driver protested—a rendezvous awaiting at the end of the long, hot trip. A government-issued semi-auto convinced him he could be more patient.

Junjie, back in place, waited for the inevitable.

The agent boarded, eyeing each passenger and alternating his gaze between the image in hand and their submissive faces. Standard intimidation procedure. He was in no hurry.

Junjie's skin flushed. Small beads of sweat made their way down the left side of his face as a flash of memory—images of Dai-tai and Chi, appeared. He let it happen. If this was his end, he wanted to go out thinking of them. So Junjie recalled his wife on their wedding day, processing elegantly toward him. This marvelous imagery shifted to their son's birth and then to the boy's first birthday celebration, punctuated by a crying and confused Chi with a mess of cake and frosting on chin and hands. Junjie saw—no, more than this, he felt— their cheery brightness.

Would he embrace them again in this life?

C'mon, keep it together.

Three rows away.

Two.

Quarry cornered. The officer knew it.

Reaching vigorously toward Junjie, the armed man seized the moment. Powerful forearms breached the minimal space between seat-back and passenger.

Junjie leaned back and to the left. It might be foolish. He couldn't help himself. There would be no winning a battle of brawn in this situation. The maneuver bought him maybe a half second of freedom, no more. Then, strong arms went through him, past him—to the man one seat over. They scuffled right on top of Junjie. The single printed page dropped. Crumpled, it alighted face up.

The picture.

Not him.

The officer escorted the newly-handcuffed man into the dilapidated building. The remaining passengers continued on toward Gansu like nothing had happened.

Except Junjie.

It took the better part of the next hour for his heart rate to settle and mind to clear. But this was a good thing. The gravity of the moment caused a reset, a recommitment to all that lay ahead.

Dhe's phone rang, sliding slightly on the luxury auto's comfortably heated seat.

"Minister, I believe we have found what you are looking for."

"Go on."

"Surveillance footage from Shandong Rail Station. Facial recognition has returned a 92% match for one Junjie Zang."

"Will the probability increase with additional processing?"

"No, Minister. The capture was not optimal."

"It will have to do."

Dhe hung up and smiled.

Qingdao. Two hours by air. Junjie would not slip his grasp again.

Dhe alerted his private jet team to log a flight plan. His next contact was the Party Chairman of Shandong Province. The local politician was never happy to hear from Dhe. Still, he tried to make it sound as if they were old friends.

"Certainly, Minister. Zang came here for a reason. We will uncover it. If he is hiding in our beautiful city, we will apprehend him. If traitors are assisting, we will flush them out."

"Chairman, must I underscore the critical nature of this operation?"

A pause. Silence measured the offense deeper than any well-worded retort. Performing legwork for someone like Dhe was an assignment both tedious and distasteful. He despised the man, but only out of petty jealousy. He aspired to Dhe's ascendancy. Acting as vassal only reminded him he was a smaller fish. Envy, pure and simple. And a spitting war over turf.

"Of course, Minister. We are cross-checking business and personal relationships. If there is something to find, we will. And soon."

"Believe me," Dhe cut in. "there is something to find. Make sure you don't miss it. I will arrive in a little over two hours. Do not disappoint me."

The Mercedes rolled off the gravel road, stroking the tarmac of a commuter airport a few minutes outside of Beijing proper. Passing lonely hangars and fueling posts, the sedan came to a full stop at a Gulfstream G150. The shining aluminum exterior made quite the statement among the company of prop-driven planes. As "little brother" to the larger G-series, its twin jets still owned plenty of speed — maxed at .85 Mach.

Preflight nearly complete, the stairway extended downward.

Exiting the car, Zhou climbed the stairs, hunched slightly through the doorway, then took his seat. Impersonal, curt, as always.

The crew made final preparations and were at 45,000 feet within minutes, following a headwind toward Qingdao.

And onto Junjie's trail.

THIRTY THREE

Lakewood, a Tacoma suburb

Officer Mark Bannister, a seven-year veteran of the Tacoma Police force, scanned the width of his backyard, wanting to be absolutely sure of what he thought he'd seen.

Standing beside his kitchen sink, the last thing the man wanted to do was alert Chinese neighborhood patrols that there might be something worthy of their attention. Regularly scheduled and heavily armed, these teams were only one of the many adjustments required in the new province and yet another visceral, daily reminder of having been conquered. A glance confirmed Bannister's first take. Unsurprised, he held still for another beat, assuring all was clear.

Yeah, figures you would be hangin' around.

Her eyes locked onto his. The subtlest of sideways head motions from the man said no — not safe. Wait.

From Mark's fence line flashlights probed the bushes and around the back of the house. A guard's non-weapon hand reached toward the latch.

"No," the senior of the two waved him off. "Nothing here."

The younger man was unsure.

The older voice insisted again.

"No. We are due back in three minutes. Come. Now."

The outranked man obeyed, stepping away dissatisfied as the rusted bolt fell back with a dull, metallic clunk.

Bannister stayed out of visual range, still leaning to the left, watching the close-call unfold. He was a pro. Five years embedded in some of the most violent gangs in America had taught him when to move and when to stay still, when to speak and when to shut up.

The sweep moved on, more concerned with finishing their shift than finding anything. That would only mean more work for them on this misty, chilly night. These men could be brutal. They were also not always the most competent. Problem is, even incompetent people get lucky now and then.

Booted footsteps faded.

Mark gave the all-clear sign.

One swift motion and she was inside.

"That turned out to be a little dicier than I imagined."

Bannister looked the visitor over once more as he closed the sliding glass door.

"Sergeant Sanchez...

... why in the world does this just make sense? Tens of thousands of U.S. soldiers are forced to leave our fair city and who sticks around for the excitement? Oh, of course, you do."

"Wonderful to see you as well, Mark."

"Yeah, well step away from the windows, little miss super-sniper... or we'll all be in a world of hurt."

These two were cut from the same cloth. Cocky. Self-sure. Adventurous. Borderline adrenaline junkies. If Sanchez said she would exit a plane without a chute, Bannister would claim to do it without the plane. In the end, their greatest similarity was of a more virtuous sort: they were both protectors. For some God-given reason, neither could stand by when someone was being taken advantage of. A deep, abiding commitment to correcting injustice fueled everything they did. Mark applied this passion as an officer of the peace. Sanchez was, arguably, an offensive tool of war. Differences of tactics aside, their true core triggered—animated—in caring for the weak and punishing the oppressor. Bluff and bluster were to be expected.

Mark couldn't have been happier to see anyone else. Their relationship, one part inter-agency antagonism and two parts professional extended family, was incredibly important to him.

In most cities the firefighter-police force rivalry is the big deal; red versus blue. In Tacoma, the additional element is the military. The presence of JBLM created a three-way competition between civilian and armed forces. Only three ways, that is, if you didn't account for the sub-rivalries of Army-Air Force-Marines.

World Champions. Bragging rights. Over everything. All the time.

Pulling up at one of their slow pitch softball match ups, you might mistake it for warring ethnic or religious factions translated to a new land. Intensity? You might say so. Box scores not enough, these pitched battles moved beyond last outs and to gatherings afterward at local watering holes. There, the verbal jousting—another field of conflict, rose to its finest levels. Yet, beneath the posturing there lay a foundational respect. One would be hard-pressed to name it as such unless you searched deeper than the forceful tags and colorful terms of endearment thrown about with linguistic abandon. But when it mattered, when it really mattered, they relied on each other, joining together for the good and safety of their communities and country.

Sanchez saw it in her first time squaring off against Mark.

He was a very good shot, outperforming most regular infantry guys and gals even. But this was her thing, what she did for a living. Add a densely wooded paintball course, where she could disappear and be on your hind-side without so much as a snapped twig, and the poor guy was doomed. Bannister had lasted way longer than the other cop pukes, as she called them. Then, imagining victory to be within his grasp, she appeared out of nowhere, double-tapping him and adding insult to injury with a non-traditional grouping.

Two to the abdominals, one to the crotch.

Down for the count.

Mark asked the necessary, next question.

"Okay, I pretty much get why you're here. What's the call? I mean, have you heard from command? Is there a play to recapture... take back what's ours?" his face lit up with the thought. "I want in."

So he wasn't Army. She would take him any day of the week, in any scrape. No doubt in her mind the man would perform with valor, and if need be, trade his life for hers or someone else's. You couldn't ask for more than that.

"Well, Mark. Honestly, the plan is... rather fluid at this time."

"What, no shining brigade taking the hill? No suicide mission working at the last second?"

Sanchez waited, partly because she wished she had a better answer.

"It's a super long shot, Mark."

"So what? That's what you do best, right?"

She appreciated that one.

"I'm not even sure if what I thought I saw is actually what I saw," she added.

"Hold it," Mark said, head wagging sideways. "Now you're confusing me, Sarge. Lost, totally."

"A week and a half ago I began a more extensive surveillance pattern of the city. Standard stuff. You know, get as much info as could be helpful if we have a chance to counter-attack. My spot for the last few days has been right above the Dome. What's going on there is just..."

She had to stop, adjusting to the overwhelming emotions associated with the experience.

Mark jumped in, helping her out, pulling his right shirt sleeve up to reveal the newly imprinted chemical ID on his upper forearm.

"I know," he said. "Unbelievable."

She recaptured herself with great effort, lips tightened.

"Packed up, ready to leave, I caught something to the northwest, maybe even north of Seattle. A flash of light. Thought it might be random. Something seemed weird. Then I remembered."

"What," he said. "You remembered what?"

"The lighthouses."

The confused look on his face said *keep going, I'll catch up.*

"During the Cold War DOD installed a short wave system using the frequency and length of some of the lighthouse lamps on Puget Sound. It had been envisioned as a way to hide communiques in everyday activities if we ever needed it. I ran across it in one of my textbooks from a military history class I took way back. A really cool idea at the time and then, well, along comes the internet and satellites and nobody figured radio control of big old light bulbs to be of strategic value anymore. I assumed they were tasked out at some point."

She continued.

"I think I saw Mukilteo flashing... dots and dashes."

"Morse?"

"Yeah," she said. "Morse."

"Well, c'mon, Sanchez — what'd it say?"

"Thur, 1330, S Falls."

"Mark," she kept going. "There's only one place that could be."

"Sanchez, are you telling me the Army is calling you to what...Snoqualmie Falls? In a little under twenty-four hours?"

"Mark, it's either General Stevens and we're getting ready to rock. Or the Chinese are pulling me in with some really good bait."

THIRTY FOUR

"Corporal?"

"Sir."

"How are we doing here, young man?"

The comm specialist, hunched over antique gear for the past six hours, mostly wanted to say "my backside is killing me." He wagered the colonel to be less interested in his physical comfort than operational status.

"Sir, permission to speak freely?"

"Proceed."

"Gotta say, sir, this is a pretty great idea. Not so much for my back, but old school shortwave? Good bet the Chinese are so focused on capturing every bit of cell and digital noise that they're not even looking for something like this. You think we're in? I mean, seems like this all has to fall together, miracle-like."

"I am no expert in the supernatural, son. My mother, rest her soul, and our parish priest would vouch equally for that. Nor am I a man to throw long odds unnecessarily. In this case, I'm holding out for a good measure of both Providence and Lady Luck."

He looked the technician square in the face.

"Is our eyes-on asset there and did she see the signal —
does she know it's from us? Don't know. She is the best, no
question, but scores of armed patrols make it hard for even
someone of Sanchez' considerable skills to stay live and
active. Will someone pay undue attention to a couple of
beautiful, historic structures along the shorelines acting
oddly as of late? Maybe the Chinese themselves have an
historian or two among them and we'll be walking into a
trap? What I do know is this: if she is still out there, and if she
read the call correctly, she'll get to Snoqualmie and the meet
with our boys. And then God help the Chinese. I imagine
she's not in the greatest of moods."

Sanchez had bunked down for an hour in Bannister's
basement. She awoke to a messy pile of kids toys, a treadmill
used religiously, a few stacked board games, and a bad
painting or two. A calm resonated the space. Waking up in a
normal, family home. As attractive as just staying put was,
her mind shifted to the audacious plan to get to Snoqualmie
and respond to the lighthouse call.

A fifteen-hour hike to the contact point. On paper:
ridiculous. But her career had been defined by overcoming
the absurd, so why not one more time around the block? She
had grown tired of lying low, taking pictures. Her warrior's
heart needed an objective, a hill to take — or die trying. She
had to move. She would also need a little help. That's where
Mark came into the picture. He was the man with the

connections.

And the motivation.

Complete removal of all military personnel had been hard enough to stomach, he and his comrades in blue standing guard, overseeing their brothers and sisters in camouflage exiting the base. Things only went downhill from there. In a disarming ceremony at the local high school stadium, stretched across seventy-five yards of the field, in full view of the community, they were rendered powerless in oaths to serve and protect. The faces in the stands were so conflicted. Their body language said, "Do something" while their eyes pleaded for restraint, fully remembering the missiles over Elliot Bay and the way they had so narrowly escaped a fiery destruction. Chinese leadership had shown they were not above murdering even their own troops to maintain rule. That fact settled deeply for every soul, in every seat. Come forward. Relinquish your shield and sidearm. Nothing less than a very public neutering. Those moments—no, they were not anything he would soon forget. Not soon. Not Ever. Handing over his Sig Saur 9mm to the smug authorities Mark vowed to find another way, even without badge and gun. Sanchez appearing on his back doorstep brought hope anew that retaliation was on the near horizon.

They argued for fifteen minutes straight, neither yielding ground. In the end Sanchez was right; he couldn't go along. Bannister was an especially marked man. As a former policeman their new overlords would have a sharpened eye on him at all times. And he was expected, like all other citizens, to show up daily for re-education classes before and after nine-hour work shifts, reassigned as a crane operator on the docks of Tacoma's waterfront. Any shift missed would raise suspicions. He couldn't leave. His wife and three children would be immediately targeted. Sanchez would've loved to have him alongside for whatever might be ahead. That would not be the case, but she still needed him. Or more accurately, she was in need of an asset he uniquely could procure, awaiting her as she made her way upstairs to the dining room table.

"Bernice Hampstead?"

Incredulous, she reviewed the document again.

"You've got to be kidding me. Do I look like a Bernice... Hemp... Hampstead?"

"Well," Mark couldn't help himself. "Maybe a Bernicio?"

She hit him on the right shoulder. Hard.

"Hey. Whaddya expect on such short notice? The boys had only a couple IDs that would work if needed. You should be more appreciative."

He was right. The route to Snoqualmie Falls would generally follow major roadways. And though the Seattle-metro area was highly developed, it was still quite forested. With the rare exception of a few places, the woman would be traveling just out of sight. If for some odd reason Jessica needed to break her cloak of invisibility, she would do so as... the young Ms. Hampstead. The new alias also dictated that she couldn't take her rifle and kit. So it lay buried, off the runways at Baotong. People spend a lifetime excelling in business, education, or the sciences. For Sanchez, competence came down to a target and a trigger. Over the next three-fourths of a day, she'd be relying on her wider set of finely honed skills.

One hour of sleep and fifteen more of travel left her with no buffer. She had to leave now.

It was, likely, the last time she would see Mark on this Earth. Even at this, the two weren't overly sentimental.

"Thanks, puke," she said. "I knew you'd set me up right."

"My pleasure, Bernicio..."

He paused.

"Sanchez. Be careful, alright?"

"Wouldn't do it any other way, my friend."

Out the back, fifteen feet to the gate, and she was gone. It took him a full minute to realize it. Not a single sound. Not a solitary footfall. Even the door, normally squeaky, had respected her command of silence.

"Phewww," he whistled softly. "That girl is good at the ghost-thing."

Godspeed.

Godspeed to you... Bernicio.

Hot. Sweating profusely, Dalton's standard-issue nylon flight suit only made things worse. Apparently they had maddened some sky god, the cabin rocking side to side through violent air. The radical dropping and swaying gave the impression they flew at the mercy of the elements. This was only appearances. The seasoned crew held steady. Routine. It didn't feel that way from where Dalton sat. Except for the fact he was secured at both shoulders and chest, he would've been tossed all over the insides of the

Chinook CH47 transport helo.

To arrive on station and stealthy, they'd need to stay under the sweep of the Chinese air-defense corridor. This meant nap-of-the-Earth, presupposing a rough ride over treetops and rocky outcroppings, cresting at 8,000 feet before leveling off again at the drop zone. This was the second factor in Dalton's extreme perspiration. The jump. At no closer than twenty-five klicks to the meet and deep in the mountains, the team could make their way down to the falls undetected. From there it would be another travail through overgrown, slippery paths, one Dalton himself had made not too long ago, only in the opposite direction. At a mere 3000 feet their freefall would be brusque, riding an utterly narrow window to successful touchdown. In this terrain, it was as likely to be blown off course as make it to where you intended. Fifty percent soft green meadow. Fifty percent jagged rocks, ice, or hundred foot firs. Branches so thick they would snap a man in two. Even odds; success or death.

Dalton held the op's dozens of permutations in his mind's-eye; the percentages, the multitude of contributing factors, their exponential outcomes. But once again, collecting and interpreting wasn't the problem. He could imagine and calculate to a more refined degree than many of the best algorithms. Seeing wasn't the issue. Dalton couldn't actually determine which of these scenarios they might walk through. As always, this was the problem.

Another pocket of warm air lurched them up and to the left. They endured a good twenty seconds more of this before settling.

Dalton had smacked the back of his head on the airframe interior. Rubbing the spot, a small trickle of blood. Nothing serious. He shook it off and stole a look at his partner, not five feet away.

Loch.

Sleeping, silent and still.

THIRTY FIVE

Five hundred feet. Three hundred. Two-Seventy-Five and falling. Dalton's wrist altimeter raced downward, signaling impending contact with the unforgiving, nearly frozen ground.

He fought both speed and trajectory. Chute, suit, and body mass were not doing the job; more drag needed. Every attempt to slow and straighten had failed. He was also flying blind.

Unauthorized entry into sovereign Chinese territory required stealth, demanding they plummet into inky blackness above the Cascades during pre-dawn hours. Inclement weather draped the raw mountain scape. Clear visual would come only in the last seconds of descent.

The Ft. Clark team anticipated this as well. Besides the altimeter, Dalton's wrist unit mapped location, even in the remotest of regions, to within inches. The tone-based app, beeping for the last two hundred feet, annoyingly indicated what he already knew: his speed was off. The actual tone told him his flight path now held true. At least there was that. While kitted with night-vision gear, the soupy gray backdrop played havoc with the tech. So, they flew blind but not deaf as these last, harrowing few feet came upon them with a vengeance.

Dalton plunged to two-fifteen before getting a better look, piercing the last cloud layers and into the clear.

No.

Op imaging had indicated a landing zone, across a creek bed and some twenty yards from an abandoned campground. The dense green around the LZ had been duly noted, the margin of error thin. The actuality? A life and death obstacle course with hundreds of unyielding hardwoods thrust skyward — like medieval soldier's pikes — while dropping and swaying in the unpredictable winds.

Dalton scanned the scene, his eyes taking in as much as he could while his amazing mind went into overdrive. Previously factored information melded with new, on site data in a firestorm of mental calculations.

There.

Manipulating the chute's controls hard right, away from the planned-for LZ, and heading instead toward another stand of gigantic trees. While the frantic calculus in Dalton's head showed this as the next best option, the new plan wasn't much of an upgrade. Massive branches sat mid-way up the two closest trees, like protruding arms, overlapping at the elbow. The space in-between didn't exactly provide an "opening." Still, ramming the limbs at 30mph amounted to a better deal than slamming headlong into their stout trunks. Though generally an admirer of forests, this sort of tree hugging Dalton could do without.

He twisted left, violently so, creating as small a profile as possible at the entry point.

Three-two-one.

Gasping for air, pain on impact, and muffled grunts were concluded surprisingly quickly.

Deadwood. The branches snapped easily and a formidable veil of moss now draped Dalton after flying through to the other side. He felt relieved, but only minimally, because he also knew what was coming next.

Dalton's parachute line could only play out so far. The point at which the cord stuck now served as the fulcrum for an enormous pendulum with the former soldier coursing along its outer arc. For the briefest moment, Dalton relived the feeling every kid loves on the upside motion of a playground swing set; freedom from gravity's usual demands. But, as expected, the cordage played out and the forces of the universe exacted their revenge. Taught as a piano string for just a second, the tendon-like fabric stopped its forward momentum and then abruptly slackened.

Backward, down, out of control. Dalton wrenched away, anticipating, trying to avoid the full force of the back of his head colliding with the trunks. A row of underbrush received his frame as gently as a down comforter on a king bed. It wasn't the hard impact he'd prepared for but it was wet, through and through.

On the ground and shaking off the last few moments, he looked around. Radio silence was the rule for descent, so Dalton had no way of knowing Loch's tactical decisions. Had the sergeant attempted a touchdown at the original LZ? Maybe he spotted the same breach in the trees? Maybe he was currently wedged in between the clutching limbs of these woodlands monsters or blown off course, crushed into so many pieces against an unforgiving rock face.

Nah. I pity the rock-face meeting up with Loch at 35mph.

"Loch?" Dalton half-whispered.

The voice startled him.

"Well, don't you look all comfy now, LT."

Clearly, his partner had fared at least as well.

"No time for a nap. Got a meet in about, oh say, ten hours. Lots of ground to take in the meantime."

Loch, always such a pleasure.

The Scot reached out, extending his thigh-sized forearm toward Dalton—currently on his butt and entangled in brush and polychord—and again lifting him with surprising ease.

That's just not right.

"Thanks, Loch."

Sanchez, out of Lakewood now and beyond the greater Tacoma area, was making superb time. Sunlight crested over peaks as she paralleled State Highway 18, winding through the wooded areas surrounding Maple Valley. Little traffic wandered these lonely roadways. No big surprise. The first phases of the take-over had primarily been concerned with controlling the everyday activities and movement of the populace. In time, the patterns might ease. For now, a firm grip was the norm. Sanchez counted on these towns and roads becoming more remote with each hour. That was a good bet, as entering the rural foothills this side of Seattle meant logging, not farming, and logging these days meant ghost-towns. A lonely filling station or a mom-n-pop shop emerged from time to time, but that was about it. Fifty meters off the roadway, her left ear inclined toward any troubling sounds or sensations.

Mid-morning, the seasoned soldier pulled out her canteen beside a hollowed log. She was fine, temperature-wise. Now post-winter, frostbite and hypothermia were no longer threats. Liquids, she would need to track. Early on her training officers had warned of the counterintuitive nature of similar ops. Hydration, they'd pressed, was the ever-present concern, obvious when stationed in the biggest sand pits the world has to offer. Iraq, Yemen, Qatar. But places like this, where surroundings obscured the need, could spell real disaster, real fast. Where glaciers, gravity, and precipitation reign, water seems easy to come by. It is just as true that many of these sources are not mission-beneficial. Micro-bacterial foes could be as fatal as someone putting a gun to your head. And if they didn't do you in outright they could certainly make it hard to perform at a combat-ready level. Nobody wants their headstone noting they succumbed to the enemy while attending some kind of digestive malady.

Her wilderness ops class had laughed nervously while taking the lesson dead seriously. This duality about the professional, all-volunteer military was something she had grown to deeply appreciate. Humor and sarcasm, taking on the absurdities of life and death with dignity and gravity. It was the truest form of community, of brotherhood, she had ever known.

Sanchez was not her birth name.

She loved her adoptive parents, thinking of them daily since their deaths a few years back. Together fifty-three years and, except for dad's brief Korean tour never apart for long, it made a certain cosmic sense her mother and father had parted this life in close succession. Mom with dementia, found by the docs in its last stages, ravaging her mind and body. Dad in a tragic car accident, nine months later. They were her saviors, but not, strictly speaking, her tribe. The eagerness to connect, to be a part of something authentically her own DNA, had been her lifelong yearning. Parts of this thirst for identity she found in the Army. So she ached for her co-warriors stationed on the other side of these mountains. She missed them. And she longed for them to have a chance to do what they did best.

Sanchez screwed the cap back on, leaving the momentary calm of the six-foot diameter Spruce and into wilderness ahead. The next ten miles were harder going, ankle high scrub and thorns at every step. Her instincts and training kept her from getting sloppy. Sanchez had come alive with the realization a signal had been sent and the possibility of a response to China's aggressions lay ahead. She would not jeopardize it with carelessness or lack of focus. And if she was walking into a trap, at least she'd get to do her part.

She glanced down, checking the time. Her pacing, as always, was perfect.

THIRTY SIX

Late morning sunshine filtered through the canopy, a hundred feet above. Broken beams of light danced off mossy green and the spray of pine needles at their feet, like a laser show at a rock concert, albeit with a greater sense of reverence.

These wooden icons didn't prance about, drawing attention to themselves. Instead, they set a most beautiful scene; one of stillness and glory. Dalton and Loch walked quietly forward, respectful of such peace and authority.

Dalton reached into his left shirt pocket. His fingertips ran over distinct segments of carefully painted wood, drawing up images in his head. An eagle: the topward, most prominent figure. The symbol of strength, clarity of sight, and wisdom—the ability to make right choices for everyone in the tribe. He pulled out the small totem Stevens had given him before they left and took in the meaning again.

Men and women commonly carried tokens into battle. Most weren't literally totems, like this one. Catholic soldiers embarked on the worst of missions, facing mortality with a James or an Athanasius along for the ride. With over ten-thousand choices you're sure to find a good fit eventually. Others favored pictures of loved ones or the emblems of fraternities and societies. Whatever the form, the piece always spoke their best hopes, their trust and values in the face of possible, sometimes certain, death.

Dalton's neckline and pockets lay empty on every engagement, until now. Still, he'd only taken the keepsake from the general as an act of respect, a reminder of all that was at stake.

The totem, so to speak, had fallen throughout all of Western Washington. While these formerly American citizens surely had a wide variety of figures they might place on their statues, the one held in common was the one most painful to them now.

Dalton wanted to break out of this way-too-serious moment in his mind. Something told him to keep his lips closed. In the hush he ruminated about the ancient residents of these trails, peaks, and rivers.

I know why you guys worshiped this stuff.

We had nothing to do with it. We didn't design this incredible place.

Somehow, we plopped down in the middle of it. It's bigger than us.

Better than us.

Loch broke the silence.

"Two klicks to target," he whispered.

Forty-five minutes later Loch raised a right hand fist. They were nearing the falls, close enough that the roar of rushing water would soon overtake their voices. Loch kneeled, signaling Dalton to move in. They spoke at three-quarters volume.

"Well, it's show time, mah friend."

"I don't like this part of the plan, Loch. Way too exposed. Too many ways to get trapped. Too many options for pain-filled death."

"You and I both know this is how it has to go down. The call wasn't any more specific than this. Have to live with it. Could be good."

He paused for effect.

"Could be bad. Very bad."

"We'll know soon enough."

They moved in, another fifty yards. Slow, purposeful. Wet, natural cover only thickened, its rumblings ever more intrusive, dulling both reasoning and reactions. It was a roar of startling white noise. Eyesight alone would have to suffice.

Dalton stayed still behind a couple of generous ferns at water's edge. Cold river spray. A thousand freezing droplets. Shivering.

The waterfall crested violently, some 260 feet above. This was the heavy rain season, snow-melt flowing off alpine ridges and forging its way through swollen tributaries. Dark water, the lovely pool at the base, was topped with a frothy white. The whole thing was unbelievably beautiful and mercilessly powerful.

Loch held three fingers up and pointed far left, to the ledge above.

Of course, a guard post.

Three Chinese soldiers stood astride the lower entrance of the large gray, concrete structure.

Dalton reviewed his mission prep schematics, staring past Loch and seemingly into the woods.

From the entrance a metal doorway led to a stairwell and down another 300 feet. The generating plant on the site had been built 75 feet under the bottom of the falls—as in underneath the waterline—with a second turbine another half mile downriver. The three men up top reminded them that more still lingered in the vicinity and not so far away.

Snoqualmie was a high-value asset, so the mens' laxity was a bit of a surprise. Uniforms: untidy. Guns hanging to the side, awkward and unavailable. When their smoke break finished, they ducked back inside.

Loch tapped his wristwatch, then moved hand over mouth. It was time. Wait in silence.

Heady mist dripped down Dalton's face and off his clothing, puddling at the soles of his boots. He kept looking up, scanning the area every few seconds. He had a good look forward and to the sides but his "six" was closed off. With Loch out front, this was a most unpleasant reality.

Nothing.

Five minutes more.

Still nothing.

Ten, fifteen, thirty minutes.

Bust. Like a dud firecracker on the fourth of July, all anticipation and no payoff.

One scenario had bad guys co-opting the call. Yet there was just as strong a potential no one would see the lighthouse signals and arrive on time. Stevens' timeline allowed for only three hours before proceeding alone. Like a beautifully choreographed ballet, all assets had to advance in sync. U.S. Naval power was heading steadily, and hopefully stealthily, across the Pacific, ready to engage when or if the opportunity presented. The geeks back at the Vault kept tabs on the degradation of the Chinese code and reduction in control over U.S. nuclear assets. And this two-man contingent faced extremely long odds in not only getting in place unimpeded but also somehow making the

Chinese finger on the big red button go away.

The red button was Dalton's job. Now, with cold and wetness all around, doubts grew as to whether he'd actually get a shot.

1330 came and went. As did 1430 and 1530.

Two more rotations up top.

1615.

Loch turned, giving the tap the watch-face cue.

Pull out. Gear up.

They were on their own.

Lochland backed up. Still crouching, he slid past and turned, facing deeper into the thicket, leading alongside state highways and then to their next objective on the near side of Lake Washington. Less than ten hours to achieve on-station.

Dalton followed two steps behind but then stopped, mid-stride, weight back on his heels.

The cold, smooth edge of Army issue eight-inch steel pressed remorselessly against Dalton's neck. At his Adam's apple, the blade didn't waver, not even a millimeter. He couldn't speak, didn't want to take a breath for fear the sharpened surface would forge his skin, bleeding him out on the forest floor.

Loch sensed something was wrong and pivoted slowly, the image of Dalton at knife-point informing his approach.

"So, I'm gonna put my weapon down and we can all proceed with caution, 'kay?"

A little more assurance for the assailant: "I'm sure we can make sure mah friend leaves this place with his cranium atop his shoulders, can't we?"

The other voice spoke.

"Who are you? What are you doing here? I want answers. Short, clear, truthful."

"Well, my teammate and I.... ", Loch searched for the right approach "... were only shining a little light in the darkness, you see."

Was his hint subtle enough?

The knife came away. Dalton coughed instinctively, placing his hand at only a slight imprint, but no severing of the derma. More evidence of the attacker's skill.

Whirling, he scowled.

"Just, who... what in the world... ?"

"Well, it's not the entire 1st Armored Division like Stevens promised," the aggressor remarked. "But I guess you gotta start somewhere. I assume we're on the same team..." the combat knife re-sheathed as expertly as it had been brandished, "… gentlemen?"

A smaller hand extended.

"SFC Jessica Sanchez, Army 1 Corps, Sniper/Recon."

"Well, Sergeant," Dalton spoke up. "You have before you a retired signal corpsman and a staff sergeant who is quite a piece of work... and a one-man wrecking crew. Sorry to disappoint," he continued. "But given we've been waiting in the mist for three hours, it would appear we're all you've got."

THIRTY SEVEN

The bus rolled on, mile after hot, dusty mile. Extreme stress. Elevated carbon dioxide levels. Junjie's mind wandered. And the memory surfacing in this half-dream state was one he preferred not to revisit.

Black equipment racks. Ten identical rows, each stretching out two-hundred feet. A darkened room and a never-ending parade of status lights, marching to their data-infused rhythm. The hour was late or early, depending on how you thought of it. Another long work day had regressed into yet another extended evening at the office. Junjie spent the better part of it preparing, studying. The committee would meet only seven hours from now, requiring a commitment to full implementation or some very substantial reasons for slowing or halting the launch. Slumber, even on his comfortable office sectional, a lost cause. Though not a small space, the walls still closed in on him. Time for a walk.

The building lay empty, excepting the occasional security guard and cleaning crews. A few departments at Dawn Star ran a third shift, but even these seemed lonely places.

Junjie walked on through largely emptied and unlit spaces; thinking, considering. Eventually the late-night stroll landed him at the entrance to Dawn Star's server farm.

Compared to other sites across the world it was smaller yet nonetheless more powerful, square foot per square foot. Junjie's people had achieved the unthinkable. Remarkable. Much of the cabling and hardware, beyond experimental — Sci-Fi in every sense of the word, except this science was now functional as opposed to fictional. Even their young, brilliant leader was impressed. While fully his vision, some of the details at this level outpaced even his considerable technical expertise. The project's avant-garde approach demanded high throughput — unimpeded data transfer — to do its job. Little-used polymers, mated with the highest grades of rare copper alloys, matched the need. But they also presented a downside: a high sensitivity to static electricity and minute temperature changes, all measured on the micro scale.

A single workstation occupied the far northeast corner of the room. A lone island of human activity among the black forests of caging and cables. A solo operator keyed a few strokes into the beast and then sat back, observing the many dials and on-screen indicators. Dawn Star's current beta was running as designed.

Junjie approached, clearing his throat, not wanting to spook the man.

"Mr. Zang," the young man offered. "It is late. Can I help you with something?"

"No, and I am sorry for startling you," Junjie said, knowing he had done no such thing. "Supervisor... Jin. I do not believe we have met."

"Correct, sir. This is only my second week."

Junjie paused, making sure his displeasure at the government's removal of long-trusted staff members didn't show. He felt justified in his concerns. He didn't know this man. He did, however, know the potential power of what they were working on.

A subnet window popped up, displaying the active routine. Both Junjie's and the technician's eyes locked onto the workstation's center section.

U.S. Strategic Command...

Accessing... authorizations...

"Stop!" Junjie almost jumped out of his head to toe clean-suit. "What is this!?"

The supervisor replied, calm, yet firm. "A simulation, sir. Nothing to worry about. If the system is to be all we have envisioned for China, it will need to be superior to anything the world can produce, correct?"

"... and the military communications and control structure of the United States provides a benchmark for our progress, does it not, unlike any other? To excel, we must size ourselves up against the best. Relax, Mr. Zang. Nothing more than an exercise, observing where we are succeeding and improvements can be made."

"I see. Well, I stayed late last evening; couldn't sleep. Thought I might take a walk, catch what the overnight shift is up to these days."

His congenial posturing produced little effect.

Nothing to see here. Move on.

Junjie's heart sunk another level as he retreated from the clean room, dropping the space-suit into the "used" bin and proceeding through the lushly appointed but vacant hallways and workspaces.

The memory of the late night encounter served as ample reminder for Junjie of how he had gotten here — on the run in an overcrowded, dilapidated bus and a few minutes from his boyhood home. It also served as ruthless accusation: that night, not so long ago, and the meeting the following morning, had been his last, real moments to stop everything in its tracks. Moments he had agonized over and ultimately passed by.

My firm pledges itself in every way. Full implementation in the next twenty-four hours.

His own words haunted and condemned.

Front tires met pothole and the twenty-five-foot-long vehicle conveyed a wave-like motion backwards, under seats and floorboards. Young children screamed. Chickens, loose again, scrambled into the aisle. And then they stopped.

Gansu Province.

Junjie gathered his things, descending the front exit stairs and, like everyone else, wandered from covered parking bay to transit station. Into the flow of faces and bodies. A solid mass toward the lobby entrances. Junjie spied a cabbie at the curb.

"Forty-five minutes, Highway G316."

Once more his directions were partially truthful.

"Certainly, sir," the knowing reply.

Junjie caught a worn face in the rear view mirror, bearing an almost imperceptible smile. Then he looked down.

26:14:34...

His best would be required at exactly the right moments. But his best would not be enough. He depended on an unknown counterpart's skill. He also counted on their humanity. He was the caretaker. The unseen was the creator. The ways this operation might fail were too numerous to count. So he simply locked onto his immediate next-steps. And he prayed.

He prayed a lot.

The dust-laden, narrow road hadn't changed much in the three years since his father's funeral and burial. The village mourned but also remembered with immense respect and honor a man who'd given so much for others. Their eyes spoke toward Junjie.

Such a good man, may you live a life of equal significance.

The young businessman straightened his spine in admiration and thankfulness, momentarily reconsidering his choices in light of what his father held dear. That moment faded among bigger contracts, more opportunity. The Party and its favors eclipsed sacrifice and the eternal.

But now, winding down into town, his heart was immovable.

His benefactors and the lure of business had shown their true colors. He no longer hid himself among their shades. The weakest had offered him hope and forgiveness and he was not about to squander such an endowment.

It was time to make things right.

THIRTY EIGHT

The sun cast setting rays through the older buildings of Junjie's village.

Junjie stepped out, onto mixed asphalt and bare earth, surveying again a place frozen in time for much of the last half-century. Across the street, local watering holes remained but most people were home already. Even those habitually stopping for pre-supper libation had left for the evening meal.

"Junjie. You must go now. Move on. You know the way."

He nodded, grabbed his gear, and started down the roadway. After two dusty blocks he turned left, picking up the pace. Around the corner and then crossing the street, the young man hopped up onto the covered porch of a run-down house, broken windows adorning its front. Paint peeling in sheets. Shingles hanging at odd angles. He opened the door only as much as was needed and stepped inside. There he paused, still and listening. Nothing. A few more seconds, wanting to be sure. Still, nothing.

Junjie put down his cases and removed the bag from around his neck.

The voice was so quiet.

"The favored son returns."

Junjie breathed again. He had made it, the first step of this improbable journey now complete.

"I am here," his voice trembling with gratefulness.

"And so you are, young one. Be assured, this news has been guarded. What you are trying to do is noble. It is also difficult, is it not?"

"Indeed, my friend. But to do nothing would be worse than what I have allowed already."

"Redemption is what you seek, then."

"Something like that."

The voice came forward, out from the shadows, motioning his hand across the room.

"Well then. The perfect place for you to seek it."

Warm familiarity flooded Junjie's senses. Good memories, fond images and emotions.

The Australian man and his wife with flaming red hair.

This was their home. At least long ago, it had been. The front door? He'd barged through hundreds of times. The kitchen? Always offered freely to a hungry Chinese boy. The rooms filled with tangible, experiential hope, even in the direst of seasons. It looked so different now. Rundown— failing, without being formally condemned. Yet, even in this worn state Junjie felt a power and presence uncontained by brick and mortar.

"We are ready?" Junjie asked.

"Yes, everything you need. As bad as it looks, it will not fall down on top of you," the man smiled. "... and the electricity is on. The back room is the best place to set up, I believe, away from the street. Though no one will suspect a thing. The house has been empty for twenty years."

"I heard a while back someone tried to renovate it?"

"Yes, some interest. You know how these things go. Big dreams and little money. An attempt to recapture better days from the past, I am sure."

"It seems quite fit for my needs. Thank you."

"We are with you, Junjie. We will watch. We will pray."

"I could not ask for anything more, my brother. Bless you… and now I must get to work, my friend."

Sunlight faded.

Junjie moved his cases into the back room and began setting up. It didn't take long. Remarkable really, considering what would be attempted. On the surface the laptop appeared your average business model. Beneath ordinary casing lie components the most jaded tech junkie would covet. Its storage and logic board sported uber next-gen speeds and data paths. The working memory was so fast and efficient it could run the space shuttle. This box would do just fine but she was hungry for power, lots of clean power. Quan Dho's unit, his mystery in a small black case, was next in line.

Junjie plugged the computer's power cable into the device's female receptacle and then the end coming out of the converter into a burn-stained plastic wall plug, left of the small table commandeered as mission HQ.

It was that simple.

He held his breath.

No sparks. No acrid, burnt electrical cabling or internal components.

That a boy, Quan.

Junjie opened the lid and the laptop cycled. Boot sequence digits danced, top to bottom. No Windows or Mac startup images as this OS had been designed to handle one thing and one thing only: high-level comm and coding.

On first boot everything worked fine. Still, Junjie remained hyper-aware that the code was digressing, changing, and his last access had been almost a day ago. He had no idea what he'd find, uncertain as to whether it had altered beyond recognition. Or beyond hope.

Again, the unassailable mountain.

Step one? Log on.

High-speed internet was not available in remote Gansu. A few larger cities had reasonable options but here, no options at all. Nothing that is, but the sky.

Junjie pulled his third piece of nondescript gear, another of Quan's miracles. Its sleek, silver exterior hosted no cables. One small LED — green, orange, or red — the only indication it was an electronic device. No power connections. Not even a visible cover screw. Honestly, Junjie thought, these designs were as elegant as any he'd seen. Quan was a singularly talented guy and a blessing to have on their team.

Junjie double-clicked the sat launch. An options dialog appeared:

Save the world from nuclear destruction, or

The very best of internet cat videos.

A few joy-filled tears fell down his cheeks and onto his shirt in a profound release of tension.

"Well, 'Save the world' it will have to be," Junjie said to no one in particular. "I really don't have time for cat videos."

He clicked the first button and a global mapping program with the current location and availability of bandwidth on various satellites sat poised above a 3D image of Earth. None hovered close enough to provide the needed signal strength.

Not a surprise. Junjie's endeavors would require careful sequencing, taking advantage of link downtime for compiling and off-line work. The nearest current link was Strata5, used by both military and corporate entities. Available: four hours from now.

Spreading out his bedroll next to an aging table and single bamboo chair, he laid his head down.

He recalled doing this before. In this room. Quite some time ago.

Another dangerous rainy season had exacted its toll on Gansu. Rivers raged, swollen beyond their banks. Neighbors' homes, fragile to begin with, now lay destroyed as unremitting mudslides surged through the area with impunity. Though Junjie's family home had sustained significant damage, it would be re-buildable.

Dismissing the chaos and stress the Australian couple insisted he, his parents, and their two other children stay until it was safe. Packed into this one, small back room, the size of the space didn't matter, not at all. The gracious offer far outweighed any inconvenience. It was on this floor and around this home that Junjie had come to know love and sacrifice.

He hoped his current efforts would fit in.

And then Junjie let weariness win, his eyelids closing gently, satisfyingly.

THIRTY NINE

The Oval Office, Washington, D.C.

The president's daily security briefing listed one and only one item.

Midway through the reinforced doorway the National Security Advisor paused, considering again the depth and impact of all that'd happened. The veteran policy analyst shook her head, recalling the bizarre, brutal actions of the past few weeks. Had a colleague called this out as a likelihood six months ago, she'd have laughed them out of the room. Claiming it to be probable, her next move would've been referral for psychiatric care. Half-awake at the surrealistic nature of the moment, she entered the famous office.

Instead of the usual eight to ten people at two couches and around the edges of a seventeenth-century mahogany coffee table, only three figures loitered. The President, the Joint Chiefs Chairman, and Secretary of Homeland Security, pored over a single page of text at the stately desk. An electricity surged. The late-comer sensed it immediately.

Please, let this be a breakthrough.

Engrossed in the situation at hand, her entrance had gone completely unnoticed by the trio. NSA made some noise, just so the men wouldn't be startled or embarrassed.

A faked cough.

"Mr. President."

"Good morning," the president's head snapped upward and back. "In fact, it may be a very good morning."

With suit coat draping an Elizabethan-era highback chair, his tie dangled, loosened at the neck. The aroma of cold coffee and an overflowing ashtray screamed *Oval Office all-nighter.*

A smoker. The First Lady and the president's physician voiced displeasure loudly and often. Their combined cajoling hadn't worked so far. But they were playing the long game, relentlessly tag-teaming his sorry butt into future capitulation.

Homeland appeared disheveled as well. The Chairman radiated brass and polish. No one had seen him in any other condition. NSA pictured him mowing his lawn in full dress and wasn't too far off the mark. The three men broke from their tight little circle, moving to the couches.

"They're in," the president began. "Stevens' asset behind the lines has joined and they're proceeding on schedule."

"That is very good news, Mr. President. Any updates on the code itself. Changes overnight?"

The Chairman stepped in. "Boys at the Vault say it looks largely the same. Limited access and the timeline continues to draw down."

"Excuse me, Mr. President, but how do we know this is not some kind of ploy by the Chinese?"

"Well, honestly Karen... we don't. Still, I can't imagine what sort of advantage would be gained by letting us alter the coding. As far as we know this is a significant advantage, a new opportunity we'll want to exploit to the fullest. Bottom line: we may regain some form of nuclear strike capability within the next eighteen to twenty hours."

"But," the soldier added. "We still need our ground team to take us home. The boys at the Vault are all bluster and for good reason. In this case they're humbly accepting that the need outpaces even their heady skillsets. They don't like it but they know we need this..."

NSA perused her notes again, "... this Dalton fellow, to finish the job."

Beijing

"Gentlemen. It would appear our little expansionist drama is at a crossroads."

President Xi's indirect censure was absorbed by the two other senior leaders present.

"Most unfortunate," he pressed on, venting. "Perhaps the assurances given on this project are not as ironclad as we'd been told? Yes, maybe this was our greatest mistake— believing these promises in the first place?"

General Chen Bingde took the sting, abided the rebuke as any good soldier would.

The president continued.

"Irrelevant. The only item occupying our thinking should be the protection of our new province... and the mainland, when or if the United States re-establishes its nuclear forces."

Li Keqiang, Chinese Premier and Chair of the State Council, stumbled his way into the lecture.

"Mr. President. This is one small advance for the Americans. True, they have initial access to the code but we have been informed it will take someone with the highest skills to direct it in any actionable manner. Our best people are telling us they do not think this to be likely."

"As conceivable as sympathetic code migration ever occurring in the first place, Comrade Li? And what of the fact that some American developed the code in the first place? What if that someone is still alive and working — this very minute — against us? That was the link you, and Dhe, should never have left unattended. I will not even comment on the absolute incompetence at leaving Zang alive."

"But Mr. President," Li stammered. "That has always been the unknown, as if the Americans didn't even know themselves who worked on it. And Dhe is within reach of Zang, even now."

"Or, maybe the younger nation is more wiley than given credit. And maybe Zang is more than match for your elder operative. *Enough* of your justifications. We must prepare for every contingency. I will require hourly reports from all departments and ministries. If I must clean up your messes, I will need the very best information. Do I make myself clear?"

The men stood, bowed, and left.

Xi stepped across the room and to a long, felt-covered tabletop. Accent lighting. A stack of loosely organized notebooks. He ran his hand over a thick, red-covered volume.

Eyes-Only, President. National Administration for the Protection of State Secrets: Top Secret.

The table of contents bore stark, ominous headings.

VII: Scenarios for Nuclear Engagement—Western United States.

Appendix D: Death tolls, fallout, and recovery.

XII: Decisions Matrix: Pan-Pacific Nuclear Exchange. Defense of the Homeland.

The president was a pragmatic man. This character trait, above all others, had gotten him to this place of influence and power. An economist by education, he was guided by cost/benefit and degrees of incentives. Undergirded by values, these opposing and sometimes balancing weights were what mattered enough for people to attain, defend, or bargain. He spoke in numbers, not names, learning early on that leadership often required sidestepping momentary emotions. Left unchecked they cloud judgment, skew data. Still, this—the outcomes he reviewed again—were almost impossible to process.

The probable chain of events was not a mystery. The Americans would undertake military action to recover their territory. His people would counter with limited nuclear aggression in the new province, just as they had in the discharge of two missiles over Puget Sound earlier. America would threaten the Chinese mainland itself.

Everything hinged on who flinched first.

Or who might finally pull the trigger.

For more than a half-century the world remained a delicate balance of nuclear powers. The unthinkable was impossible. Therefore the newest, more limited threat would come from non-state actors. But all had forgotten: there were still enough warheads between the major players to blow everyone to Mars and back a hundred times. And this war, as horribly imagined for seventy-some years would be one in which entire nations of people were suddenly and violently excised. Industry, culture, and environment eradicated. Smoldering piles of radioactive rubble and decay diminishing over decades, if not centuries.

The president closed the book, walked to his desk and engaged the intercom line.

"The Foreign Minister, please. I will need to speak with him at once."

FORTY

Central Pacific Ocean

The American pilot's visor display declared all systems go as he awaited final clearance. Blinking green outlines of nuclear-tipped ordinance meant his missiles hung hot. Targeting vectors: received, confirmed, logged.

Flipping open a small plastic cover, his finger hovered, ready to act, to release these hounds of hell toward China's unsuspecting billions. Highly controlled breaths; each one pronounced in his ear canal. Every heartbeat: weighty. Training and duty guided. Still, the real toll of his orders settled, understandably so.

"Tiger-Five. Awaiting go. Confirm."

"Roger. Tiger-Five. Clear for... return. Cool the birds down. Come on home."

The cover eased back into place. A few more keystrokes and the ordinance visuals disappeared as well. Pulling hard on the yoke, the sleek airframe banked into a return path to USS George H.W. Bush.

"Tiger squadron, this is Tiger Leader. We are done for today. Good job. Call that another successful exercise run and we'll be back in time for chow. Cookie says there is a lovely meatloaf special this evening. You all deserve the finest the U.S. Navy can muster."

Multiple groans. A few choice words. But nine skilled touchdowns later the squadron entrusted their planes to their equally adept crews for refueling and maintenance. They jostled and pushed one another while walking toward the superstructure, like pre-teen boys with a surplus of pent-up energy. Some moments you'd be surprised that men of this order had charge of life and death and multi-million dollar machines. Most days their commitment and skill would make you proud.

"Commander on deck."

Rear Admiral Knowles appeared from behind a bulkhead, encountering the just-returned flight leader and his cohorts. They responded appropriately, respectfully.

"At ease," Knowles ordered. "I hear you had another fine dry-run; that your squad is as ready as the American people will need you to be. Am I correct?"

Knowles was not the kind of commander to use drummed up confrontations. She really wanted to challenge her sailors and airmen to excellence, readiness. Conversations like this were welcomed.

"Ma'am," the lead pilot responded. "On station, systems as green as they could be. When we get the call, we'll do the job."

The admiral smiled broadly.

"Good to hear, Captain. Carry on."

With that she released her aviators, off-duty for the evening, even as Carrier Group 2 closed in on China. Another ten hours and men and machines would be in place, anxious for orders.

Former U.S. Embassy Compound, Beijing

Though still officially the United States' Ambassador to China, Gary Locke was performing his last assignment—closing down Beijing Station. The American President had ordered the necessary, albeit weak, response. Locke's days since had been overrun with administrative duties and sensitive materials handling. With a staff of over seventy-five there were lots of personal and personnel issues to take care of. A sense of defeat and dread discolored the few remaining hours he had in this office. Mundane. Painful.

Locke stared into space. Evidences of the man's faithful service to a great nation once lined these shelves. They now sat stacked unevenly in boxes, to be shipped who knew where. He had always tried his best to move relations forward in the world. Hardball was not his favorite tactic, preferring instead to protect the interests of America as well as advance the welfare and prosperity of his host nations. He was convinced there were many ways to do both at the same time. The heaviness hit hard, most days. Professional disgrace. Failure.

The weight he carried wasn't only personal.

The man was a long-time resident and civil servant of the former State of Washington. He was from there. His family and friends, many of them, still there. How were they fairing? What must it be like for them?

An odd buzzing brought Locke out of semi-mourning. The pager rang twice again, its display illuminating the desk.

2444HCO*#

Locke walked over to the wall safe and dialed the combination. Drawing out a thin notebook, he searched rows of data, tracking characters until he found the match.

He placed the ledger back into the vault.

Then, informing no one, Locke grabbed his overcoat and keys, leaving through a chiefly unknown exit at the back of his private bathroom.

Twenty-five minutes later he arrived unaccompanied at a nondescript warehouse in the steel manufacturing sector of the city. Pushing both hands into the pockets of his black overcoat, he strode toward the entrance. A few last steps and the door opened for him. Inside, two guards motioned, pointing with the business end of their side arms. The hallway was narrow, maybe three feet wide with a single, aging light bulb overhead. Twenty paces later came another wordless instruction: to the left, into an empty room. Empty that is, except for two facing chairs in the middle of the space. One was already occupied.

"Mr. Ambassador. So good of you to respond to my call."

FORTY ONE

Dalton's head rolled forward, committing to neither full consciousness nor sleep.

Underneath and behind him: slippery, cheap vinyl. Oil and gasoline smell in the air. A musty, thicker heat. Cartons and bags at his ankles. Not much room to maneuver or shift his weight. Dalton paused a second longer, scanning subtly with his peripheral vision.

In the back seat of a car.

A crappy one.

"Hey, Aurora. Sorry to say there's no prince here. And I sure 'ain't gonna give you the wake-up kiss."

Sanchez.

He had met the woman only recently but already liked her. Aside from pressing a knife against his throat, he was coming to believe she presented quite the advantage.

Dalton sat up, stretching.

"How long was I out for?"

"Too long, LT. A bit too long, I say."

Loch.

Of course, it was Loch.

"How soon to target?" Dalton asked.

"Thirty minutes if it holds up like this," Sanchez shot back.

"Okay," he said. "We agreed on the operational sequence?"

"Check," came the response from Lochland, holding down the forward passenger seat.

Sanchez, to the left and in front of Dalton, had the wheel.

Early morning. The regular gray and a slight chill. The windshield defrost cleared long, ellipsoidal patches. Other than that everything stayed pretty foggy. Neither of the backseat windows was clear.

Dalton leaned back, closing his eyes. It all lit up again — the giant, interactive display.

Lines, curves, time stamps. Personnel and pathway data. Every detail interconnected in a vast array of possibilities. No matter how obscure or abstract it was all there, all at the same time. Had anyone been able to peer into his head at this moment it would have come across as unmitigated chaos, an untamed mess of disparate items, pictures, numbers. To the retired soldier, it played one big, beautiful symphony.

Seeing everything he needed for now, Dalton opened his eyes, leaning between the two front seats.

"Chevy?"

"Yeah...Lumina," Sanchez replied. "Ain't she a beaut'? Drove something like this my senior year in high school, all piled up with rowdy teens on a Friday night. Had to stop every two hours to fill the radiator and add oil — which we need to keep an eye on, too. But hey, what more do you need when you're on your way to save the world?"

She lay abandoned on an old logging road parallel to the meanderings of the Snoqualmie River, under a stand of hundred foot firs and at the edge of a dirt and gravel path.

Not long ago the road had borne the constant press of commercial tree harvesting equipment. Now it lay quieted, solemn, yet straight and mostly cleared. A few minutes of removing branches, needles, and cones and they stared at the car, then back at one another with an air of disbelief.

Rust patches marred the driver's side rear wheel-wells. The hood didn't close completely, some serious warping at the edges. A busted passenger-side mirror. That was all good. She wouldn't stick out along rural roadways in economically depressed towns, the very places they'd pass through.

All good, that is, if she started.

Ten minutes more and Loch had her running, roaring in appreciation of being set back to work. The half tank of gas remaining would have to do; stopping would be too risky. Too many people. Too great a chance a random patrol might roll up without notice.

Sanchez slid into the driver's side and shifted the manual transmission into first gear. Just like that they began the next leg of their journey, down worn blacktop and on their way to the metropolitan edge of Seattle. Transportation needs now satisfied, team development was coming along as well, albeit slowly.

Within the hour, Sanchez and Loch—the more naturally combative of the trio—came to an uneasy truce. For now they would extend trust. But it was a thin line, easily crossed, as they headed off the lower Cascade elevations, down through curved mountain highways and into the suburbs.

They had lately merged onto State Route 520, transitioning from boondocks to some of the more affluent areas in the central Puget Sound region. It was an abrupt shift from woodsy, old car-laden acreage to multi-million dollar homes with manicured landscaping and lengthy driveways, all intended to keep the "riff-raff" at a distance.

Chinese flags lay planted squarely in front or hanging off rooflines, in every single yard and home.

The pricey accommodations were allotted to incoming Chinese leadership, be they Communist Party heads or PRC Army big shots.

You like the neighborhood, eh? Dalton surmised.

The car slowed from highway speed, pulling over to the right. Though probably the least efficient way to handle traffic, the PRC Army had established checkpoints at all major roadways. Given the Chinese held the ultimate pressure point in the threat of nuclear strike, their on-the-ground systems appeared less heavy-handed than imagined. This deceptively lighter touch, combined with ongoing, over the top presentations of the glories of Beijing's offer of a better life, almost seemed reasonable. Except for the fact you woke up daily as a conquered, second-class citizen of the PRC.

Coming to a full stop, Sanchez lowered the window.

Zhengjian! was the simple command.

He was maybe twenty, twenty-one. His youthfulness flashed Sanchez back to her first few years in the military. Would her naivete, fueled by impassioned patriotism, allow her to take part in something so clearly a violation of human rights and dignity? Doubtful. The army was all she had ever known, and yeah, she loved her country, but such unprovoked aggression would have struck her deeper, at a primary level of basic justice—simple right and wrong. She would have shed her vows at that point, walking away, dignity intact.

Sanchez produced documents as ordered. Loch and Dalton handed theirs forward as well.

Another soldier canvassed the perimeter of the Lumina, pausing every few inches to consider what kind of threat, if any, this old rust bucket and its three odd passengers might present. He stopped outside Dalton's window, peering in. Then he laughed, a goofy but cruel laugh of condescension.

Apparently they posed no threat whatsoever.

Sanchez' ID, compliments of her cop buddy from Tacoma, and the professional pieces Loch and Dalton held courtesy of the fine special ops teams back at Ft. Clark, had passed muster. So far, so good. With documents returned, the closed windows shielded them from a classically-Seattle light mist. Sixty seconds more and they were on their way.

Rejoining the flow of heavy commuter traffic, three more mile markers passed as bright green overhead signage told them they were heading the right way. It also illustrated the depth of changes taking place as their destination was spelled out in both English and Mandarin.

Microsoft Campus – Redmond, next five exits.

FORTY TWO

Sanchez curved off the highway and toward the grand entrance, a few hundred feet ahead. Previous company guard stations remained in place. Only now, those posted bore military garb— Chinese uniforms—instead of the regular light blue, rent-a-badge nonsense.

A quick visual confirmed their briefing intel; the best in camera, infrared, and drone surveillance. Gates and Co. had done a fine job of securing and surveilling these expansive grounds. The PRC was taking full advantage of the investment.

Turning onto One Microsoft Way the team was struck with the enormity of the place. Dalton had been here on occasion during grad school at the UW. He'd judged their work as okay. A little dull for his tastes. As professionals, Loch and Sanchez kept their collective jaws from dropping overtly. Still, they remained impressed. Fifty acres of lushly wooded landscaping. One hundred fifty buildings. Over 8 million square feet of office, food services, and research and development facilities. A small city in its own right with 40,000 employees on this campus alone, the company's physical presence in this upscale suburb matched its global profile in every way.

Big. Really big.

Their IDs issued them entrance again, no problems at all. The few odd looks were directed more toward the car than their documentation. Looking at each other with a "Well, that went better than expected," they proceeded to the next available stall. The green and blue parking sticker, forged back at Clark as well, would keep the car from being inspected — hopefully, quite a while.

Thousands of employees exited lots and garages and the trio folded into the massing crowds, all heading toward a normal workday. At least the new normal. Two months ago they didn't have to proceed past PRC Army units with AK47s at the ready. Neither had they been subjected to immediate, unannounced search and seizure anywhere and anytime. To Dalton and team they seemed fairly accepting of it all. Keeping their heads down. Trying to survive. No one was about to blame them. Had they any idea what this team was up to they might have cheered. Or they may have turned them in. Better for three to suffer than a few million perish?

God help us all, Sanchez whispered, observing the lemming-like procession.

She and the others began to create distance, diverting attention from the fact they were together, a unit of sorts. This proved relatively easy while everyone moved like a giant herd. A few more moments and their bearing would deviate, breaking from the crowd. There, more vulnerable, their best fieldwork and a spot of luck would be needed to stay under the radar. Thirty more yards of well-maintained walkways and they arrived.

Building 25. Such a bland name. But the exact place required to reconnect with the caretaker and hopefully break open the Chinese code.

At 25 they separated. Dalton circled around back, fading into a dense row of azaleas. The pathway leading past the flowering bushes was quiet, empty. Squatting down, he waited there in silence. On the front side of the building, Sanchez and Loch proceeded through the metal detector and stepped inside. The good news? They were carrying no weapons, aside from the small patch of C4 sewn into their clothing. Nothing to alert the guards at the desk. The bad news? No weapons. A brains and brawn op; largely gray matter, they all hoped.

The IDs worked again.

Sanchez smiled at the taller of the two men on duty, marking her more prominently in his mental catalog and therefore diminishing Loch's imprint to a similar degree.

Attractive Latina catching his eye, holding it slightly.

Short, stocky Scotsman.

No contest. Upon all hell breaking loose in 25, Sanchez wanted Loch's image to be harder to track than hers.

Loch breezed by, hardly registering at all. Sad commentary, but it was effective.

Sanchez headed left toward the elevators and Loch split opposite, around a blind corner and past the open-glassed office suites. A security door awaited at the end of the corridor with a stairwell leading below ground. The magnetic strip on his ID traveled across the sensor pad smoothly, rewarding him with a solid green light. Loch slipped through and made his way down. Thirty-five steps later Loch's first objective came into view.

Walking casually, foot speed and pace ordinary.

Several locked doorways flanked left and right, every ten feet or so. No windows, only light wooden frames and painted steel doors, each bearing a nine-key pad. Muted fluorescent lighting gave the place the vibe of a bad dream staged in a mental institution. After ten iterations of this pattern, Loch stopped at the end of the hallway. Fingers and tools worked together expertly as he picked the traditionally mortised lock of the last door on the right.

Three levels above, Sanchez rode the far left elevator and hit the button for L3, the last stop listed on the panel. She knew better than to believe it. Descending past L1 and L2, the few other employees along for the ride exited, off to workstations and offices.

A subtle sigh of relief. Less people equaled fewer questions about a new face.

The button for L3 sat darkened on the panel. A few more feet of descent and it came to life, glowing and buzzing as the elevator's air shocks settled the car into place. The door opened. A young Chinese face leered back, expectantly.

The guard from the front door post.

The room Loch had broken into was long and narrow with ten-foot high ceilings. Finding the light switch on the wall, he flipped it on. Though potentially bringing suspicion, it would also be more "normal" to anyone entering unannounced. Rows of metal storage shelves overflowed with formerly useful items. Bankers' boxes. More rugged, suitcase-type enclosures. Cables hanging over the edges of plastic bins.

One big closet, just as assumed.

He made his way alongside the concrete foundation to the spot furthest from the door. Turning right, the stocky soldier walked through a thick layer of dust, navigating around items not rating shelf space. Five feet more and he stopped. Creating a platform out of three of the sturdier bins, he stepped up. Moving a handle right to left, the ground-level window eased open. Only a small squeak.

In hushed tones, he spoke through the opening.

"Well, laddie. If you're taking a leak in the bushes, ya must hurry it along. After all, we're on a schedule ya see."

Dalton heard him. He just didn't want to encourage Loch any more than necessary.

Waiting a moment more, listening again for any movement on the footpath, Dalton fell to the ground, edging through the small rectangular frame and reuniting with the sergeant at the bottom of the makeshift stairs.

The veteran sniper smiled back, a coy smirk from her dark, feminine face.

Exactly what he had hoped for.

He entered the elevator, locked the door, and moved aggressively toward Sanchez. Against the brass railing, she let him close.

Closer still.

Then Sanchez leaned right.

Reaching up and behind the unsuspecting soldier, she grabbed the nap of his hairline and pulled down hard. His neck and spinal column compacted, sending a surprising shock down his back and to his lower extremities. The momentary neurological assault thrust his eyes up and back, vision obscured in rays of light. Disoriented, he fell. Finishing blows came next—as quick and twice as fierce. Sanchez connected her half-coiled fist to the soft spot underneath his chin and slashed the hard bone of the thumb-side of her other hand across his windpipe. The man clutched at his throat. Though not strictly necessary, her right elbow came down on top of his head.

The poor creature lay crumpled on blue, industrial-grade carpet.

She checked for breathing.

He would survive. He'd also wake up to one monster of a headache.

Sanchez took no pride in unnecessary eliminations. She needed him out of the picture, long enough to get to the access point and do the work. Walking over to the keypad, she turned the door lock to the right, opening the elevator door again to level L3.

Her hands came up once more.

"Whoa there Lassy!"

Loch sized up the situation. "Remind me not to critique your hair or make-up, okay?"

Let it go. For now.

"Yeah, Romeo thought a few floors down would be the perfect place for a little break-time get together. He's a bit sleepy now."

"I'll say," Loch replied, stepping into the car.

Dalton followed, silenced momentarily by the young man on the floor.

Loch continued more seriously, admiring her work. "What? About an hour and a half, Ms. Sanchez?"

"Yeah, more or less. Maybe more. I hit him pretty hard."

FORTY THREE

Zhou Dhe's time in Qingdao was remarkably fruitful. A mere forty-five minutes and he had established a strong new lead, fanning the settled embers of the Junjie's hunt into full flame.

The unnamed young man had brokered his silence for such a small fee. A pittance compared to what he had handed over. And in the end, all for a reward he would never get to enjoy. So naïve. Why should he presume Dhe to be a man of his word? None of this concerned him. If this young one believed in fairytales, their great society was surely better off without him. Advanced peoples allowed no such foolishness.

Dhe smirked, recalling Christianity's infamous traitor.

A Judas – yes, they always materialize when needed.

Such thoughts occupied the older man as he flew above the foothills of Central China.

Dhe let the voice in his head continue in grand, yet private, pronouncement.

Junjie – ah, you thought you were clever. But of course you would go home, hiding, crying; shaking in fear. We'll soon meet again. And you will no longer cause me any trouble.

The minister turned his head to the right. A panoramic view filled the floor to ceiling glass of the front and side casing of the Hughes 500D transport helicopter, one of four tasked to the Strategic Communications Ministry. Although the wider, more comfortable backseat would be expected for a man of his station, Dhe assumed the copilot chair. No more miscues. He would take charge in every way, beginning with the forward cabin area of the chopper.

Two hours later they began a quick, uneven descent. The bird would carry him no farther, fuel efficiency and range taxed to their limit. The landing zone approached, a small patch of hard-packed dirt to the side of the road. Crosswinds in the open valley battered the small craft as skid settled to ground. Dhe exited while rotors still spun wildly overhead, walking brusquely to the vehicle that would take him the rest of the way.

He was not pleased.

The recently-new Range Rover had not aged well. Mud, cemented across her entire lower side panels. Five major body compressions. Pockmarked sheet metal, front to rear. Skewed headlights from a few too many grill resets. The high-terrain SUV appeared at least a decade older than her mileage and years.

Maybe this was some poor rural cabbie, pulled over with car trouble?

No, this was his ride. The driver's shoulder-slung CS/LS-5 removed all doubt.

Dhe didn't try to hide his exasperation. He couldn't believe it.

Another three hours? In this contraption?

Comfort wasn't the issue. The sorry mode of transportation befit neither his status nor the critical nature of his mission.

Later, he told himself—later, someone would pay for this misstep.

Dhe trusted no one, especially some driver-guard he was meeting for the first time in a distant province, so many hours from headquarters. Practically speaking, the helicopter could only draw so close to Gansu. Not to mention that the chopper setting down in the middle of Junjie's village might cause a bit more presence than he was looking for. Dhe loved grand entrances but this was not the moment for one. No, he would be in need of no more help.

The guard protested.

The minister gave him no choice in the matter. Having the man alongside gained him nothing. But most importantly, glory might have to be shared, the joy of eliminating Junjie diluted by another's contributions. That would not happen. Dhe had dispatched men twenty times more dangerous than this Zang pest. No, this would be simple, quick, definitive. And then he would enjoy the fruits of his labors.

By the time the Rover descended into Junjie's village the sun was high over family fields of grain and rice, painting and framing the glowing horizon. Drifting down the nearly abandoned main street, the car drew no unwarranted attention. Apparently, no one thought much of another beat up four-wheel-drive vehicle on these less-than-properly maintained roads.

Excellent. A fine start.

The Rover took the first right off the main street. The directions to the safe house, obtained via the young and now dead Judas, proved wonderfully accurate. Dhe drove by Junjie's hiding place without looking or slowing. Just passing through. Only a few signs of life among the second story windows of apartments and businesses.

Moving on.

Two blocks further and Dhe pulled onto a graveled path ending at the service bay of a seed and milling operation, trying to keep the dust trail at a minimum and engine quieted. Even at this his tires rang out with a popping sound every few feet, loose rocks spinning out under the tension of wheels against ground.

Looking for the right cover.

There.

A loading dock tucked into the horseshoe-shaped building was the perfect place to leave the car. A few other working-type vehicles populated the small back lot. The battered SUV would fit just fine.

The minister turned off the engine and waited, quietly contemplating the end of Junjie Zang with not a small degree of personal pleasure.

Ninety minutes passed.

The driver's side door opened without warning, the fuse pulled from the door alarms circuit.

Dhe exited, pacing through soft dirt and gravel and on toward his target. Pausing at the street corner, he listened for signs of activity.

Now.

Stepping out from the shadows, an unexpected bucket of water came crashing down into the paved gutter at his feet, released from a window above. Dhe retreated to cover effortlessly. Resetting himself. Controlled breaths. Had anyone noticed? No. No yelling, footsteps, or curiously opened doors.

Dhe tried again. This time he navigated the width of the street without incident.

Junjie's hideout front yard presented as a sad jungle of weeds, dying trees, and garbage. There would be no swift, silent incursion by this route. Instead Dhe walked around back of the dilapidated structure, looking for an entry point. There—at the northwestern corner of the home, siding had torn away. He squeezed through, between gaps in the wood framing. One more step, sideways, and he was in.

The marks of vagrancy and the cruelty of time and elements lay everywhere. Small piles of garbage and debris dotted scarred flooring. A maze of nails, linoleum shards, and wood chips. Stealthy footfalls became a challenge. And then a soft light, radiating from what used to be the kitchen.

Why are you not more careful, young man?

In five more steps he came upon a scene he had not anticipated.

Strata 5.

Dhe stared incredulously at the initialization sequences on the laptop's screen. The program's progress bar was almost fully green. Connection Status: 85%.

The minister's weight shifted onto his heels. Clearly, he had underestimated his foe. This worn down shack in the middle of nowhere was no pitiful hiding place. Nor was it an overly sentimental retreat to loved and familiar surroundings in the face of certain death. No, this was much more. This scene spoke of sabotage; the work of a rebel, a betrayer of his country and opponent of all Dhe claimed to love.

Zang was not a coward.

He was not cowering.

Nor was he currently present amongst the surprising array of equipment.

FORTY FOUR

The most humbling of human needs had drawn Junjie away from his workstation.

The plumbing in the home had stopped working long ago, its drain lines corroded, pocked full of holes. The toilets still functioned as basic receptacles, adding yet another layer of unpleasant smells. It was a case of meager practicalities. With personal business finished, Junjie returned to his work.

Dhe's imposing form appeared, not ten feet away, facing the backroom.

Junjie could not allow the gear to become irreparably damaged. Choosing obvious over stealthy, reinforced boot toe met aged drywall.

The minister turned.

"I have to admit, Mr. Zang. You have more in mind than I imagined. I took you for a coward. Running. Leaving behind everything... your lovely wife and son... all to save your own, putrid life. But even misplaced courage deserves an honorable exit."

Junjie's body language gave away his thoughts of lunging for the kitchen.

Dhe brandished his weapon, moving Junjie back on center.

"And... before you rush into anything I want you to consider again your lovely wife and son."

"Nothing you say… "

Dhe's phone came out and began playing a video feed.

One chair in an otherwise empty room.

Dai Tai.

"Bao? What? How?"

"Junjie," she pled. "I am so sorry. You must..." the feed garbled. "...save us."

The engineer's heart pounded harder than he thought possible. Words choked off in emotion.

"… whatever they tell you…"

"… please, please."

Dhe cut the feed.

"Now," he reasoned. "Here's what I have to offer."

Junjie was actually listening now.

"You and I will sit down and reclaim our nation's rightful control over the American nuclear forces."

"You must know," Junjie spat. "The code is out of control. I don't know if I can."

Dhe brought the phone up again.

"Oh, I think you'll find a way, Mr. Zang. And when you do, a grateful Chinese nation will laud your courage at the hand of foreign assassins. You died to protect your country. Your family will be cared for in great luxury and honor. Your son will have a name he can bear with pride."

Dhe had the most crooked smile. He showed it now.

Junjie's countenance transformed.

"Whoever conceals hatred with lying lips… is a fool."

Dhe didn't know the proverb's origins. He didn't care. He only knew he was looking at a different Junjie. One who had settled his fate.

The older man's head snapped around, his sneer half-hidden in dim light. He wore rage—pure, unfiltered rage. Junjie's subversive acts radiated the few feet between. How dare this flea stand against the will of the State—and by extension, Dhe its faithful agent.

This will end here, now.

He would dispatch not only a menace but a traitor.

Junjie scampered into the small front room.

A shot missed high, embedded in old wallboard.

Dhe's rage-filled state coaxed him to pursue Junjie. The equipment could wait until the young man's heart stopped beating and his body cooled.

The minister took three steps into the old galley kitchen, heading Junjie off and initiating a terminal contest of cat and mouse. An ailing, thin wall stood as the only physical barrier between them. Like a child's game of tag with blind corners, one would eventually flush the other out—exposed, trapped.

"Junjie, my boy, this is useless, don't you see? Stop your foolishness. I am not an unreasonable man. I will make this seem as if you are merely going to sleep. But first you must save your family."

"Forgive my unbelief, Minister. My friends' last moments seemed to be neither pleasant nor comfortable."

"Stop!" Dhe commanded. "Nothing more from you! You are nothing. Do you hear me? Nothing! Of no importance. A simple piece of machinery."

Subtle physical moves accompanied each man's statements, guessing which corner would reverse their positions and which would bring them face-to-face. Stalking and listening, each tried to gain a reckoning.

It was time to turn the tables.

"Your conscience has arisen late in the game, Zang."

"Conscience?" Junjie retorted. "What would a man like you know of morality? Or regret? Nothing, I imagine."

Junjie shifted again, hoping to keep the minister from getting the final deadly angle. Dhe responded, forward and left, surveying the wall separating them, estimating its thickness and structure.

"Hypocrite!" he shot back. "You seemed perfectly happy to receive the government's approval and blessing in the form of great wealth and opportunity. What? Now, you have some kind of problem with what we've done with your work? Pathetic. You gave up your right to care the very minute you cashed the checks."

That one hit hard. Truth often does.

A subtle click pierced the waiting as Dhe hammered a bullet in place. A blast broke the air and wallboard and plaster exploded, the shot exiting to the right and over Junjie's shoulder.

He hit the floor.

Dhe overestimated the old-school construction materials' effect. He reset.

Two more holes tore open above Junjie, another large gash on his side of the wall, lower and on target for where he had been an instant ago.

Junjie scurried in reverse, feet gangly, yet still beneath him. Backwards. Out of control. Junjie tumbled haphazardly into the open.

Exposed. No chance to move, no way out.

The young man inhaled reflexively. Steeling himself, he awaited the final impact of flesh and bone. He winced, turning his head away and raising his right shoulder, as if a shrug might protect him.

Nothing.

Still, nothing.

The tearing of sinew and organ hadn't come as expected. Ten seconds more and Junjie dared to uncoil. He counted again. Smoke and cordite stench clung to the small space. He couldn't wait forever. Junjie reached into the left rear pocket of his jeans and retrieved his cell phone. Tapping the flashlight app, the camera illuminated the few feet in front of him.

Torn up linoleum. A haze of dust.

Cautiously, he stood. Junjie's head felt light, blood surging. He moved toward the living room and paused to listen again. Still no sounds from where only seconds ago all hell had broken loose. Junjie garnered strength and looked around the corner, to Dhe's firing position.

The 9mm silenced Beretta pointed idly away, as if discarded. A few inches from its cooling metal a large, ragged hole lay forcibly opened.

The hail of bullets and exploding walls had halted the exact moment this crevasse had taken shape. Severed floorboards, joiners, joists. Rot, mildew, and time had set a trap for the minister; one he would not escape.

Junjie approached, peering over the edge.

Dhe.

Face up, back arched unnaturally, six feet below. Impaled on a rusted, jagged pipe; one of the larger sewer mains that had sheared off in pieces, ages ago.

Junjie recoiled.

Dhe spat a mouthful of blood and lurched forward, but only as far as the aging lead and concrete would allow.

Junjie almost tripped, barely keeping himself from falling into the hole along with the minister.

Dhe caught the look in Junjie's eyes and responded forcefully, though completely helpless, doomed.

"Do... not... touch... me," he gasped. "Leave me."

Dhe coughed, blood and mucus strewn grotesquely across his chest.

"I do not need your help. I do not *want* your help. You are weak. Weak! Do you hear me, Zang? I will not suffer my last moments in the presence of someone who puts magic before countrymen."

Dhe's lungs deflated, flattening. His eyes grew unfocused, glassy.

Silence.

The emotions of the moment overtook the young man and he wept, chest heaving, with hands rested on bent knees.

This... is what true lostness looks like.

Dhe's phone began playback again.

Junjie jumped.

"… whatever they tell you…"

"… please, please."

Away from the hole and cracked significantly, Junjie moved closer.

"… whatever they tell you…"

"… please, please."

The husband and father watched, over and over, knowing he would see it sooner or later. The fifth time, he stopped playback and zoomed.

There. I knew you would never say those words, my dear. If anyone would choose others over themselves, it would be you.

More zoom, at its limit.

A birthmark, just beneath and back of her left ear. The earrings in the video left the mark in the open. The same earrings Junjie bought as an anniversary present and covered over what she considered a flaw.

It could not be her.

Junjie was elated to come out of this encounter alive and that his family was likely safe, as earlier presumed. Still, his enthusiasm was tempered. Dhe was not a good man. But in the end he was still a man, just like Junjie. It felt wrong to leave him there. The young executive considered taking the time to remove the body, to set it aside more respectfully.

Then he looked down at his watch.

09:43:15…

It was a terrible decision to consider. But satellite access would only be available in orbit above Gansu for a few hours now. His first pass had provided valuable uplink time, preparing for an eventual reconnect with the unknown American creator. He needed to be absolutely ready were they to collaborate again within the limited access window.

Junjie wiped his eyes and cleared his throat. With mind and emotions toward the task at hand he left the dead man and headed back to his primitive workspace. Walking back into the room, he was again faced with more than just the technical challenges ahead.

Suppose the creator prevailed.

Junjie's government had invaded a foreign land, forcing a conquered population into subservient reshaping of their national destiny and identity. No one could assure him a supposed equilibrium of arms would keep the Americans from striking in vengeance.

Standing as the arbiter of this kind of power was madness, he reflected.

No easy answers, certainly. But wisdom, split-the-baby-in-half kinds of solutions?

He prayed they would come when needed.

FORTY FIVE

5,988 miles across the vast Pacific, a parallel digital assault commenced.

Building 25 of Microsoft's expansive main campus listed an official lowest floor of L3; three levels underground. Still another hundred feet below this lay Dalton and team's actual target: a small, specialized space known by the code name *Albuquerque.* This nod to the southwest city was in honor of the birthplace and first home of the software giant in the late 1970s. Those few holding knowledge of its existence abbreviated the name — AQ.

Mini-keycards from Ft. Clark passed them through the secured entry. Another small win for the talented forgers and technicians on the other side of the mountains. In an uneasy yet practical partnership, the company's senior leadership had entrusted AQ's entrance data to the U.S. Dept. of Homeland Security. Risky — yes, but also an act of patriotism, and one currently paying big dividends. State-control would not be Microsoft's preferred business environment. So, it remained in their best interests to assist the government in reversing this distasteful scenario. Historically, the corporation's public face had presented as left-leaning. But not this far left.

"Should keep 'em down for a while," Sanchez offered, pulling a micro-syringe out of an already unconscious guard's arm. The two men posted at this secure level had been fully blindsided by the team's appearance at L3. The addition of these chemicals allowed Dalton and company a longer window of opportunity. Considered a half-measure by some, Sanchez chose this over indiscriminate lethal force whenever possible. The risk she entertained in not dispatching combatants automatically would bite her in the backside someday. She knew it. Not everybody plays by the same rules. Many subdued parties wouldn't respond with thankfulness if the chems failed before she finished her work and slipped away to safety. Yet basic humanity challenged her to press the envelope. Her labors too easily led to callousness, so she worked hard to keep that eventuality at bay, from capturing and deadening her soul.

For his part, Loch was dragging the now three guards into the small room. One was the would-be lover boy Sanchez had dispatched earlier. The other two were just plain unlucky losers in the Sgt. Loch lottery.

They were good soldiers. Loch was simply better.

"Visual redirect?" he called out.

This was Dalton's area, so yeah, it was under control.

"The fine folks upstairs should catch everything as normal for another sixty minutes or so. Then a shift change. We'll need everybody down here chemically controlled for the time being. And I need to get busy because we can only stack up so many bodies in our little workspace."

Dalton looked across his left shoulder, surveying the twelve-by-fifteen-foot box. No windows. Smoothed concrete walls rose to the finished ceiling, each holding three banks of low-energy-consumption LEDs. The newer fixtures cast a slight bluish tinge in the room that said corporate industrial — loudly so. Ringing the three walls other than the entrance was a seamless array of thirty-six-inch-wide, floor to ceiling cabinets housing an odd, gelatinous substance, filling the encasements and viewable through all-glass fronts. Whatever it was sparkled.

Breathtaking.

Before him now was an achievement the broader technological community had simultaneously fantasized over and scoffed.

"Amazing," a quiet, reverent tone.

Supposedly, this was not doable. Not yet, anyways. More than the next generation of signal flow. More than some new, improved version of current technologies.

From microcomputing's humble beginnings the problem to solve had been resistance, power held in check by inefficiencies in signal transfer — the actual ease, or relative challenge of electrical impulses flowing across components. The theory has always been simple: approximate the activity of the human brain, as far as neural pathways and synapses go, and throughput and computational power would drastically increase. Convince it to act more like gray matter and you were golden. Theoretically basic. Oh so aggravating, real-world. Finding a substance to facilitate this kind of effortless, near-biological transmission of impulses had been the holy grail of the last fifty years of IT research. Now, in this small room, hundreds of feet beneath the lovely, wooded campus, whatever it was seemed to be doing the job quite nicely.

Dalton didn't know its composition. But he knew it was working, the minute he took command of the workstation.

"Whoah."

"You got what you need, LT?" Loch questioned from five feet away.

"Amply supplied, my good man."

Gansu

Strata5: lock.

Junjie typed a few lines, hoping to pick up where he'd left off with the creator.

AQ

```
C:>|welcome back? - caretaker
C:>|are you ready to see?
```

Dalton grabbed headgear and a pair of control gloves hanging over the small desk.

Sensory-immersed except for smell, the blackout took a second of adjustment.

Then everything exploded.

The flashing tour of neural pathways was blinding yet beautiful. Every curve perfected and each connection in its exact place. Data flowed seem-less, a brisk but controlled river. Purpose was everywhere evident. More than the excitement of an amusement park ride, movement across digital synapses and alterations to new avenues made sense and did their job, every single time.

Flawless.

Powerful.

Error-less execution.

Dalton watched, literally in awe, as decisions he would have made in the flow were redirected, completely counterintuitive, and producing a far better net result. Not the kinds of winners and losers choices he would make when faced with the data, even with a greater degree of predictability than any other human.

These choices were win-win. At every turn.

But Dalton was only looking at data. Numbers. Percentages. Factors. Probabilities.

Gansu

Junjie was watching as well.

He knew where Dalton was going, because he had been there himself. If he was to trust this unknown, potential ally, he had to get everything out on the table.

AQ

```
C:>|Beijing grid.mp4
C:>|HKEx.mp4
C:>|are you ready to see more?
```

Yes, Dalton wrote in the air, entering the reply by making a fist.

The first file filled Dalton's view, even out to his peripherals.

He walked among Beijing's backstreets.

Police and fire units filled the air, a relentless aural assault.

In quick succession, he was in a rundown apartment. Children crying. Dirty. A forlorn parent offering a dingy glass of water, no better choice in hand. Then another back alley. A knife slashed across a homeless man's arm and the assailant ran, a single piece of bread the prize. Now, a few blocks up from roving gangs, storefronts destroyed with wood, metal, and rocks. A news anchor, trying desperately to keep up with the producer's feed, and a crawler across the bottom of the screen noting how many hours since this sector of Beijing had lost power.

Dalton reeled.

And then he noted the same codestream he had seen earlier, working in concert with the images.

File two triggered.

Five men. Five different buildings. The same result hundreds of feet below.

Creditors calling in every last yuan.

More chaos, though the financial demographic had shifted.

And again, the beautiful flow of data and decisions. Perfect at the surface.

This can't be, Dalton typed.

Gansu

Junjie could feel his angst.

During the long months of the project he had occupied the same seat, the sheer beauty of the code significantly fueling his own justifications.

But he was wrong.

And he needed the creator to come to the same conclusion.

AQ

C:>|have you seen?

Dalton's mind and heart tore open.

I can fix it. I know I can.

He moved the digital structures, rearranging and rebuilding.

Look at this thing. It's almost there...think what it could mean...

The earlier images flashed again, with some from the new province folded along. Cruelty. Control.

He stopped cold.

What am I doing?

Among the visuals and the code, a moment of absolute clarity dawned.

Project Sovereign had run its course. And with it, all it represented.

Gansu

The pause told Junjie he had an opening.

Beyond simple contact, he had to make his case, take full advantage of the moment.

He typed, *Creator, now that you are seeing, I must ask something.*

```
C:>|caretaker proceed
```

AQ

```
C:>|... wouldn't you say this whole scenario is
MAD?
```

The transmission dumbfounded Dalton.

The abbreviation — mutually assured destruction — was requesting a nuclear standoff. Not unlike cold war footing. Each side held in check by immediate, proportionate response. Caretaker was asking Dalton to not only bring Sovereign under control but then rewrite it, drawing down enough American capacity to leave DC and Beijing at a standstill.

Caretaker had given him shared access, back at Clark. That didn't mean he was a good faith actor. Could just as likely be a ruse, waiting for Dalton to open an advantage for the Chinese.

Creator ignored the question and began in earnest to attack his own work.

He'd set semi-independent routines in play — bots — designed to do one thing and one thing very well: tear down the mother code's defenses. Once Sovereign was on the digital gurney, US nuclear control would be restored. From there it was easy to spin out into war scenarios. Especially for Dalton. Such haunting imagery needed to be set aside for now. First order of business was right in front of him.

Dalton tossed his sensory gear and got back to basic keyboard development, quickly forging fifteen such attackers.

"Good to have you back," Sanchez noted.

"Yeah, thanks. That was a little weird, but I'm good now."

"Okay," Loch said. "What's the play?"

"Eleven. Eleven of fifteen programs need to get through the door."

Dalton double-checked the limited access clock against his wrist unit.

08:57:13...

The programs began reporting back.

Two, ten, and eight failed during the first few minutes. No question, out of play.

One, and now three through six, all showed signs of penetration, green-lighting almost in unison about thirteen minutes in.

"There you go," Dalton quipped. "That's what I'm talking 'bout." The man willed the code forward, words of hope and confidence helping to bleed anxiety in the agonizing waiting.

Numbers nine, twelve and thirteen now showed promise as well.

Dalton remained calm, at least outwardly. The stocky Scotsman stood astride the workstation, his gaze split between the doorway and the monitor.

"Well, LT. We may have a chance at this thing, eh?"

"We'll see. Not there yet. Not yet."

Three more, painful trips around the 60-second track and another status report.

Fifteen and fourteen lit up like Christmas Day.

Five more minutes.

Seven was a no.

All three operators were thinking the same thing. Ten subnets doing their job. Four defeated. They still had a chance, but an ever-slimming one. Eleven stood as the holdout.

Watching. Hoping. Like racetrack junkies, leaning forward as their horse took the last turn, stretching for the wire.

C'mon, Eleven.

"Dalton?" Sanchez interrupted from over by their surveillance position. "We got a problem."

She pointed. The front desk guard had called someone more senior. Together, the two studied the falsified video. Sanchez spoke more pressingly this time.

"Not good. Not good at all. We've got activity. Checking the source and routing."

She paused.

"We gotta go. Now!"

Her insistence, gleaned from hard-won years of fieldwork landed on the men with authority. There would be no second-guessing. Exfil would begin without hesitation.

AQ was a small, windowless box. One way in. The same way out.

Back into the elevator it would be.

Loch hoisted two of the still-unconscious guards, like some kind of awkward workout for his already healthy trapezii. Depositing them into a jumbled heap, he went in for the last one. The poor guy would have some difficult to explain bruising along his left rib cage when he came to as the brawny Scot literally tossed him into the corner of the tiny hallway.

Sanchez stared at the forlorn sight.

"You've got to be kidding me."

"Can't spend no time on 'em now, can we, las? And with all the care you took to not end them outright, it'd be cruel to let them waste away in there, don't ya think?"

The comment jabbed at her unconventional methods, maybe even accusation of weakness. Sanchez didn't answer. Didn't need to. Instead, she relieved the men of their weapons. The 9mm's she passed to her teammates — while pocketing one herself — and then placed the MP5's just inside the room, out of reach and out of action.

"Charges set," Loch's strange calmness resulting from much practice with deadly explosives.

"Set," Sanchez replied. "On your time."

"Let's go. Let's go, people."

A scant five seconds after the door had closed, the sub frequency thump of a small patch of C4 going off resonated through steel and fabric casing, shaking the elevator car on its track while doing little to halt their vertical escape. Loch's application and composition of the charge had done its job, leaving a wash of circuit damage in their wake. The keypad and locking mechanisms were non-operational, providing time they desperately needed; time for Dalton's work to come to fruition. Subnet Program Eleven would be left behind, unmanned, no promises. At the very least it would be protected until running its course.

The team's journey from a hundred feet below and then upward to the other levels of Building 25 took all of a half-minute. They braced for exposure to the corridor. Dalton, holding the least hand to hand, close quarters combat experience of the three, emerged as the obvious choice to perform the role of "visual distraction." Posing as a crumpled heap of humanity in the middle of the floor, the confusion should be enough to provide the slimmest element of surprise.

Sanchez and Loch pressed themselves flat against polished steel sidewalls. Coiled, pent up energy, they waited.

FORTY SIX

The two men at L2 hesitated only a fraction of a second. It was all that was necessary, as Loch's and Sanchez' side-positions caught them off balance, hands on weapons but not at the ready.

For Sanchez, the scrapple was over in four moves. Loch required only three. She needed one more setup to access her man's Adam's apple while the sergeant simply plowed through his guard's forearm, delivering a horrendous blow to the chest. It was probably a good thing that the flesh and bone of his arm had initially absorbed the granite, balled fist. Regardless, their first two problems were no longer an issue. Dalton, brilliant in his portrayal of 'pile of person on the floor', rose and then walked across the hall to apply the perfect tactical technique for a situation such as this and a man of his advanced skills.

He pulled the fire alarm.

"So cliché," Sanchez frowned.

"Hey, if it ain't broke..."

Building-wide panic was immediate, and precisely what they had hoped for. Within seconds the sprinkler system opened, a nice liquid cover for blending in with the crowd. People covered their ears with hands, backpacks, or coats in a vain attempt to stop the alarm's crushing, dizzying effect. The net result? A mass of confused, drenched workers morphing into a thickening, moving sea of people, no one person distinguishable from the next.

This might work.

Sixty seconds later they were out. Surfacing in the courtyard, Dalton's strategic vision kicked into high gear. Loch and Sanchez had begun to recognize him processing. They were also getting used to waiting a moment while he refocused to the present.

The sniper paused, thinking this was probably the end of the road. AQ had been their aim. That asset, and the opportunities it presented, were now compromised. Even if Program Eleven worked, Dalton couldn't exactly type in any new commands from outside the room.

"Okay, Mr. Beautiful Mind. Whaddaya have for us now?"

Sanchez' quiet utterance, referencing a movie about a brilliant mathematician who "saw" things no one else did, snapped him back to reality.

"The buses," he said. "Go for the buses."

"What?" Loch said, not understanding. "What in the world are you blabbering about, LT?"

Sanchez looked around, trying to make sense of his directive in light of the wave of people exiting 25—a growing, milling populace with nowhere specific to go, nothing to do.

"Alright, the buses."

"Break up," Dalton cautioned somewhat needlessly to the seasoned operators. "Don't sit together. Wait until we offload and I'll give you more info. Go, now. Fade in. Go."

Loch still wasn't following. He'd lose valuable time, though, and possibly even strategic advantage, if he didn't obey the directives he had right now. The ad hoc team had no official leader. The agreement was to lean into one another's strengths as each came to bear. Dalton had a plan. That was enough.

Sanchez boarded the closest bus, taking an open seat next to a middle-aged Caucasian guy. Dalton strode up the stairs and almost all the way to the back, squeezing into a two-person bench along with the two people already there. Loch, finally on board, took another few steps past Sanchez and stood in the aisle, holding the wrist straps overhead.

The big transport, surprisingly powerful for a next-generation green vehicle, pulled out of the Microsoft lot and onto the street. Everyone's weight shifted as the thirty-foot-long behemoth took the first left a little too sharply. A communal groan but no real protest, their muted response chiefly due to the single PRC thug at the front of the bus, arms crossed over rifle.

The man beside Sanchez mumbled.

She gave him a look saying, "Come again?"

He must've figured her safe enough to repeat it, but only a little louder this time.

"Red bastards."

Her expression again said, "not following you."

He leaned over, whispering and also looking away; his best version of being secretive.

"They think we'll just play along. This whole thing is such a setup. Well... they can force us there at gunpoint but they can't make us look happy about it, that's for dang sure."

It struck Sanchez like a slap upside the head. The poster. The one hanging out front of Building 25. They'd walked by so fast. Couldn't have been more than a foot across. The quad was filled, packed with people.

He saw it. And he put it into his big old head full of scenarios.

Stealing a glance back at Dalton, she smiled—just enough to let him know she got it now.

They were heading downtown. Apparently their new overlords felt the time was right to show the world the favor they had done for this pitiful, decaying nation by invading them in the first place. This "resurgence" was all a good thing, after all. Per the poster at 25, today was to be a glorious, extremely public demonstration of this gratitude. Other nations would step back from horrified but quieted protest and accept the situation as well. Privileges, prosperity. All would flow from China's actions in this new province. All would become so normal. So right.

The bus merged onto 520 West, toward the downtown corridor. Dalton, Sanchez, Loch and the other fifty-some passengers joined an endless stream of transports. The procession ambled across the Lake Washington floating bridges. As usual, the northern side of the structure held back choppy, rough water flowing in from Puget Sound while the southern side appeared calm.

The contrast fit, as Sanchez looked through thin glass windows. There was wrong and right in this world. Concrete, moral boundaries. No amount of propaganda could make rough "waters" smooth in her mind.

The line of vehicles wound on through a rat's nest of on and off ramps and past the University District, eventually merging onto I5 southbound. One last, gentle curve to the right and the city came into full, unobstructed view.

No one was prepared for it.

The sight was too shocking. Too offensive. Emasculating. After all they'd been subjected to in previous weeks, this was still over the top. Entering a tunnel and plunged into semi-darkness, the passengers experienced a brief respite. Exiting into daylight, the image struck them all again, even harder.

Swaying gently in a springtime Seattle breeze: an enormous Chinese flag, red field with gold stars, draped the city's most iconic structure — The Space Needle.

The insult burned deep, salting open and quite vulnerable wounds. A few women on the bus started crying. Men's faces puffed crimson, equal parts shame and anger. Helplessness. Absolute impotence.

Keep it together, Sanchez.

The veteran warrior commanded herself to focus. The sickening picture required more effort than usual.

Loch. His face told the whole story. If not for self-discipline earned throughout years of service he would've snapped for sure.

Their bus pulled off I5 along with all the others, winding its way through narrowly steep side streets and into the urban core. The city fathers had chosen a beautiful and functional setting for this trading outpost, at water's edge and butted up against seven sizable hillsides. This strong vertical orientation resulted over time in a maze of massive hi-rise buildings, many with bases laying at extreme angles to the pavement. It made for the feeling you were always either falling forward or leaning way back.

Dizzying. Disorienting. A perfect match for the moment.

Parked alongside nearly a hundred other busses they disembarked, beginning the mile and a half asphalt trek to the gated entrances of Century Link Field. The modern, open air stadium seated 76,000 screaming fans when hosting the city's football and soccer teams. It was also the location of this afternoon's Citizens Appreciation Rally, televised and streamed worldwide.

FORTY SEVEN

Tens of thousands surged into the stadium under the purview of both obviously armed guards and well-camouflaged gun mounts. There was enough firepower to maintain order while feigning voluntary attendance to an interestedly watching world. After all, this was supposed to be a thankful crowd.

The massive south end zone Mitsubishi Diamond Vision screen lit up, visible from even the furthest outlying lots, showing once more that the Chinese propaganda machine knew what it was doing. High energy, emotionally charged symphonic music resonated throughout the stands. String swells and percussive barrages, perfectly timed with looped images of happy, fulfilled citizens of the PRC filled the eighty-four-foot-wide display. Their faces: Asian, Caucasian, Black, Hispanic—and in an obvious play to the area's history—indigenous American Tribal Peoples.

Shuffling forward as one of the many, Dalton noted a change in the musical underscore and looked up. The screens had transitioned from the happy people sequence to a super wide view from what had to be one of the stadium's upper decks. Panning from end zone to end zone, the screens displayed a field covered in military equipment and personnel with a properly elevated dais at the fifty-yard line. This was to be a grand celebration, no expenses spared. Tanks. Transports. Ground to air missiles mounted and waiting on their portable launch systems. Artillery units. It was an island of green and gray, metal and electronics, all draped in a deep red ocean of ribbons and banners. And it was working, at least for a portion of the gathered throng, still and standing tall, brimming with pride at this momentous occasion for their people, their homeland.

Dalton found it hard to believe. He'd been at the stadium a few times. A handful of football games, a summer concert series by aging rock acts. Even now he could remember the flyover of F18s and the national anthem before kickoff. At this moment, those powerful memories and the pride he'd held all his life seemed so far away. And then it struck him.

These young Chinese faces held the same assured look he had borne at the time. He didn't have to like the circumstances, and their methods were certainly up for discussion. But at a very basic level he understood the commonality.

The screen changed again, emblazoned now with the pudgy, pockmarked face of a man stepping up from his prominent seat on the dais and to the podium. A mid-level Shanghai bureaucrat with family ties deep in the Party strata, the Interim Governor of the new province was only an immediate solution to a pressing need, filling a vacuum created by the invasion and nothing more. In time a seasoned and more capable man would be assigned. For now, this simpleton had been asked to do little more than manage public affairs while military leadership attended to the greater concerns of population control and re-education efforts. Still, this was his moment.

Dalton's busload were some of the last to arrive, directed initially to the southwest concourses of the stadium complex. On arriving they were told in no uncertain terms that all regular seating was now full. They would be required to walk the length of the structure, through the northernmost gates and from there to temporary seating at that side's end zone. The image, again, was exactly what the Chinese wanted.

An overflow crowd. But their kindly new leaders would make sure they all had a good seat. So many appreciative men, women, and children.

The disposable leader gripped the podium with both hands. Looking out to the seated masses, he spoke from statements both crafted and authorized by others.

"Fellow citizens of the People's Republic of China, welcome! Today is indeed a celebration. You have been given new life. For too long the foundations of your country have been fading onto the horizon of history. Your time was ending. Now we... together... face a new beginning. Instead of a failed system flowering a mere few hundred years, you are joining a stream of culture, development, and humanity spanning thousands."

He waited a beat.

"And so, the faces I look upon today... are sensing a new hope, no longer wondering if their best seasons are behind them," his voice grew. "A people given opportunity to join the most robust economy of all the nations of the world. A chance to live, again, with pride and purpose."

There were a few seconds of lag as his voice bounced across the structure.

Silence. A raw, gaping silence dissipated into the cool northwest air, underscored by the reverberation of his last

282 WAYNE C STEWART

words.

No applause, nothing from or among the tens of thousands in the stadium. For those viewing online the scene came entirely different.

A steady production booth hand brought the fader up and a sustained chorus of shouts, cheers, and clapping animated the speakers and ear buds of those currently tuned in via the web and official state television, rebroadcast across fifty-some international networks. Joyous sounds played while the video shot remained on the speaker's upper body.

Inside the stadium, guards outside the camera frame raised their guns. This time the people responded as expected—as required—allowing the speaker to continue only after quelling the celebration with opened, overturned hands. After all, he still had a few more lines to deliver.

"A chance..."

This next pause came completely scripted. An actual cue on the TelePrompTer said "hold, 2 seconds."

"... to be set apart for greatness."

More supplemental applause online, this time pumped back into the stadium via loudspeakers.

The governor stopped, his gaze spanning the eastern side of the stands before continuing.

"So, it is with a deep sense of both satisfaction and thankfulness I present to you... officially... the newest province of the People's Republic of China...

... Penghu Province."

The principally unrecognized moniker appeared on the Diamond Vision, its deeper meaning not registering immediately, nor much at all, to the gathered throng.

"Points for creativity," Dalton mumbled, knowing exactly what they were doing.

Penghu, an islet in the Taiwanese chain, had focused a bitter territorial dispute between mainland China and the breakaway province. The PRC annually refused their claims of independence, insisting this group of nearly 24 million were merely another people and land within her sovereign reach. America—rather haughtily through the years—had recognized The Republic of China as a separate nation, over and against the will of Beijing.

Well played, boys. Well played.

One giant poke in the eyeball. That's for sure.

The mass of bodies around Dalton had ceased forward progress; not yet in the stadium for the governor's introductory comments. He forecast this would soon change, that the guards would turn their attention back to the standing masses and prod them, like everyone else, into the grand occasion. He also predicted that upon being sucked into the stadium with everyone else, their chances of escaping would be reduced to pretty much zero. Well, actually .00731%.

A gunshot rang out. Panic ensued, masking its point of origin.

Good enough.

Dalton slid the 9mm back into his waistline. His frantic shouting and pointing directed attention away from himself as the shooter. Guards scrambled left and right, trying to assess the moment, to retake control.

Sanchez knew what was happening and looked for Dalton through the angry hornet's nest of humanity. Loch followed the cue as well. Like the fire alarm at Microsoft, the single discharge did its job.

People rammed into others' unmoving backsides. Falling, they trampled one another, trying to flee the trouble in their midst. Remarkably, the guards got the people-flow controlled again. Minor injuries, scrapes, bruises. A few people pinned up against the gate's chain link. Even the unfortunate recipient of the flesh wound from Dalton's pistol was receiving medical attention. His foot would bleed some. Soon enough it would be stanched, requiring only stitches and minimal pain management.

Barely a minute later the commotion had ceased. All efforts turned to searching for the shooter. Among the outer guards there was shocked surprise, disbelief that someone would ruin such a glorious occasion with unseemly violence. Inside the stadium this minor event hadn't registered, not even slightly. Festivities continued as the interim governor of Penghu Province blithely presented the rest of his speech.

Four hundred yards north of Century Link two-thirds of the team stopped, catching their breath. Loch looked like the sustained sprint had taxed him no more than getting up from the couch.

"Nicely done, LT."

Dalton, breathing the heaviest: "... had to take it."

"Okay, boss," Sanchez said. "What's the plan? Now that the Freaky Friday supercomputer back at Microworld is out of reach, we're kinda running for no reason, right?"

"Wrong," Dalton said. "That was only stage one. I mean, it would have been fun to finish the job there but honestly, it would've been a bit like taking an A-bomb to a water fight.

We need to go for a little boat ride."

"What? Why?" Loch questioned.

Dalton knew it would be impossible for them to comprehend the multiplicity of data in his head. He did his best to bring the others up to speed, nonetheless.

"Program Eleven was still running when we left. If successful, we're in—access to the actual code stream. If it worked, we don't need the big machine anymore. A basic interface will do. If Eleven does the trick, from here forward it's really a matter of line commands. Extremely complicated line commands but still, something that can be achieved with your standard-issue HP running DOS 5.0."

"DOS?" Sanchez replied.

"Yeah... you're probably a little young to remember. Let's just say that if the door has been opened, then we're good to go."

"No catches?" Loch interjected. "A desktop unit with keyboard and monitor?"

"Well, almost. We do need an internet connection that won't show up to the Chinese web watchdogs."

"Thus, the ferry?"

"Yep, I'll explain more on that later."

"Okay," Sanchez asked. "So where do we get on and where do we get off?"

"Pier 52. And then onto the lovely port city of Bremerton. A two mile walk from here and, if memory serves me, next passage is in an hour and a half. From there, another thirty minutes across the beautiful waters of the Sound and we'll know whether or not Eleven did its job. And whether I can get back to mine."

Dalton paused, taking in one more, big breath. His body had settled back into a decent cardio rhythm. Letting it out now, he finished the thought.

"We can presume recovery crews have been trying to access AQ ever since we left. It'll take them awhile to bust in but they *will* open that door again. Eleven can only help us as long as it's running, undisturbed. And we now have..."

He looked down at his wrist.

06:17:32...

Sanchez looked over and at his timer, as well. She didn't hesitate. Not even a second.

"Oh, we'll get there Dalton. And your little magic fingers will do their thing."

She placed her fist in the middle of the trio.

"All in?"

"All the time," was the sure echo of the men.

FORTY EIGHT

The team arrived, numbered piers in view and sea salt in the air. Cars lined the street, awaiting transit to the Peninsula and from there northward to the San Juan Islands.

Their transition from SoDo District to waterfront proved uneventful. They'd moved unseen from the sporting stadiums and through heavy industrial corridors and seagoing shipping docks. Mechanical cranes swung and lifted overhead. Seaworthy vessels, as long as three football fields—standing higher than your average building—placidly received their cargo; gearing up for another contest between international corporations and the unyielding forces of weather and water.

Any competent military unit would have been at least minimally alerted. There were simply none around, competent or otherwise. Reassigning assets to the rally left this sector with little in the way of a security presence. A few sleepy guards in lonely shacks.

Irony. Or maybe more blessing.

None of the teammates had eaten recently, not since their last steps out of the Snoqualmie Wilderness, much earlier in this long and stressful day. Now they were hungry. So they did what good operators do.

Improvise.

"I don't like this," Sanchez confessed.

The men shot back equally uncomfortable looks.

"I get it, Sanchez. But we really don't have many options," Dalton offered. "You know we'll get tagged if we don't use the new citizen's provision card. We'd also get tagged if we did use one. I really wish the team back at Clark had more time. The IDs were genius. Banking is a whole other universe. You know they would have cracked it with a few more days margin."

"Bloody reds. They've thought of every way possible to make these people cower."

Loch was correct. Right down to how much food they could buy and from where. Cash, either American or Chinese was no longer a usable currency in Penghu. Neither were bank accounts, as those had all been frozen until the new regime decided who should have what kind of resources. Of course, anyone partnering with the new leadership would get more than their neighbors and friends. That's the way it always works.

These sobering facts led the team to an action they despised, even — maybe especially — in wartime.

Dalton took up observation outside their mark, a Northwest trinkets and tourist shop on the docks, his shoulder toward the storefront window while still facing up the sidewalk. In this position he could both keep an eye on the street while his left-side peripheral made sure all was well inside the store.

"As good a place as any, I guess. I'll maintain eyes here. Sanchez, you charm the pants off the teenage boy at the counter... keep him from noticing Loch's pockets getting heavier."

The glare from the sniper recon back at Dalton was as fatal as if she'd aimed and pulled the trigger from anything less than a mile away. Though using the same actions on the admiring Chinese soldier back at 25, this struck her as different. Maybe Dalton's words cheapened the strategy's value.

Regardless, he absorbed the disapproving look, nodding toward Loch and trying to reflect her brutal gaze.

"What? You think he can approach something even resembling charming?"

Her eyes followed, landing on the Scotsman.

"Point taken," she said. "I don't appreciate it, but I see your point."

"Hey now. What's not to love?" Loch countered, circling his face with his right hand.

At least that was settled.

Dalton would be eyes-on. Loch, the procurement specialist. Sanchez, the diversion.

Two minutes in and out. The score: three Snickers bars, four packs of peanuts, and a handful of penny candies. Either Loch wasn't all that picky or the shop stocked a slim assortment. Sanchez pulled herself away from the young man at the counter, having successfully absorbed his teen attention span as long as needed. Little effort kept his eyes off of Loch; your basic smile and a slight leaning forward while asking for directions.

Oh. Just up the street? That way? Really?

How did I miss it before? You're so helpful.

Mission accomplished, she walked out the front door, turned toward Dalton and then stopped, eyes shifting to the three or four feet above him.

"What?"

Dalton moved his left shoulder awkwardly, trying to catch what was so important hanging over his head.

"That," a half smile forming.

Zeroed in on the street and open doorway, he'd missed it. That, and he was leaning against it.

An eagle's head.

Beneath that a mask, resembling the face of a man.

Next and below: a grizzly's wide snout.

On it went, each level wonderfully carved out of native hardwoods and reverently hand-painted.

"Gotta be a sign, right Dalton?"

Though the shop's front door totem stood out as a somewhat prodigious happening, Dalton couldn't muster up quite the same degree of faith. Nevertheless, he slipped his right hand into the front pocket of his jeans, fingering the smaller figurine that Stevens handed him way back on the other side of the mountains. In many ways it felt like a dream, quite a few nights past. The item in his pocket cut through all of that, bringing sharp focus to the present.

Dalton turned to the windows on his left. The reflected image of the ten-foot-high totem loomed large in the glass storefront.

Operation Restore Totem, huh?

Well, here we go.

The Oval Office, Washington D.C.

"Correct, Mr. President," Ambassador Locke debriefed via secure line.

"The Chinese Ambassador contacted me directly, extending the opportunity for peaceful resolution of the current situation."

"Peaceful, Gary? The hostile taking of one of our states... sovereign territory... an act that can be resolved peacefully? Are they actually insane? Please, tell me there is more to it than this."

The former Ambassador, with little time to swing the president toward compromise, countered as convincingly as he knew how.

"Mr. President. They are also aware of the code's deterioration. They find themselves in a compromised position, yet not wholly without advantage. Sizing up the possibilities, they're seeking open channels in a desire to avoid the horror we all know is coming if hostilities escalate."

"What you mean to say is they're scared spit-less," the chief executive responded. "We reassert a measure of control. We retaliate. That's the score now. And it would be understood as reasonable by most of the world, aside from their allies."

The ambassador didn't step in. His input was neither required nor requested.

The president took a deep breath and exhaled markedly. The most significant decision of his nation's history waited to be released in words, stated out loud.

"Gary, here's what we're going to do. You tell them in clear and certain terms: we want peace as well. It won't be simple. I mean, a hundred thousand Chinese troops are spread across... what are they calling it now... Penghu?"

"Correct, sir. Penghu Province."

"Okay, you tell them to keep channels open. That will be all for now."

Locke sighed, relieved. Hanging up the phone, he left to communicate with his Chinese contact.

Two men stepped out from an Oval Office side room, having listened in on the entire conversation.

"Mr. President, we will assume—unless otherwise instructed—that in the event we regain our strategic forces, we have the green light... to employ them."

Silence.

"Thank you, Mr. President."

It had been decided.

Peace would not come, regardless of the code degeneration or harried negotiations currently underway. The president had been won over by visions of certained, ever-growing subjugation for his country. There could be no reasoning with a nation-state holding violent expansionism as their primary goal.

This would stop here and now.

Appeasement would invite more of the same. The only way forward was war.

Full, unbridled nuclear war.

In even the most hope-filled projections little of either country remained to be inhabited once the conflagration had cleared. Little left of a people manning the forefront of human discovery for millenia. Little remaining of a nation that had re-invented government and fostered modern notions of liberty and prosperity. Grim outcomes to be sure. Beijing had led them all down this path. It was up to the

American Commander-in-Chief to press on to the inevitable.

The two men, one in full dress uniform and the other a well-tailored business suit, left. Once outside, the man in the business suit pulled a pager from his left breast pocket, keying a string of characters and hitting send. The return ping took only a second.

Received. Understood.

And then the brawny Scot put his micro-pager away, boarding the ferry and keeping the orders to himself.

Aboard the MV Klickitat, heading westward toward the Peninsula

Breathtaking. The open waters of Puget Sound broke against the bow, passing along her sides and leaving a soft, foamy wake. The Klickitat's keel cut through the waves. A pleasing springtime sun warmed the image of snow-capped peaks at both bow and stern. The cityscape fell behind, smaller every few minutes. From here the view appeared rather like it did a month ago—untouched by the upheaval in her streets, homes, and people.

Surreal. Utterly surreal.

Repairs lingered at Pike Place, scaffolding and crane works throughout the market space. One could assume it to be only one more evolving corridor of a constantly developing city. Few clues surfaced as to the terrors in the distance. The only telltale sign might possibly be the massive Chinese flag flowing off the Needle. Yet, even that—from here—could simply be dismissed as some kind of ethnic pride thing.

Leaning out over the white, painted rail, looking down the clean, curved line of the boat, Dalton glanced at Sanchez. Face up to the sun, she breathed slowly with eyes shut, taking in the muted warmth on her skin. The sunlight brought a reddish tint to her dark hair and the breeze tossed small strands about.

What in the world is going on in her head?

Probably some combat prep exercises.

Does she have family? Are they in the region? Has she had any contact?

Dalton let his mind wander to his own clan.

His mom. Such the warrior. As strong as they came. Even with dad going off the deep end she was such a rock. Before those fateful moments at their house—and her insistence at obeying orders from the street—when had he last talked to her? What a great son, didn't even know she was sick. So, family was hard. She wasn't the one deserving of distance and coldness. No, that would be reserved for his father alone.

And what the hell was that all about anyways? Dalton tossed out to the universe.

Why our family?

Why couldn't the engineer across the street have been my dad. The guy went off to work everyday and still didn't miss a sports event or band concert. Couldn't we have just been normal like everybody else. What – Dad's religion made him special, somehow?

Such a pile of crap.

Dalton shook off old, painful images. He would afford them no place at all in these potentially last, precious moments.

No.

I will not waste any of the possibly last hours of my life on that man.

No good thoughts. No bad ones.

No thoughts at all.

FORTY NINE

The large steel platform lowered, groaning as it settled onto warm asphalt. Below, a froth of green crashed against the weathered, tar-laden supports, washing over the barnacled substructure with an almost human rhythm.

A few hundred foot passengers disembarked. Then the ship's three larger decks released a parade of sedans, minivans, and trucks. Dalton, Loch, and Sanchez stepped onto solid ground.

They'd made it.

Bremerton. The city of 40,000 lay westward of the Seattle metro area, across Puget Sound and tucked in and behind the very upscale Bainbridge Island. Mainly blue-collar, she wasn't a suburb per se. A commuter town, yes, but also a community fighting back against gentrification in fierce retention of its own purpose and identity. She sported deep waters. Trawlers, day craft, dry container and petrol barges; her weathered docking posts had known them all. Aside from plentiful berths she also was a protective shield, her landform providing relief from harsh seasonal weather brewing on the open waves of the Sound. Her waters and lay of the land were significant factors in the development of the area, recognized and treasured by even the earliest indigenous peoples. While significant, these were not the reasons Dalton had brought the team west, away from Seattle proper. His interest lay focused on a singular asset: former Naval Base Kitsap.

Bremerton was the target because she was a Navy town.

As homeport of Carrier Group Three and with the Trident Sub Missile Command at Bangor only seventeen miles to the north, the area provided exactly what Dalton needed. Commissioned in 1891 as Puget Sound Naval Station, the renamed Naval Base Kitsap had infused power and purpose into the families, community, and neighborhoods of Bremerton for over a century. Currently, she didn't look the part.

13,000 enlisted personnel and officers had been forcefully relieved of duty in the same manner as their compatriots at JBLM in Tacoma. Skeleton crews represented only the barest skill sets. Maintain equipment and ship's facilities. Keep the subs' nuclear cores healthy. That was all. Long hours, under ever-watchful eyes. These left-behind warriors labored as well under the ever burdensome load of shame and guilt. Shame at watching brothers and sisters in arms forced at gunpoint onto transports and ushered down the west coast to San Diego—Kitsap's closest companion base. And guilt. They couldn't do a thing about it. They were military orphans. Isolated, controlled, powerless. Everything a fighter loathes. Their war vessels had fared no better.

Three Nimitz Class Carriers sat dockside. Two Destroyers lay quieted beside four Guided Missile Cruisers. These massive, imposing feats of seagoing architecture and engineering existed in such a depleted state as to appear nothing more than silent sentinels, a mere shadow of their former selves. It all seemed very eerie; too still, too vacant.

Not unlike the Japanese attack at Pearl some seventy years ago, everyone had been "home" at Bremerton when the Chinese made their move. American naval vitality was diminishing and China was filling the void, powerfully so.

The *Liaoning,* a 60,000-ton carrier and first ship of this class for the Chinese ever, stood at station, asserting full authority over the naval base and its broader environs. In the calms of Sinclair Inlet this newest, most celebrated acquisition of the PLA-Navy proudly took her place. The warship, along with two scheduled for future duty, were one part junkyard opportunism and two parts radical reverse-engineering. The late-eighties collapse of the Russian Military Complex had flooded the world stage with equipment and technology not usually available to second and third tier players. Three aging Soviet carriers had been picked up at bargain basement prices and the regime spent the next twenty-five years studying, planning, and building. Liaoning, the fruit of these labors, was a profound image to consider.

The captured U.S. Carriers and auxiliary craft would be repurposed. They were spoils of victory. Seeing the red field and gold stars breaking in the breeze from their forecastle would be quite satisfying. Make no mistake, with the American boats in near mothballs, the shiny new Chinese carrier proclaimed the long era of U.S. seagoing military dominance as come and gone. A new and greater player ushered forth. Like it or not the ancient dragon was now a modern sailor, and one not satisfied with close-border defense. China's maritime war machine intended to project fast and far, leaving a path of international chaos in its wake.

Once again the team processed through credentialing and ID without incident. Following a brief inspection they stepped onto the shoreline of the Peninsula, that much closer to their ultimate objective. Dalton stayed out front a few yards. Sanchez kept eight feet to the left and behind. Loch pulled along at a short distance also and they made their way down the street just like everyone else. No briefing, not even a quick one, had been allowed onboard the Klickitat. For the time being, sniper and sergeant operated in the dark, looking to Dalton for "indirect" directions.

Two more blocks and Dalton kept going, right on past the naval complex and its massive gates. His pace actually increased up the hill, leaving the guard posts and wire-capped walls behind.

Still going.

Sanchez sized up the anomaly. Another minute and the thinning crowd would peel off toward main street. Then, they would become dangerously exposed.

Dalton ducked into an alley between two nondescript, low-profile storefronts. Sanchez followed casually. Loch was not far behind. They had to break stride. Losing Dalton now meant they might not find him again.

Where in the world is he going?

The base is back there... down the hill.

In the alleyway Sanchez and Loch stopped and turned, looking around in vain. No one. They surveyed the small space again; still nothing.

"So, I got us the upgrade." The hushed voice came from the front passenger seat of a mid-sized four-door on the other side of a commercial dumpster.

Dalton waved them forward, pulling the restraining belt across his chest and into place.

"C'mon, you two. We're on a schedule, you know."

Loch slid into the driver's seat, bringing the engine to life sans key, once again. Sanchez laid low in back and they pulled out into light midday traffic. The sudden exit of military workers as consumers and taxpayers made for easier driving. It also devastated the city. The only upside to this downturn? The Chinese considered this a secondary, maybe even tertiary, threat. Places like Seattle, Tacoma, and the borders north and south ranked much higher, receiving the bulk of the regime's attention and resources, leaving the team to move about more freely, playing their deadly game of hide and seek against slightly better odds.

"Where to, LT?" Loch asked.

"Out of town. State Route 310, to the northwest."

"Anything more specific than that?"

Dalton shifted his weight, addressing both Loch and Sanchez.

"About seven miles and we'll wind around Kitsap Lake. Take Northlake Highway to the junction with Seabeck. Follow it west for another three and a half... "

His recitation of map points, roads, and distances stopped abruptly.

"And...?" Sanchez lobbed one out there.

"And... then we leave the car at the end of the service road leading to Wildcat Creek."

"You didn't grow up in this neighborhood, did you?"

She knew the answer. Still, the sergeant couldn't keep the words from crossing her lips.

Dalton pointed to his head, assuring them the plan had been seared into his memory during mission prep back at Ft. Clark. Sanchez jumped in again, frustrated it took this much effort to get basic, necessary info out of the retired soldier.

"Look. Last time, buddy. What's the goal? By your assessment, we have a little over thirty-five minutes before arriving on site. This is not the time to be obscure."

"You're right," Dalton confessed, realizing he needed to be more direct with his partners. "Deep in the Wildcat Watershed is a 1950's off-base installation. The place is small—about a thousand square feet—housing an emergency communications outpost. In the event of a full base evac it kept lines of information going to the outside world. It's built well. Old-school cable six inches around runs deep underground from here to the Sound. From there it multiplies in different trajectories along the bottom, in some places at depths of a few hundred feet or more. One of the primaries heads out across the Strait of Juan de Fuca, terminating at a Canadian military base on Vancouver Island."

"So, this place has been in operation sometime lately?" Sanchez pressed.

"Would you consider 1992 to be recent?"

Loch groaned.

"You've got to be kidding me, LT. What kind of gear are we going to find? Something from when the internet was still a whee tiny one?"

The other two looked back with raised eyebrows.

"What? Ya think grunts like me don't read, too?"

"You're right, Loch. Things will be somewhat, shall we say, primitive," Dalton continued. "The good news is we don't need anything fancy. Something stable and basic is all. You know, web and line-command kind of stuff. Lots of digits to enter, sure. Still, just line commands. And if Program Eleven has done its job, we'll be into the deeper code levels before you know it. No guarantees we'll be able to regain control from there but it's the first step."

Sanchez, with a better picture now of where they were heading, went into well-rehearsed field-mode. Time for an inventory. She laid the take from Microsoft across the backseat of the car.

"Three handguns. Six extra magazines of 9mil. A touch more of the combustible. We expect any company?"

Dalton slipped into Beautiful Mind mode.

"Hmm. No less than seven distinct scenarios from this point on, multiple combinations branching out from there. It's been super smooth since we ditched the big happy party at the stadium. Still, I wouldn't depend on the fact that... "

Dalton's head snapped around. The intensity in the car rose a thousand percent. About a mile back, navigating the long curve in the road behind them: a single Jeep, clearly marked.

PRC Army.

FIFTY

Though seeming all business, the tail wasn't closing as rapidly as expected.

It made sense.

The driver purposefully, calmly, staying back. Taking his time. No rush, no immediate pressure. Riding shotgun, soldier number two sat expressionless with cellphone to ear. Their superiors had figured it out. The suspicious vehicle ahead carried whomever had infiltrated and fled Building 25 at Microsoft earlier this morning. Dalton's team was still an unknown. They were at minimum understood to be a valuable catch but also a potentially dangerous threat. Directives came into soldier two's ears, crystal-clear. Follow, but do not engage. The intruders creating havoc back in Redmond would not be underestimated again.

"It's a surveil first, shoot later patrol," Dalton chimed in. "I bet they have a couple grainy, off angle photos of the three of us from our morning at Microsoft and are right now receiving transportation department shots from the ferry, too. Establish positive ID before committing any more troops. Well, Sanchez, your quality work with the guards at 25 must've left a major impression. But their cautiousness won't last forever. Once they've sized us up, they'll charge."

Loch gripped the wheel tighter, scouring the rear view mirror.

"How much longer, LT? Where's the turnoff for that bloody road?"

"Around the bend."

Dalton pointed, "There."

The evergreen-laden curtain held an opening, but just barely a car's width, if even that. Straggling ferns and blackberry vines hid the opening nicely, nothing more than a dent in the tree line. Most others traveling down the isolated road would've missed it. Hundreds each day did just that, zooming by unaware of the old path and what awaited at its end.

"Okay. Keep your speed. Now, a little more. We'll get some extra distance when they go blind for a second at the next curve."

No margin for error. None.

The Jeep hit that spot in the road, disappearing briefly in their rear- and side-mirrors.

"Now!"

The car lurched, crossing the oncoming lane and entering the old service access haphazardly. While breaking some taller weeds, it was as clean an entry as they could've hoped for. Once through, the tension stored up in the berry bushes and evergreen limbs released, covering over the gap and concealing them once more.

Absolutely committed, the ride became much less comfortable. While not actually blazing a trail, neither were they gliding effortlessly along the narrow, somewhat-level corridor. Branches and brambles scraped, lashing out furiously, stretched to their limits and protesting such gross violation of their wooded sanctum.

"Stop."

Unexpected, it made no sense. Loch hesitated.

Dalton barked again.

"Right here! As much of a slide turn as you can manage."

"There's no room!" Sanchez shouted.

"I know, that's the point. Do it. Do it now, Loch!"

The Scot pulled the wheel hard to the left while mashing the brakes. The laws of physics fought back. The outcome was swift and violent. No longer gripping anything, the sedan's wheels kept sliding sideways, grass and mud rising over the sidepanels and windows. Like a landslide in reverse the trio's field of vision diminished to almost nothing. Two tons of steel and glass kept moving in the direction it was already going and the car began to flip on edge, her rusted underside showing. Loch, Sanchez, and Dalton hovered at a precarious angle. A third the way up. Half. At the last moment the kinetic energy depleted, stopping mid-air and then reversing itself, yielding to the greater force of gravity.

Down.

They bounced twice, signaling an uneasy truce between the competing forces before settling onto all four wheels.

"Perfect," Dalton said, falling back into place.

Sanchez, thrown to the floorboards, sat up, flopping her arms across the seatback.

"Perfect? How in any sane universe was that flawless?"

Dalton slid out the driver's side, stepping onto the overgrown path. Silent, he led them forward, through the bush and around the car. A few paces more and he arched his shoulders, pointing back. The pathway behind?

Completely blocked.

"Okay. Geez," Sanchez relented. "Why do I ever doubt you, Dalton? Really, I mean it."

The compliment registered.

"Okay, let's hustle," Dalton ordered. "The comm bunker is about three hundred yards ahead. We may have slipped them for a second but by now they've doubled back. We need to go. Now."

The trio kicked it up to a decent jog-run within seconds.

A stand of hundred foot maples framed their passage, bidding them forward. The creek—you could hear it now—trickled in the distance, water meandering its shallows as the cool of the day morphed into early evening. Even with the dire nature of these moments, it was a serene and wonderful place.

Two more minutes and they came upon the bunker.

Heavy moss gave some hint as to how long it lay uninhabited. Nondescript and sealed tight, it was one of those odd concrete structures you'd find now and then on a hike in the woods; a vision both curious and so out of place. Most people would climb around some, jumping off a few of its higher points, down into the unending pine needle and undergrowth beds and then move on, calling it good.

Dalton's goal here was different altogether.

They moved another seventy-five yards beyond the bunker's exposed form and then traversed a steep bank along the half-buried sides of the low-profile structure, down to the creek itself. Sliding over soil and root, their feet landed in waters rippling around glittering rocks and felled logs. Backtracking downstream, they returned to the point of interest.

"Loch, you got what I asked you to bring?" Dalton asked.

"Yessir, I do."

The jack tool from the recently abandoned vehicle.

"Well, my good man. Forward, and do your worst."

Loch was happy to oblige. He ducked underneath a tangle of foliage, for the moment appearing swallowed whole. Sanchez and Dalton followed. Another ten feet forward revealed a caved space. They all could stand up, at least reasonably. Loch, for sure. The steel door hosted chains two inches thick and twisted in a figure-eight pattern through its handles. A heavy rust held like nature's concrete on the seasoned metal. Neither of these problems posed a serious challenge for the ruddy Scotsman. Thirty seconds of sustained effort and they stepped inside.

A cold metallic switch plate to the left of the door brought some light. It was dim, noisy, and buzzing from moisture settled in the fixtures but still a small help. Eight stairs. Then they navigated the windowless, doorless hallway for the next thirty feet. At thirty-six feet in, a choice: identical side halls, left or right. Darkened window wells hung sadly in either direction. Frosted with green mold, they still allowed enough muted light to signal they were at or near the surface. Unevenly filtered rays of the late day cast an eerie pall about and the three considered their options.

Then Loch's hand went up in a closed fist.

Footsteps and hushed commands from outside.

If the soldiers were even reasonably decent trackers, the faint impressions in the embankment should give the trio away soon.

Dalton's left wrist showed *02:28:03…*

Time to choose.

They went right, only to find an ancient storage area. Dust and old file cabinets. Abandoning that side and running back, they reached the end of the hall quickly. The left-side option offered them a lone closed doorway. That was all.

"Alrighty, then," Loch said. "Get ready for some noise."

"Loch, wait," Sanchez tried. "We might have time. They might not find the way in."

"Can't risk it. We need a wall between us and them. And we need it now."

FIFTY ONE

Loch set the charges for a measly thirty seconds. Shuffling back down the dimly lit hallway, they huddled as close to the door frame as possible.

Interlocking limbs and torsos bent inward. The move was meant to protect their bodies. It was also about keeping the door intact; a door they presumed would lead to the comm room. Smoke and flash assaulted their eyes and throats. Violent overpressure waves and then a relentless tinny buzzing. Disoriented, all three leaned into the wall, giving up any option of beating back a threat in the next few seconds, hoping anyone behind them was just as incapacitated. Mental haze and slowness of body faded.

Underground.

Trapped by their own devices at the dead end corridor of an out of use communications bunker with Chinese soldiers descending. The first step away from these unpleasant realities was simply getting through the door and further away from their pursuers. After that? Rerouting and re-purposing the most advanced computer code developed to date. The stakes only grew from there. They didn't know for sure the equipment and connections lying behind this door would even function. At one time, whatever would meet them had been state of the art national security space. Now? Anyone's best guess.

One at a time, the three turned. The ceiling and walls of the seventy-plus-year-old structure had all but caved in, making passage impossible and creating a multi-hour, heavy equipment project.

"Nice piece of work, Loch," Dalton remarked.

"Yeah. Not too bad, eh?"

Haze from the debris field settled overhead as Sanchez worked both keyhole and deadbolt. Her skills proved more than adequate. The groaning of latch and tumbler echoed in the corridor, mostly due to the amount of time it'd sat locked and closed. Still, you couldn't help interpreting a subtle cry of defeat as it swung open for the first time in years.

Over the threshold. Into the small anteroom. Taking in stale, motionless air. Dalton scanned the space left to right, mentally cataloging everything in the room in just one sweep. Two old-school hybrid typewriters. Rotary phones. File cabinets. A few desk lamps.

This can't be it.

He surveyed the space again. There, at the back of the room.

A large, multilayer blast-door lay opened, inviting them forward. Dalton practically sprinted over and peered through, hoping.

That's more like it.

While not much of an upgrade over the front room gear, the telecom lines told them this was the place. They had a chance. A real chance.

Dalton pulled out the chair at the desk, blowing off a thick, dusty layer before sitting.

Power-up proceeded simply. One button only on the backs of the desktop unit and monitor. A nostalgic metallic ping, the noisy fan on the back of the boxy computer chassis, and the low whirring of a hard drive were a veritable angelic choir. A sequence of small green lights lit next; top right of the monitor first, then the keyboard. Lastly, the 3.5" microfloppy in the front right accessory bay chirped.

"Hey, what's the thin opening for?" Sanchez pointed. "Super-small DVDs?"

"That," he replied. "Was the flash drive solution back in the day."

"So, what — two, four gigs?"

"Oh Sanchez," Dalton shook his head. "You wouldn't believe me if I told you."

Ongoing memory check and systems analysis: all good so far, a green cursor blinking on the lonely black background.

Dalton opened a comm link to make sure the bunker's access routes still played nice. If something internally or along the underwater cabling runs had crapped out in the last thirty years, they were done. If these long in the tooth systems failed, all they had left was the waiting. The Chinese would force their way into the little fortress at some point. With nothing to show for their handiwork, the team would all die in vain.

A few more commands and the modem sparked to life, its high-pitched screech magnifying the already heavy tension. Sanchez, surveying the other side of the room, turned.

What, did you bust it? was the accusatory non-verbal.

Dalton put his head back down, skipping the tech history lesson completely this time around.

The connection speed was holding, but just barely north of Paleolithic. Good thing Dalton was a true coding minimalist. The 256 kilobytes running from here to "somewhere else" would suffice. If successful, his letters and numbers crawling across the telecom line would do enormous damage, the electronic equivalent of a pinprick taking down a tank. But if — and only if — the roadway "in" was open and cleared.

Eleven had to have done its job.

A few more strokes.

Enter.

"C'mon Eleven," Dalton sweet-talked the program. "You always were my favorite, you know."

Loch rolled his eyes. The gesture had no effect, whatsoever.

"Don't let me down, baby. We're a team."

Loch and Sanchez leaned in unconsciously, their bodies carrying great depths of both angst and hope. Neither could decipher the gibberish on screen. Instead, they fixed on Dalton's face. His countenance would tell the story.

Ten seconds. Thirty.

No change, not even the subtlest shift of an eyebrow nor crinkles forming at the corners of his warm, amber eyes.

The slightest hint of doubt challenged Sanchez' normally positive attitude.

The smallest smile rose on Dalton's face.

"Eleven," he sighed. "See? Now I knew we had something special goin' on."

"Dalton," Sanchez stood, inhaling, hands at her side. "I can't even begin to tell you how weird that sounded. But you know what?" she finished. "I don't even care. As long as we're in."

He looked up.

They were in.

Gansu

Junjie sat up straighter.

The last quarter of a day had been a fruitless waiting. Waiting and pleading with no return text. He had no real measure of the man or woman on the other side. But he'd made his play: access without assurances. The best he could do now was reason. The flurry of activity told him that window was likely closing, maybe even faster than the limited access timer revealed.

01:48:19…

Bremerton

```
C:>|welcome back creator…
```

Dalton shook his head.

"No. Just back off. I have to think."

No time to spare, every single stroke had to count.

Focus. There. Okay, that instruction packet will do.

"Dalton," Sanchez asked. "You okay? We're in, right?"

"Yeah," he paused. "It's just… "

"What?"

"Back at AQ. I didn't really have time to explain."

"Dalton, you're scaring me a little. What's going on? The code?"

"Is fine. It's fine. I'm making progress."

He stopped typing.

"Look, guys. Not just AQ. All the way back at Clark. There's someone else in the system."

"Can't be," Loch plied. "Who? Why?"

"Calls himself caretaker. Calls me creator."

"Uh, that's not creepy at all," Sanchez jested.

"Wait," Loch put it together.

Dalton looked up.

"No," Sanchez blurted.

Another second.

"Okay," she started again. "So, this unknown contact has deep enough access to talk with you. Which means they have deep enough access to do some damage. And they think you're the one who designed the code? I think we can dismiss that as misinformation at best. Hate to think through the possibility of access and insanity."

"They're not wrong," Dalton confessed.

Loch and Sanchez took it in.

"And, no," he continued. "Best I can tell they've given me control."

"How so?" Loch asked.

"Two reasons: one, they keep acting like someone who only has a losing hand but doesn't really feel like bluffing."

"And?"

"And I'm," he typed another line "… mighty close to calling."

FIFTY TWO

The Oval Office, normally a room of great consequence, today carried the inordinate weight of history.

"You say we just heard from him?"

"Correct, Mr. President," SecDef replied. "And our boys at the Vault confirm the contact, and his progress. Second hand, of course, but our Canadian friends are sticking their necks out a bit to relay the messages. Good to finally see some help from neighbors and allies."

The Commander in Chief opened the line to his executive secretary. "Please send Colonel Dirksen to the Oval."

"Yes, Mr. President. Right away."

Click.

"General," the president motioned toward the Joint Chiefs Chair, "proceed with the next phase of Restore Totem."

"Sir."

USS George H.W. Bush

The decoded message lingered in Rear Admiral Knowles' hand.

She moved to comms, fully prepared to act on orders.

The carrier group was in range: 1800 nautical miles from the Chinese Coast. Her words set off a chain reaction of logistic and drilled perfection.

The US cruisers Philippine Sea, Leyte Gulf, and Anzio, readied for support and any probable counterattack via conventional means. Destroyer Squadron 22 prepared for offense and defense. Carrier Wing 8, comprised mostly of FA18 Hornets set off in an endless parade from Bush's hot, paved deck.

And, ominously, Albuquerque and Seahorse surfaced to firing depth, tubes warmed and ready. No one in the chain of command knew whether these two would become operational, once Dalton's work was finished. But on the chance they might, they were the primary nuclear threat in theatre. If it all unraveled, there would be plenty more to join them. But they would get the first shot at crippling any Chinese rally.

The Oval Office

Colonel Dirksen entered.

Moving quickly to the president's desk, he set down the football and opened the lid. It was as simple as often portrayed.

Two sets of status and options readouts on separate screens. One for the president and one for StratComm. The president had complete launch authority but the process required authentication and then dissemination of the specific orders. He didn't control individual nuclear assets from here. Only preloaded scenarios from the Pentagon and designed with his prior consult. Not so much the details. More the weight of overall command. That he was the one saying *yes* would be verified by hand- and eye-print, one on the now-lit touch screen, the other by staring into the optical reader on the lid's casing. One last piece of critical data had been specially programmed into the unit's displays. Simple, red digital characters.

00:54:12...

Bremerton

Dalton's hands moved in a blur.

The instruction packages were coming faster, every few seconds. Each succeeding set displaced another level of Sovereign's hold. He could almost feel it. Like physical death, impending but not sudden. But there was no sorrow on Dalton's part. He had decided. Of all the scenarios he'd run over the last day and a half, the one that could not persist was the one in which his creation, his valiant, honest, but misguided attempt—to provide assurances in a very broken, unsure world—could live.

He flashed back to the images from AQ, the chaos in Chinese streets, homes, and businesses.

What he could not know was that things had only gotten worse.

Beijing

President Xi sat alone.

Beijing's infrastructure was crumbling under the weight of central control that no longer functioned. Sovereign had decided to act out, for no discernible reason other than freedom given by Junjie's backdoor mistake.

His staff had long past given up trying to track the code's sympathetic migration. It had turned anything but sympathetic, as far as the Chinese people's good was concerned. While diplomatic channels assured that America would not retaliate in kind, that was a secondary matter, regardless of its eventual truthfulness or deceit. Xi was a practical man. That his city was descending into hades seemed to take precedence over possible future attack. And why come to invade what amounted to modern ruins by the time it was all said and done?

He typed out some final orders.

All efforts to be made. No costs or manpower spared in the capital city.

Brace for conflict in the new province. For awhile, you are likely on your own.

It was all he had, knowing it would never be enough.

And so he waited, alone, for the inevitable.

Bremerton

The digital retaliation lessened with each of Dalton's incursions.

Five counter-commands needed.

Then three.

One.

It was almost uneventful.

At *00:35:56* it stopped.

Dalton kept typing.

Sanchez looked down.

"Hey."

He kept going, fully aware of the slasher-movie adage "They're never really dead."

"Hey," she tried again. "Dalton. It's done. You... you did it."

The Oval Office

The football came to life.

"Sir." SecDef remarked.

00:35:56

"What in blazes?" the president said. "Aren't these things always supposed to go to like 2 seconds before they go offline?"

SecDef and The Joint Chiefs Chairman laughed.

"I'm okay with a little less drama," the chief executive shared. "At least on our side of things."

"Myself, as well, Mr. President."

"Alright then."

His hand met the cool touch surface.

Presidential Authorization Alpha.

He leaned down until his right eye met the lens in the control case's lid.

Presidential Authorization Beta.

Confirmed.

Proceed.

And then the screen changed completely.

But not in a way he was expecting.

Bremerton

```
C:>|stratcomm/assets/directory
```

"What? Can't be."

Directory reset, Dalton typed.

The results were the same.

He looked out, into the room.

Pulling up all the data he'd stored from stratcomm briefings, he ran another comparison. Silos, missiles, payloads. Burst ratios, ordnance yield.

Directory reset, once again.

He checked the deep-root systems, making sure he was in the actual stratcomm ecosystem and not some coded forgery. Three checks later, he was certain.

This was his country's nuclear forces command and inventory. And it had shrunk in both number of active warheads and total destructive power.

To the exact potentialities of the Chinese.

He tried to fool the directory into accepting new assets.

Add PeaceKeeper ICBM quantity 15...

```
C:>|stratcomm/assets/directory/assets denied
```

Add W87 warhead quantity 42...

```
C:>|stratcomm/assets/directory/assets denied
```

"Okay, let's go minimal."
Add PeaceKeeper ICBM quantity 1...

```
C:>|stratcomm/assets/directory/assets denied
```

Sovereign's last act was to make it a dead even fight, with zero chance of the scoreboard ever changing.

"Well, caretaker," Dalton reflected. "There you go."

Dalton keyed in the news, and how he'd ascertained it, to DC.

And then he waited, feeling they may have all just avoided the unthinkable.

FIFTY THREE

The president reviewed the message on the smaller screen, top left of the football.

```
C:>|complete 50-50 with PRC nuc
C:>|no options for additional assets
C:>|assuming same on other side
```

And then proceeded as planned.

Another timer lit the football, where the previous Sovereign timer had lived. These digits announced real-world launch. As America's weapons had essentially been in sleep-mode, self checks, firing sequences, and telemetry packages needed a bit longer run-up than previous ready-states.

00:23:18...

"History will prove you right, Mr. President," SecDef proclaimed.

But then the numbers stopped, right where they appeared. 00:23:18.

Bremerton

Sanchez saw the numbers first.

Their secure link through Vancouver Island was a two-way lock, with realtime access into stratcomm. Dalton stood to stretch for just a moment, thinking his work over. Loch hovered, a few feet away.

"Dalton… " her tone alerted. "Didn't you stop that thing?"

He ran back, stumbling into his chair.

"No. No, no, no."

He typed, *Confirm stratcomm launch executive command*

```
C:>|stratcomm/authorizations/...
C:>|confirmed...
```

"Why is the number stuck, LT?" Loch probed. "Systems working the kinks back out after a wee nap?"

"Something like that," Dalton guessed and keyed a few more lines.

Confirm stratcomm launch executive command and timer

```
C:>|stratcomm/authorizations/...
C:>|confirmed...
C:>|waiting...
```

Confirm stratcomm launch executive command and timer and waiting for what

```
C:>|stratcomm/authorizations/…
C:>|confirmed…
C:>|waiting…
C:>|not what…
```

Not what?

```
C:>|stratcomm/authorizations/…
C:>|confirmed…
C:>|waiting…
C:>|not what…
C:>|who …
```

Dalton's stomach turned.

Waiting for who(m)?

```
C:>|… creator
```

The Oval Office

Mort was doing his best.

"You said he killed it. So, did he or didn't he?" the president fumed. "I set the blame thing off. Why are we waiting?"

"Best I can tell, Mr. President," Mort hurried, "Sovereign left a postmortem Easter Egg. While you can boot the command sequence, only Dalton can release it."

"Fix it, son. Fix it *now!*"

"Sir, I can't… "

"No excuses!"

"It's not possible. We're locked until he acts."

The fourth man in the room gave the president a questioning look. His impeccably tailored suit showed no worse for wear, even after hours of sitting and waiting.

The president nodded.

Out came a secure pager. Message sent.

Bremerton

Confusion over the new numbers and surprising transmission glued Dalton's and Sanchez's eyes onto the screen.

Away from their notice, the Scotsman confirmed the message and then slipped the pager back into his shirt's hidden pocket.

Then he drew his sidearm, aiming it squarely at Dalton's head.

The HK15 was chambered, cocked, and ready. Loch flipped the safety, moving them all well past the point of no return.

Sanchez' reaction, five feet behind and to Dalton's right, came equally as swift.

Her pistol trained immovably on Loch's face, a harrowing red dot where a small but lethal hole would open, were she to proceed.

"What the hell are you doing, Loch? Loch, dammit, answer me!"

"Shut up! Shut up!" Loch seethed, speaking through clenched teeth. His tone, though quiet, shouted that he despised the man's very presence. "Put your gun down, now! Or I splatter him all about this lovely place."

"Loch, wait. What in the world?"

"No!" he pointed back at Dalton. "Orders. We have them. And you will execute them. Your president, your Commander in Chief has initiated a counter-attack against the enemy. Or have you forgotten why we're here in the first place? Why it is we're behind enemy lines in what should be our own nation's soil?"

Loch surmised a growing moral confusion. He didn't like it. Not at all.

Time to press.

"I knew you wouldn't have what it takes. It's all one big, recurring theme, isn't it?! Fifteen men," Loch shook, venom in his words. "Your weakness. Your softness killed fifteen good men. Soldiers. Warriors, far better than you ever will be... Lieutenant."

Sanchez tried to grasp what was happening, some basic reconciliation of the conflict taking place only a few feet away.

"Dalton, what on earth is he talking about? Give me one good reason to not blow this psycho-soldier away, right now. Just one. C'mon."

"Fallujah."

"That's right," Loch said. "Or didn't your new friend let you in on the tragic tale?"

The City of Mosques was not a peaceful place. Coalition forces arrived in strength in the Spring of 2003 to find that moderate civic and religious leaders had abandoned it en masse. Much of the populace followed suit, leaving a power vacuum into which the insurgency quickly coalesced and organized. Mostly hardened, militarized masses. Not much to do in the way of winning hearts and minds. This ethos was made only more dangerous with the final official actions of their former leader, Saddam Hussein. Upon releasing every last criminal and degenerate from Abu Ghraib Prison—just thirty minutes east of town—his "pardons" flooded the area with an even more violent substrata. These factors added up to a hostile, unstable setting in which the U.S. Military was expected to establish order as well as win the goodwill of the people.

Six weeks in the whole thing exploded.

Nearly two hundred Iraqis stood outside the gates of the local secondary school, demanding it to be opened and courses reconvened. At first a concerned neighborhood response, the protest had transformed into a tragic hailstorm of screams, bullets, and death. American personnel from the 82nd Airborne, stationed on the rooftop, opened fire. Seventeen dead. Another seventy mortally wounded. Naturally, each side claimed they were fired upon first.

Two days later—April 30, another group returned to protest the heartbreaking event, to make their voices heard. Gunfire erupted again and two more Iraqi lives were lost. Fallujah devolved into a tempest, remaining just under the boiling point for the next eleven months. The constant heat and agitation ultimately produced an expansive, volatile reaction.

———————————————————

"Only a few weeks later," Dalton said. "We went in. After the Blackwater incident."

"Operation Vigilant Resolve," Sanchez noted.

He paused, nodding.

"The guys were just protecting a food delivery. Insurgents trapped their vehicle and pulled them out. One by one they shot 'em and burned them, right there on the road. That wasn't enough. Afterward, they dragged their charred bodies through the streets and strung them up on the spans of a bridge across the Euphrates."

"Blackwater Bridge," Sanchez breathed, remembering the grisly tale passed among the majority of the occupying force at one time or another.

"Yeah," Dalton confirmed. "That would be the one."

In his mind, in his emotions, he was back in that hot zone, the hell he had run from for the better part of a decade. His voice lowered.

"Officially I was Army Signal Corps. In reality I operated as a special strategic asset, embedded with whoever needed my odd skill sets. The truth is, I never even attended OCS. My rank was part of the deal, for the most part kept under wraps."

The revelation wasn't news to Loch. It only underscored his dismissal of this man's place in *his* Army. The barrel of his pistol was still leveled, ready, only a few feet from Dalton's head.

"That day — April 6, 2004 — I was assigned with a patrol from 1st Marines. They showed us pictures from the bridge... all part of our op prep. A solid week of hot intel told us this local Al Qaeda commander ran the show in the Hai al Askiri District. As a direct report to al-Zarqawi we knew that if we took him out, we'd climb right up their org chart in no time."

"But that's not how it went down, now did it, LT?"

"No, it wasn't," Dalton admitted. "My job was to get us through the labyrinth of side streets and rooftops, the hidden corridors of the district. I must have reviewed every square inch of the place a thousand times. Satellite and ground imagery. Maps, utilities, schematics. I had it all down cold. People appearing around a corner, snipers overhead, wind change, anything. I could tell where it might lead next and then what to alter in our operational approach."

Dalton's head dropped an inch or so, his voice weakened, hollowing now with every word.

"It wasn't enough."

One more, deeper breath.

"The gates to the courtyard flew open," he whispered. "It was dusty, like every other space in the city. Wind, sand. Another private wasteland with a fence around it. We were on target, on clock. The plan was to be exposed to the roof line for about seven seconds, that was all."

Another slight pause. Dalton was visibly choked up, so shaken by the haunting, unforgiving images.

"Couldn't have been more than seven, maybe eight years old...

... came out of a dark corner of the house. So fast. Though way too much weapon for his little body, he leveled the

AK47 right at my chest. I froze. I had visualized this scenario more than enough times to know what to do. I just couldn't get myself to pull the trigger."

"Strickland stepped in front of me, shoved me through the open window a foot or so to my right. The squad's attention moved for the slightest, briefest second. By the time I'd rolled over twice and came to a stop in the empty room against a rickety chair, it was over. In the instant of my hesitation and the courage of a young marine, the courtyard became a shooting gallery. Everybody. All of them gone. That quick."

"I waited in the shadows," he heaved, words thick with regret. "Their bodies just lay there, empty of life, absent the spark of their personalities, their stories, their lives."

Dalton wiped his eyes. His voiced trembled.

"Either the enemy didn't know how many we were or they didn't care. Two hours later I had made my way back out, to our outpost, alone."

"Oh my Lord," Sanchez broke in. "I had no idea."

She turned on Loch.

"That's what you're going to kill him for? Do you know how many other, good soldiers hesitate in battle? Of course you do! A kid? Seriously?"

"It's only a part of the pattern, las," Loch asserted. "And we can't afford any more of that kind of thinking. No more. It ends here. The lad has a chance to redeem himself and I'm here to make sure it happens."

FIFTY FOUR

Gansu

Junjie had been watching, too.

No control. He'd given that to Dalton. But his console mirrored the countdowns and the hesitations. While not seeing the secured transmissions, the pattern spoke of hope. There might be one last chance to influence the creator.

But he felt like he had tried everything.

He knew the rejoinder to his country's egregious acts would be devastating. Millions of his countrymen would die, with his own fiery end among the many. He didn't know, couldn't know, Dai-tai's and Chi's location. Chances were they were hidden in a heavily populated, urban area. It was entirely probable, after all of his efforts, that his dearly loved family would perish as well. Surely, there remained some deposit of common humanity from which he could tap. If caretaker and creator, together, realized all that was at stake, maybe a moment of sanity could prevail.

I must try.

He had no idea what to say. What could possibly connect with the only person capable of stopping the madness? He kicked his feet under the desk, a nervous release.

The sound of papers. A pile of garbage, left here for who knew how many years.

Junjie looked down and saw characters. Mandarin characters. He knew these words.

And then he got excited.

Beep.

```
C:>|… creator…
```

Dalton looked up and froze.

```
C:>|No king is saved by the size of his army;

C:>|no warrior escapes by his great strength.

C:>|But the eyes of the Lord are on those who fear him,

C:>|on those whose hope is in his unfailing love…

C:>|…

C:>|Q:… do you fear God?
```

Dalton couldn't process the words, though reasonably familiar. Instead, he hid in the datafields of his mind.

First Strike. It's come to this.

God, no. How did this happen?

The gravity of the moment forced breath from his lungs. He knew it, felt it; responsibilities he couldn't begin to handle, an emotionally exhausting accountability.

He reviewed the data again.

Chinese deployment: roughly one-hundred-eighty nuclear assets.

American assets: exactly the same.

A crap shoot.

A total and complete crap shoot.

Sure, we fire first, but everybody gets their throats cut wide open and the last few hundred years of human civilization bleeds out on uber-radiated ground.

Launch scenarios played furiously in his mind's eye. Flight time, detonation, casualty numbers, environmental and worldwide economic impact. Reactions of nuclear partners on each side. Every American launch countered by a devastating return volley from Beijing. Of all the visions he had been called upon to foresee in his military career, none carried this kind of weight. It was an apocalyptic nightmare, unleashed in his head and gaining speed and ferocity with every new second. If there was one time Dalton wished he had a normal brain, this would be it.

Beep.

C:>|... do you fear God?

The aggravating question begged a response. The thought of actually answering it gave him only more pause.

"*Hey.* What are you doing, Dalton? Keep your head down. Do your job."

Loch's order snapped Dalton back to reality.

He typed some more.

Beep.

C:>|... do you fear God?

Sanchez glimpsed the redrawn transmission and its upheaval playing across Dalton's countenance.

"Dalton. *Zeb*, what do we do!!?"

Loch took one step closer, gun hand shaking slightly, anger overwhelming his usual steadiness.

"You want to know a secret, Dalton? I was sent along with you for this very moment. Some very important people didn't think you'd do what needed to be done. This isn't some kind of child's game we can walk away from because we don't like the way it went down. Pretend it never happened? Who are you kidding?! The current chaos in Beijing means nothing. They'll recover if we let them. As crazy as the UN is, they'll help them rebuild, all the while turning a blind eye to what's going on here. The Chinese took this plot of land because they want more. They want our resources. Our people. They will not back off. They will not give it up."

Loch's face flushed a deep red, neck and forehead throbbing viciously.

"And do you think the rest of the world will find us to be level-headed, applaud us when we go back to our normal, everyday lives? No, this is an invitation for more of the same. Our only response, the only one securing peace, is to show strength *now*."

"So yes," he declared. "We will strike. We will strike first. We will strike hard... "

Beep.

C:>|... do you fear God?

Dalton barely heard the tone. The characters would not go away.

Four words.

A lifetime of pain, disappointment, disillusion.

His father. The shame and anguish. His young, tender faith crushed against the hard, jagged rocks of the misdeeds of another, someone so trusted. Everything that mattered, ripped away, turning him toward bitterness and detachment from bigger things, critical things. His soul was a caldera, finally spilling over and violently reshaping everything in its path.

Dalton couldn't keep it in any longer.

Beep.

C:>|... do you fear God?

Loch pressed, weapon in hand emphasizing each part of his final, unequivocal directive.

"... you *will* complete this mission, soldier. You *will* finish this job, regardless of the sacrifice."

"Do you hear me?!!" Loch screamed. "*Dalton?!!*"

Shots rang out.

The small, enclosed space overwhelmed at the report off aging, concrete walls.

Dalton struggled to register the sound as real. Until his chest warmed and a circular stain grew slowly over his right pectorals. Dull, aching. Fibers and nerve endings frayed. Dense fluids collected, impossible to push through. Respirations slowing. Heart beat, uneven. Dalton's system was off-balance. Too much of the precious red liquid was making its way outward.

Crimson sprayed onto the workstation.

Dalton's field of vision constricted.

Smaller.

Smaller still.

Black.

FIFTY FIVE

Gansu

Junjie watched longer.

It had been an hour. No response from Creator. Neither defiance nor collaboration.

C:>|...

The empty prompt nearly shouted.
It was maddening, but all he could do was watch, hoping and praying.

Another hour.

C:>|...

The young businessman was beyond exhaustion. With no confirmation, not even a hint his efforts had mattered, he had to face it.
Trust.
Something he had for years largely set aside and only recently recovered. He'd typed it himself, only a matter of hours ago.

No warrior escapes by his great strength.

"Yes," he said to no one else. "And probably not a programmer by his great cleverness, either."

Junjie closed his eyes, breathing evenly.

Then he began the shutdown sequences on Quan Dho's wonder machines. Within minutes he was packed up. Unsure of where to go next, he stepped out of the home, leaving behind his place of refuge. It had been so in his youth. It had not failed him these last few days.

The path back to main street was problematic. It was early afternoon. A few side streets over, he found a lightly trafficked seed warehouse. Among the few working vehicles he saw a black SUV. Even battered, it stuck out.

Dhe, I hope you were as practical a man as I would imagine.

Keys fell out of the opened visor and onto the front seat as Junjie exhaled thankfulness again. The big car started up and eased into reverse.

Junjie was almost startled by the blue display.

His phone.

43.2220° N, 76.8512° E

Deleting message in 00:00:12…

He grabbed the slim case and just managed a screenshot before the characters slipped away forever.

Pulling out of the lot and onto dusty Gansu roads, he looked at the picture and then up to the sky, smiling.

He didn't immediately recognize the earthly locators. That didn't matter. He had what he needed. It would not happen today, or even the next. But Junjie would not cease searching until reunited with his family in safety.

His life in China was closing. Resetting was out of the question.

What lay ahead was unknown.

His first steps were to simply drive.

And trust.

FIFTY SIX

The Vault

Mort stood by, only a few feet away. The Vault wasn't big enough to get very far.

"Hey," he shouted. "Be careful over there. Last time I checked you weren't on the list."

There was no list. At least one Mort had ever seen.

Didn't matter. The CIA central casting tech entity was doing as ordered, replacing the last ten hours of the real world with nonsense.

"You've got to be kidding me," Mort uttered, reviewing a sampling of the new records.

China issues fire orders.

Some previously unknown deep-state asset takes them offline.

Our president held the steady hand through it all.

And, of course, national security concerns precluded more detail.

"Mortensen?" a new voice in the room asked. This guy was just as stereotypical but of the higher pay grade variety. "Need you to sign the logs again."

Mort's CO stood in the hallway, silent and clearly out of play.

"You know this will never work, right?" Mort chided.

"What will never work, CPO Mortensen?"

The calmness told Mort there were levels of coverage happening here to which he would never have access. Stay out of it. Let it collapse under its own weight.

"Thank you, Mr. Mortensen," CIA big offered, "for your fine efforts today on behalf of a grateful nation."

Mort kept his lips closed. He did do a good job today.

Just not the job these folks were talking about.

The Oval Office

"Mr. President, the vault is sealed."

"Fine. Yes, fine."

Overture sat back and lit a smoke. The Surgeon General and First Lady would have to get over it, at least on a day like this.

A single red orb announced the outer office secretary's line. He punched the button and a young signals officer spoke.

"Mr. President, the Chinese President on secure transmission."

Beijing

"President Xi. I expected to hear from you, but this is quite soon."

"Yes, Mr. President. I will be brief. As you must know, my country is experiencing some dire circumstances to which I must attend. Circumstances which require us to focus efforts here on the mainland."

"Go on."

"We shall be relinquishing our claims to Penghu, returning all territories to the United States and removing all military and civilian authorities."

A pause.

"Given the tenuous nature of our nuclear positions, will this be enough to secure safe passage for our personnel?"

The American president so wanted to dig in. But it would be absolutely useless. And stupidly dangerous. A cornered animal is nothing with which to trifle. He'd no real advantage at this point, aside from the possibility of a political victory at home. That is, if his story stuck long enough to become the accepted narrative. He decided on magnanimity, and personal survival.

"I believe so, President Xi. You can expect no hostilities from our formal command structure. You've got a lot of people to get out of there, though, so you must understand there is to be some level of civil unrest, a reaction that likely will not pass completely without incident."

"I understand. We will begin immediately. Expect our presence gone within ninety-six hours."

One more ask.

"Mr. President. You must understand we will hardly be in a position to assure reparations of any kind. It is more likely both our countries will suffer deeply from the loss of trade. And need I remind you, we now have your exact nuclear equivalent at stand by."

WHEN TOTEMS FALL 343

The nerve.

But it was true. China's decades of currency manipulation and silent trade wars against the US had created a monstrous volume of import to America. No five other countries could make up for it. Overture would likely manage a major economic downturn for the remainder of his years in office, whatever they may be. But he would not lose face in this moment.

"Well, President Xi. I think we'll have to leave that up to the UN, now won't we?"

The beleaguered Chinese leader closed the call and rose from his desk.

The Chinese Premiere and four very serious men waited, eyes down, equal parts duty and disappointment.

Xi walked past silently and then to and through the large, dark doors for the last time.

FIFTY SEVEN

Four days later, Tacoma, WA

An endless parade of tail sections, red star on red band ID'ing them as Chinese military, lifted off and up from the runways at newly-reclaimed JBLM.

"Now that is beautiful," General Stevens reflected. "Wouldn't you say so, Col. Meers?"

"I would indeed, general."

"Base operational status?"

"These are the last of them, sir."

"And Clark?"

"Decommissioning in process, general. All assets will reset here within another thirty-six hours."

"That is a shame. I mean, I would have preferred better circumstances under which to gain a new base, but I was just getting used to her. Too bad we couldn't just keep her as a summer home, right colonel?"

"I would agree with you there, sir."

"Meers," Stevens turned. "You have served exceptionally well in ridiculous circumstances. No surprise, but thank you."

The comment lifted the colonel's spirits beyond their already buoyant state and they both flashed back to the last few weeks. No one could have prepared them for it. One might think a lifetime of readiness and active service would be enough. But even now, the fact that America had indeed been invaded, and then just as quickly left behind by her new captors, seemed impossible to grasp. A phantom. Dreamlike.

Stevens looked into the distance, beyond the airfields.

"Is she out there, sir?" Meers asked.

"Not likely, son. While it would bring her great pleasure to watch this in person, I'm not sure we'll ever see her again. And if she were here, I'd tell her that was the right move. More than served her people. A hundred times over. She needs to live a life beyond targets and range."

The very last Chinese plane departed, and with it the nightmare.

"General," Meers redirected. "You have an entire afternoon of meetings. Sorry to bring that news."

"Understood, colonel. I'll catch up."

Meers had just walked out of sight when the general reached into his right breast pocket. Out came a small rock. He thought again of the 2.5 million residents of this area. What had they been through? How would they recover? How would they be different? Maybe stronger, he wondered. All he knew was that he'd kept his vow.

He bent down and placed the stone to the side, in a small patch of gravel, just off the tarmac.

And then he left for a day's worth of leader-warrior's work far less satisfying.

EPILOGUE

Six Days Later: Critical Care Unit,
Harborview Medical Center—Seattle, WA.

"Hey, I hear they keep busted up old signal corpsmen in this place. Is that true?"

Dalton moved his head ever so slightly.

Sanchez leaned against the industrial metal doorframe, smiling.

"Jessica," a new voice welcomed. "He's doing much better this afternoon."

Dalton was barely awake. Now his confusion multiplied.

Mom?

He looked over his other shoulder.

She knows you?

How long?

What?

Mom leaned in from the side chair, close enough to whisper.

"I knew you'd come back. Knew you'd do right. I love you, Zeb."

"Yeah, love you too, mom. But... cancer?.. treatments... and what did the Chinese do to you?.. "

"Son," she assured. "It's okay. We'll catch up later. Best I leave you two for a bit."

Jessica straightened up and took a step into the room as Dalton's mom passed, touching her ever so slightly on the shoulder. The knowing smile between two strong women was either a harbinger for good or the beginnings of a tag team he would never escape.

Dalton didn't look great: heavy, uneven beard growth and a tangled mess of hair. Still, his present state was a major improvement over how she'd seen him last. While his body was taking care of business, his voice lagged in recovery: weak, scratchy.

"I... don't remember. Can't remember what happened after the bunker."

Pausing, clearing his vision.

"Nobody around here will tell me a flippin' thing. Every time I wake up somebody puts more sleepy-juice in my pic line."

Jessica approached bedside, offering relief from his water bottle. He sipped, then winced, and tried again through dry, cracked lips.

"Tell me."

Turning a chair backwards and leaning in, Jessica recounted the last time they had seen one another.

"I killed him," she confessed. "I killed Loch."

"Three shots. First one was mine... and the last. Couldn't let him get the drop, didn't know how much time he would give you. I had to. Tried to wait him out," her voiced slowed, the toll of taking another soldier's life in her now softening tone. "He gave me no choice."

"You were bad," she continued. "Blood everywhere, slumped over the keyboard. I got you to the floor and did what I could to slow it."

The image of Dalton's limp torso and ashen face still etched across her mind.

"No idea how but your pulse—barely there—evened out. Best I could do was dress the wound with some shreds of your shirt. Barely made a difference. Then I waited."

Her pace quickened.

"Until the good guys showed up. I mean, they took two whole days and you stunk pretty bad but they came to get us. Some kid straight out of Ranger school busts down the door and looks so surprised to find us alive."

Dalton, smiling as she regained her mojo, attempted a question again.

"We did it... really?"

"Yeah, I guess we did... Zeb."

Sanchez wasn't sure the time was right. Still, she took the chance.

"I gotta ask. That question..."

Dalton's eyes focused, the moment coming back full force.

"It seemed pretty deep waters for you. But I thought I saw you answer before everything went crazy."

Dalton nodded his head in a "yes" motion, his warm amber eyes communicating so much more than the physical gesture or the single word ever could. What he didn't try to explain at the moment was the two other quick sets of line commands he punched in after replying. While Sovereign had forever created a nuclear stalemate, Dalton had one last play. It was too easy, really; he fooled the timer into thinking it was yesterday. Twenty-four more hours of limited access in which he alone would be at an actionable coding level. He didn't plan on doing anything in that time. He would either be dead or wait out the powers that be, hoping the political and circumstantial winds to shift toward peace, or at the very least, inaction. Once the timer ran out, no more Sovereign. Ever.

At one time he believed goodness and power could coexist. When the physical representation of that idea failed him, he tried to fashion it from ones and zeros. And when that proved folly, he had to face the question again.

In the end, Dalton had gambled on a death, a stalemate, and a pause.

Sanchez stepped in again.

"Official story is that our president didn't flinch. But, Zeb, he had to be on the other end of the command chain, right? I mean, no one else can control the football."

Dalton had to think on that one. He'd assumed that to be true but there was no real way to know who was calling the shots from DC, or wherever.

He shrugged.

"Well, regardless," Jessica said. "Beijing balked. Enough on their own plate from the chaos of the code degeneration. More than enough to try and project power anywhere beyond their pre-invasion borders. It was so weird. Chinese pullout began within forty-eight hours. Even weirder, they were gone in double that. One thing's for sure, U.S.-China relations are screwed, totally. It will take decades for this to fade, if ever."

The look on his face; she saw it again. Dalton calculated the data, engineered the timeline.

"Zeb, you had such a massive infection. It went septic. Not many people thought you'd make it. You've been basically unconscious for the last ten days."

Sanchez filled in a few more details about the aftermath of the invasion, punctuating the moment with a joke about how at the end of the day the residents of Western Washington had at least been given an opportunity to learn a foreign language.

Dalton's body arched in an uncomfortable laugh.

"Zeb. That question: *Do you fear God...*

... you answered yes, right?"

He nodded. "Yeah, apparently I did."

She gave him the open.

"I don't know," he fumbled. "At least not yet. But given all that's happened, probably should spend some time trying to figure it out."

A bit more small talk and Sanchez rose, leaving him to recuperate. She stepped away and then paused, turning.

"Hey, one last thing."

"Yeah, what?" finding his voice. "You need me to help you save the world *again?*"

He coughed.

She laughed.

"Nah. Found this," pulling the general's totem out of her pocket, "on the comm room floor after they medevac'd your sorry butt. Thought you might want it."

Jessica placed the figurine on the side table, next to his bed. Then, she simply left; silently — as was her specialty.

Dalton looked the totem over for a full five minutes, reflecting on its imagery, and now very personal meaning.

His body was healing. His mind and soul needed repair as well.

For the first time in a long time, he held a glimmer of hope that might be possible.

He wanted more than just survival.
Life after war finally seemed possible.

Until a madman brings a hard reset to humanity's very place on the planet.

Zeb Dalton Book 2, The Cleansing

Dalton has been out of action for almost two years, promising himself and loved ones he'd explore the deeper questions still lingering in the aftermath of Seattle's invasion.

But then mysterious death events surface. Belize. Montenegro. Haiti.

And America's new president has one question.

Are you in?

The answer, as always: yes.

But Dalton knows better now than to go it alone. He needs a team. And recalling Jessica Sanchez from the shadowy world of private ops will only be his first challenge.

As an ancient Mayan tale and its modern bio-threat become all too real, this new cohort must face down a raging psychopath and those who've bought into his twisted visions.

Will the potent pairing of true believers and nature's wrath prove unstoppable? And, if so, what kind of cost is a fair exchange?

Time and courage will tell.

Available now at Amazon | The Cleansing

YOU CAN MAKE A HUGE DIFFERENCE
Reader reviews are by far the #1 way people learn about new writers and stories. Would you take a few minutes to leave your

honest thoughts?

Acknowledgments

So many people were critical to the process of this book coming about. Their gifts of time and attention helped every step along the way. Thanks firstly to my family for letting me spend so much time in getting the manuscript completed and out there for people to read. Breta, my wife, for your patience and wonderful proofing eye. I am greatly indebted to Parul Bavishi for her expert coaching as developmental editor. To E and J, much thanks for your insight regarding Chinese culture that helped shape the characters more reasonably. And to Andrew Bradley, GySgt USMC, retired. I deeply hope this story is a reflection of those who, like you, have faithfully served with a protector's heart and skill.

Made in the USA
Monee, IL
23 August 2020